THE NINE:
ORIGINS

KES TRESTER

OWL HOLLOW PRESS

Owl Hollow Press, LLC, Springville, UT 84663

Library of Congress Cataloging-in-Publication Data
The Nine: Origins / K. Trester. — First edition.

Summary:
Eighteen-year-old Blake Wilder discovers her ability to see pivotal moments in other people's pasts and futures, forcing her into a centuries-old paranormal society where she witnesses a series of bizarre murders before they occur. She must decide whether to trust her head or her heart in a race to unmask the killer before she is the next to die.

Cover: Pocket Hollow Designs

ISBN 978-1-958109-06-9 (paperback)
ISBN 978-1-958109-07-6 (e-book)

For my mom, Betty Sullivan
Our Fearless Leader

The Nine Gifts

Elementalists: *Those who influence the natural elements*

Empaths: *Those who read or influence emotions in others*

Enchanters: *Those who influence thoughts, memories, and actions of others*

Evanescents: *Those who channel living energy*

Materialists: *Those who conjure from the material world*

Phantomists: *Those who commune with the nether world*

Telekinetics: *Those who move objects with their minds*

Telepaths: *Those who hear the thoughts of others*

Voyants: *Those who discern the future and/or the past*

...

Sentinels: *Those who are immune to the Nine Gifts*

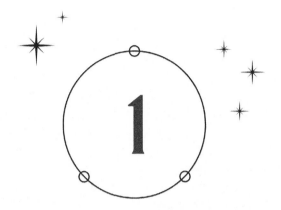

Out of the Shadows

I just *knew* today was going to be a bitch, though my ability to see disasters before they happened had nothing to do with it.

Professor Stein charged into class, late as usual. In one practiced move she tossed down her battered briefcase and snatched up a dry erase marker. As she scrawled out a chemical formula that looked alien in origin on the room's giant white board, she called out, "Yes, this *will* be on the test."

The guy on my right swore under his breath. "Can I borrow a pen?"

Scuffed Vans and floral board shorts marked him as a member of the skater crowd. His shoulder-length, tightly waved hair had probably been black once, but long hours in the sun had left it tipped with blonde. His one concession to the cooler fall weather was to throw on a hoodie. This being Southern California, "fall weather" was a relative term.

He reached for my spare ballpoint with a grateful smile, but the moment his brown-skinned hand grazed mine the classroom disappeared, and I slipped out of reality.

That was my secret and my curse, what kept me on the outside looking in. I saw things—emotional, important events in peoples' past or future. And like it or not, I was about to spy on Skater Boy.

The image was faded and jumpy, a sure sign what I was about to see hadn't happened yet. He loitered in one of the school's parking lots, and as if by magic, a red car appeared next to him at the curb. Skater Boy leaned into the driver's side window, his hands resting on the roof. Maybe his girlfriend was about to break up with him. A tragedy as far as he was concerned, but nothing I'd lose sleep over.

The vision flashed forward again. The paint on the car began to bubble like soup left simmering on the stove, and little wisps of smoke curled up from the hood. Then with a start I was back in Chem 101. Only a fraction of a second had passed, but it always felt much longer.

Future visions were often tantalizingly obscure, and usually more annoying than disturbing. It's why I always brushed them aside. You try telling someone to cancel a rager because her parents would be coming home early from vacation and see the grief you get. Besides, it wasn't like destiny needed any help from me.

I suffered a pang of regret when Skater Boy returned the pen at the end of class. He had warm brown eyes and a delightfully lopsided smile, the kind that put people instantly at ease. I would just have to hope he had the good sense to avoid red cars.

The warmth of the midday sun helped burn off the uneasiness that troubled me the rest of the morning, and it felt good to stretch my legs on the way to the food court. I passed buildings with coral tile roofs, graceful archways, and stucco walls the color of old parchment. A game of lunchtime Frisbee had sprung up on one of the rambling lawns, and a few girls had even stripped down to shorts and sports bras to catch some rays.

"Hello, Blake Wilder." The guy who fell into step beside me came out of nowhere. He was tall and lean with short dark hair framing a handsomely angular face. His navy cashmere sweater over a pair of dark fitted jeans were a definite step up from the just-rolled-out-of-bed look the rest of us strived for.

"How do you know my name?" I asked.

He smiled with such warmth my body heated up in response. I might not have much experience with the opposite sex, but it wasn't for lack of interest on my part.

"I know a lot about you," he said in the same posh accent as the actors in my favorite BBC shows. "For instance, I know you saw something today no one else did."

The blood drained from my face, and I stumbled to a halt. The main reason I'd applied to a small state college almost three hundred miles from home was for a chance to reinvent my life. If my new set of classmates found out they went to school with the main character from a Stephen King novel, I'd go right back to being a social reject faster than you could say Carrie White.

"I don't know what you've heard, but it's not true." The lie sounded weak even to my own ears.

"Don't worry. I won't tell anyone," he said.

"That's because there's nothing to tell. Now leave me alone." I bolted for the food court. My best friend Scarlett would be waiting, but I'd suddenly lost all interest in lunch.

She'd staked out a booth by the café's windows, a glossy magazine open on the table as she took yet another of those ridiculous quizzes (*Good Girl/Bad Girl: Which One Are You?*). I threw myself onto the padded bench across from her.

"What's wrong?" She calmly checked off another box on the questionnaire.

In another era, Scarlett would have been a battlefield nurse, dodging bullets and slapping on bandages without breaking a sweat. She never blinked at all the drama in my life, and as a theatre kid, she once joked being clairvoyant was easy; it was comedy that was hard.

My fingers dug into the seat cushion. "I've been recognized, and somehow he knows what I can do."

"Could be worse. According to this," she said, tapping the magazine with her pen, "I'm a 'caged tiger waiting for someone to show up with the key.'"

I scowled at her. "I'm serious."

"Me too! You try living on skinless chicken and carrot sticks, and then we'll talk about what's important." The diet she'd started months ago had resulted in curves I envied. She'd always been pretty with vibrant red hair and a dusting of freckles across her cheeks, but now her figure turned heads.

"There was a guy," I reiterated. "He knows what I am."

She raised a brow. "At least tell me he was hot."

"Scarlett!"

"Okay, okay." She dropped her pen and leaned back in her seat. "We'll figure something out, but let's order lunch first. Caged tigers think better when you throw us a naked green salad with a scoop of tuna."

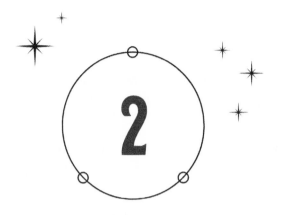

Walk with Me

"I've got improv next, so I can keep my phone on," Scarlett said as we exited the cafe. "If you need to text, I can make it part of the scene."

There was no sign of the guy who'd freaked me out. Though we hadn't come up with any brilliant solutions for preserving my anonymity, her threat to go caged tiger on anyone who crossed me made me feel worlds better.

"You're the best."

She made a face. "Tell that to my scene partner. He's always telling me to die at the beginning of every scene."

I laughed as we began to go our separate ways. "Maybe you should. Just make it death by the slowest poison known to man."

Her grin told me her classmate was about to regret his suggestion.

I was halfway across campus when I spied the stranger eyeing me from the shade of a towering eucalyptus, and my heart sank. If I had any chance of holding on to my new life in Santa

Carla, here was the defining moment. I ground to a halt, forcing him to step out into the autumn sunshine. He approached more cautiously this time.

I shifted my backpack with impatience. "What do you want?"

"To offer an apology. I didn't mean to upset you," he said as students dashed past to make it to class on time. "My name is Nicholas Thorne. Can we please talk for a minute?"

If I was about to be blackmailed or extorted, better to face it head on. "You have from here to Art History to tell me what you want." Without waiting for a response, I continued on my way.

"You're a voyant," he said as we walked, "or a clairvoyant if you prefer."

The truth of his words sent a jolt running through me.

"You may have the ability to look into the past as well as the future; some voyants do," he continued. "In recent months, you've grown stronger, allowing you to see more clearly, more selectively."

My shocked gaze locked with his. It was true I'd once been at the mercy of my visions, but I'd gained more control since turning eighteen in May. I could now turn away from the secrets of strangers who happened to cross my path—for the most part, at least. Physical contact, like with Skater Boy, made it harder.

I lifted my chin a notch. "Let's say I can do all the ridiculous things you think I can. What of it?"

"I want to help," he said.

I lurched to a stop outside the Bell Tower Building. "Look, I don't know what you're up to, but I'm fine. Really. Now leave me alone, or I'll call security."

I reached for the door, but he beat me to it. I frowned at him, but he shrugged. "I have to get to class too." He followed me down the hallway. "Would you at least tell me what you saw today? Please?"

"What does it matter?" I asked, realizing too late I'd just confirmed his suspicions. "Nothing's going to stop it from happening."

It was true I had tampered with fate a handful of times, but only for members of my family, which included Scarlett.

"Have you ever tried to change the future?" He lowered his voice as we walked into class. "Sometimes you may see something because you're supposed to interfere."

I navigated through the packed room to the empty seats in the back before saying in a low voice, "Sorry to burst your bubble, but that only happens in movies."

I dropped into a chair while he helped himself to the next seat over. I sorted through my backpack for the appropriate notebook before risking a glance in his direction.

"Please," he said again, flashing a brilliant smile.

I'd never had anyone fanboy over my weirdness, and I weakened. "*If* I had seen something, it would have been of the guy who sat next to me in the last class. He *might* soon be in a world of car trouble, but since I *didn't* see anything, there's really nothing else to say. Don't you have a class to get to?"

Nicholas's mouth stretched into a grim line, but the startling arrival of Dr. Hamilton prevented further conversation. The middle-age professor was big on presentation with a style that often straddled the fine line between trendy and ridiculous. Today he was at risk of becoming fashion roadkill in embarrassingly tight pants, a striped shirt that had aged way past retro, and a lime green velvet jacket.

He strolled to his desk and plugged his laptop into the projector. Like the born showman he was, he stood with a finger hovering dramatically over the keyboard before he theatrically announced, "Caravaggio!"

A giant image splashed across the classroom screen followed by a handful of groans from the audience. After a few moments, he launched into the brutal history of the famous painting, *Judith Beheading Holofernes,* which depicted the Israelite widow Judith dispatching the drunken General Holofernes as her maid looked on.

"Not the kind of threesome I usually go for," the teacher sniggered, eliciting laughs from several of the guys in the room. He might be a college professor, but his sleazy jokes had yet to graduate high school.

"I wonder what would have happened if someone had been there to warn Holofernes," Nicholas murmured loud enough for me to hear. The general's army had laid siege to the widow's city, so in my opinion, he'd gotten exactly what he deserved, but Nicholas had made his point.

I half-listened to the rest of the lecture, growing more worried as the class wore on. I'd foreseen Eugene Rogers, one of my chief tormentors in high school, break an assortment of bones on his first snowboarding trip, but he'd recovered. What if this time the subject of my premonition didn't walk away?

With a start I noticed class had ended, and people leaving the room. Nicholas watched me put away my unopened notebook. I was still irritated by how easily I'd confessed a vision to a complete stranger, so I left class without a glance in his direction, hoping he'd take the hint.

Before the college sprang to life a few years back, the isolated property had been a state mental hospital hidden away from polite society by miles of farmland in all directions. Scarlett and I always parked our car in the lot still bordering acres of orange groves, and we met there every day after school.

"You never go anywhere slowly, do you?" Nicholas matched my strides. This guy wouldn't give up.

"It usually keeps people from following me," I said pointedly.

"Maybe I just happen to be going the same place you are."

I pinned him with a stare. "And where might that be?"

He took in the collection of buildings ahead, which included the gym and the food court. "I'm going to work out. This is California, after all."

We neared the gym, but I powered right past. "Have fun with that."

"Oh, I just remembered," he said, not missing a step. "I already went running this morning, so maybe I'm hungry?"

"You're not sure?"

"Well, you know," he said as we went by the food court. "Jet lag completely screws with your head. Do you know I once woke up fully dressed and holding a cup of tea?"

"Jet lag? Really?" I raised a skeptical brow. "Are you saying you fly in for school every morning?"

He grinned. "Don't you?"

"Then there's no reason for you to follow me to the parking lot. Planes are parked on the other side of campus." I kept a straight face, but I couldn't hide the amusement in my voice. Never had anyone worked so hard to get my attention.

The unmistakable sound of skateboard wheels clicking along the sidewalk from behind sent us both skidding off the path and onto the grass. I stumbled when I recognized the rider as the guy from my premonition, and Nicholas reached out a steadying hand.

The vision struck again without warning. It was still a fractured glimpse of the future, but there was nothing ambiguous about it this time. Flames danced on the hood of the red car as my classmate stared curiously at his hands as they too sparked and ignited. He lifted his gaze to meet mine only a moment before a raging fire engulfed both him and the car. I pulled out of the premonition with a cry.

"Is that the guy?" Nicholas stared at the boarder's back as he cruised past.

I nodded, my stomach churning as the skater zipped to the curb where his two friends waited and bumped fists in greeting. They too were dressed in variations on the beach theme. One was short with dark stubble shadowing his chin, and the other's head sported the fried blonde frizz of a dedicated surfer.

Behind them stood a shiny, red Mustang.

"Were the other guys in your vision?" Nicholas asked, his voice low and tense.

"No," I ground out, but that didn't matter. The more intense the vision the more quickly it came to pass, and this was one of the clearest premonitions I'd ever had. The car was fated for destruction. How could I justify holding my tongue when keeping silent could very well be a death sentence for those guys?

I wanted to scream in frustration. The minute I opened my mouth, the whispers would start up again, people would stare as I passed through the halls, and classmates would suddenly find a reason to change seats. I might as well face facts, adopt a dozen cats, and call it a day.

With a resentful groan, I started forward as the guy with the whiskers whipped out a set of keys and popped open the trunk. My classmate stomped on the end of his board, causing it to flip neatly into his hand so he could pack it away.

"Excuse me." I focused my attention on the guy from the premonition. Maybe if I could speak to him first, he could somehow convince the others not to get in the car. A few days should buy them enough time. "Can I talk to you a minute?"

He gave me a friendly smile. "You're the one who loaned me the pen. I gave it back, right?"

"Hey, Warren, who's the babe?" The bleached blonde guy looked me over with friendly interest.

"I'm Blake." I edged up to Warren and hoped the other guys would take the hint, but it only served as an invitation for his friends to gather closer. "You know," I said with a small laugh, "this is going to sound really funny, but what if I were to tell you that sometimes I can tell fortunes? And what if I also said that maybe you were at a fork in the road, and that one choice would be good and the other one would be, well, not so good?"

Geez, I sounded like one of those fake mediums at a carnival.

The bearded guy grinned, waiting for the punchline, but Warren maintained an air of polite interest, so I got to the point. "What I've seen is it's dangerous for you to get in that car. You guys need to find another way to get around for the next few days."

The bearded one brayed with laughter. "All right, who put you up to this?" He hooked an arm around Warren's shoulders. "I bet that poser who's always hogging the ramps sent you. Probably hoping to get the pipes all to himself today."

"What? No!" I insisted. "You have to believe me! You guys could die if you drive that car!"

Warren's companions exchanged grins, but he searched my face, probably wondering why a girl he barely knew would say such a bizarre thing. Finally he said, "Guys, I really should stay and catch up on my chem labs." His words were meant for his friends, but his eyes stayed on me.

"Are you serious, dude?" The bearded guy was no longer amused. "You're going to blow off an excellent day at the pipes because some psycho chick tells you to?"

I didn't mind the diss. I'd been called worse.

"Hey, Kevin," Warren said to the blond one. "Would you pop the trunk?" Once he'd retrieved his belongings, he addressed his indignant friend. "Eddie, it's just one day. You said you were behind on your history paper. Why don't you stay too?"

"Is this some kind of joke?" Eddie took two threatening steps in my direction.

Nicholas, who'd been quietly observing up to this point, moved instantly to block Eddie's path. "She's trying to save your life," he said, looming over the other guy. "I suggest you listen."

Warren came to stand next to me, making it clear he'd made his choice. Scarlett arrived and, picking up on the tension, quietly stationed herself on my other side.

"Fine," Eddie hissed, glaring up at Nicholas who hadn't budged. "Stay with your little friends. Come on, Kevin."

Eddie slid into the driver's seat and slammed the door. Kevin stood in indecision, looking back and forth between Warren and me before reluctantly folding himself into the passenger side. Eddie gunned the engine, and they peeled out of the lot.

Maybe it would be okay. Warren's actions had altered the future, so there was no reason to believe the car was still fated to catch fire. Besides, I hadn't seen Eddie and Kevin in my vision. They were probably fine.

I relaxed as the red car picked up speed, merging onto the two-lane farm road fronting the school. They had just zoomed past the last parking lot when a truck loaded with oranges shot out from between a row of trees and directly into the Mustang's path. There was no time to react before the car smashed into the side of the truck with a horrible shriek of twisting metal and shattering glass.

The impact propelled both vehicles across the road, dropping the farm truck into a drainage ditch, the mangled Mustang landing on top. Crates of oranges lay broken and spilled across the road like a forgotten game of marbles. For the span of a heartbeat, maybe two, we all stood in stunned silence. Then one of the gas tanks exploded, and a massive fireball engulfed both cars. Tar-black smoke billowed up, tarnishing the cloudless sky.

Scarlett stared at the scene in horror while Warren gagged and staggered away. Nicholas was the first to find his voice. "Will you listen to me now, Blake?"

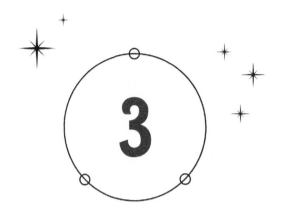

The Offer

Students and faculty poured out of classrooms, a few wielding fire extinguishers. Others whipped out cell phones and presumably dialed 9-1-1, though a few couldn't resist snapping pics like tourists at Disneyland.

I sank to the ground, tears sliding down my cheeks. A few yards away, Warren was on his knees retching into a tidy bed of nasturtiums as Scarlett hovered over him. Nicholas quickly tapped something into his phone before grabbing my hand and helping me to my feet. A jolt of energy shot through me at his touch, and reflexively I jerked away.

"You did it," he said with satisfaction. "You saved the one you were supposed to save."

I stared at him in horror. "How can you say that? People are dead!"

"You warned them. It's not your fault they chose not to listen."

I used the sleeve of my sweater to angrily scrub away my tears. "You really are a bastard, you know that?"

His eyes narrowed. "And you're living in a fairytale if you think you can walk away from who you are."

I couldn't listen to this, not while the sizzle and crack of a deadly fire roared in my ears. I made my way over to Scarlett and Warren.

"That's the guy from this morning?" she asked, keeping a wary eye on Nicholas.

I nodded. "Are you all right?" My glance encompassed them both.

Warren gazed up at me, his eyes wide with shock. "How did you know?"

"That's not important now," Nicholas interjected as he slipped past me. He extended a hand to Warren. "You've had quite a shock. I suggest you go home and get some rest. Blake and I need to talk, so maybe Scarlett can give you a lift."

Scarlett and I shared a look. How did he know her name?

"I don't know what it is you think you know," she said, her voice pitched an octave higher than usual, "but you've got it all wrong."

"I know how special Blake is, and what a good friend you are to her." The wail of approaching sirens made him raise his voice to be heard. "But what happened today is only the beginning."

"The beginning of what?" As always, Scarlett appeared composed, but there was no hiding the way her hands trembled.

He turned to me. "You can try to keep ignoring the truth, or you can hear me out."

I glared at him, recognizing the skillful way we were all being handled, but I wasn't a coward. If he had something to say, it would be in a public place of my choosing.

I handed Scarlett the car keys. The faded green Volvo we shared waited nearby. "It'll be okay."

She reluctantly helped up Warren before shooting Nicholas a parting glare. "You mess with us, and I will hurt you."

As if he saw scenes of death and destruction every day, Nicholas casually turned to face me. "I'm afraid there's nothing more we can do here. Can we go someplace to sit, maybe have a cup of tea?"

"Tea?" The acrid smell of burning tires, vinyl car interior, and something else I didn't dare contemplate filled the air. The last thing on my mind was grabbing a drink.

He shrugged. "A cup of tea is a cup of peace."

I led the way across campus to Basics, a coffee bar in the library's elegant courtyard. It was even quieter than usual at that time of day. I was friendly with the girl behind the counter, Mina, a fellow barista with hot pink hair and a ring in her nose. I'd taken a glance into her future once to find the only exciting event headed her way was the purchase of a new bong. It made her easy to be around.

"I heard there was an accident out on the road," she said, whipping up my usual vanilla latte without needing to ask and a cup of Earl Grey for Nicholas. "Did you guys see it?"

"Sorry, no," Nicholas said, sliding a hundred dollar bill across the counter to pay for our drinks. Mina raised a pierced brow, suddenly more interested in Nicholas than whatever was happening on the other side of school.

I zipped up my sweatshirt to fend off a breeze before taking a seat on the bench outside. It fronted a circular reflecting pool mirroring the late afternoon sky. I couldn't help thinking if the water were truly reflective it would have appeared murky and unsettled.

"You're not really a student here, are you?" I sipped my coffee and found it surprisingly comforting.

The bench creaked as Nicholas settled in beside me. "No. I go to school in England, which is also home to The Nine."

I squinted up at him. "The nine what?"

"The name comes from the Bible, 1 Corinthians 12:1 specifically, where St. Paul writes about the nine spiritual gifts. Among those are the gifts of prophecy and the discernment of spirits, which were supposedly bestowed by God for the common good. There are thousands of us all over the world."

I had a sinking feeling. "You're not part of some cult, are you?" I had attended church sporadically as a kid but was hardly ideal recruitment material for a bunch of Kool-Aid drinkers.

A smile twitched briefly across his lips. "The Nine has been around for centuries, ever since the European witch trials in the fourteen hundreds. One of the accused was the daughter of a rich German landowner by the name of Alder. He was able to smuggle her out of the country to relatives in England. She lived quite a long life, and even took in others who were suspected of having the sight or being witches or whatever. Her home, Alder House, eventually became the home of The Nine."

"You want me to join a club for witches?" I wondered if I should have called security after all.

"What I want is for you to know you're no longer alone." He removed the lid from his cup. "Your connection is growing stronger, and I'm here to help you understand what that means."

"So you waited until I finally had a life to show up?" Anger quickly bubbled to the surface. I'd spent years masking my emotions, but all bets were off today. "Where were you when I had no control over my visions and thought I was going to lose my mind?"

Nicholas studied the steam escaping his cup in tiny swirls. "It was my father's idea to send me now."

I took another sip of coffee and dialed back my temper. My entire life had been spent wondering why I'd been cursed. Maybe here was my chance to get a few answers.

"Your parents are in this thing, too?" Mine didn't always know what to do with me, but they did their best to understand their unusual child. I would have once said the same for my younger sister, but that changed when she started high school.

Going through adolescence as the sibling of the school fruit loop had put a big strain on our relationship.

"My mother is dead," he said as if that fact was ancient history, "but yes, my father is Henry Thorne, chancellor of The Nine."

"A voyant family?" There'd be no surprises under their Christmas tree.

"Only a few in The Nine are voyants. Others are empaths or telepaths or what have you, and some, like me..."

He focused his gaze on the reflecting pool in front of us, and I turned to see what held his attention. I leapt to my feet in shock.

The water in the pool stood. Straight up. A column of water shimmered in the afternoon light, a perfect glassy cylinder about eight feet high. Nicholas smiled as the water eased itself back into the pool.

"...are telekinetic," he concluded.

I sank back down onto the bench, stunned. "You...you can move things with your mind." Everything he'd said suddenly took on new meaning.

"Yes," he confirmed, "and there are others like me as well. Your George Washington was telekinetic, you know."

"Seriously?"

He took a sip of tea. "How else do you think a small band of farmers defeated the best-trained army on earth?"

Something still didn't add up. "You didn't come six thousand miles to hold my hand."

There was empathy in his gaze. "It's complicated, but the SparkNotes version is you will have more premonitions of people who will need your help, much like today."

That shook me to the core. "But I don't want this. I've never wanted any of this."

"It's the way it's always been," he explained. "If it weren't for voyants acting on their visions, Galileo would have been killed by religious zealots before inventing the telescope, Jonas

Salk would have died in a lab explosion before discovering the polio vaccine, and Vincent Van Gogh would have jumped off a bridge as a teenager."

I stared at him. "Are you saying that skater boy will somehow change the world?"

He shrugged. "We can only wait and see."

How easy it was for him, having an ability that didn't mess with your mind or your life. What I wouldn't give to be able to completely control and channel my energies. From doing chores to stopping...

A chill gripped my heart. "Can you move bigger things?"

He shied away from my accusing stare and gazed into the distance. "That is not my purpose here."

Anger warred with grief. "You could have stopped that car, but instead people died because it's not your *purpose*?"

His expression remained infuriatingly placid. "If you didn't see them, then their fates were sealed."

"That's bullshit! I'm supposed to put myself out there because you tell me to while you just stand back and watch?" I jerked to my feet and grabbed my backpack. "We are so done here."

"Blake, listen to me." He leapt up as well. "You need to know how to survive being what you are, how we all work together to live normal lives, free from interference and exploitation."

I glared at him. "I'll tell you what I know about survival. You keep your mouth shut because when people find out you're different, they turn on you. Unlike you, though, I will do what I can to save people like Warren and his friends." I drew a ragged breath at the raw memory of Kevin's and Eddie's tragic fate. "But the rest of you can go straight to hell."

"I don't blame you for not trusting me," he interjected before I could turn away, "but what happens if the next Nine you meet isn't quite so reasonable? What if the next one decides a powerful voyant could be incredibly useful and uses any means necessary to make sure you cooperate?"

I searched his face, trying to discern if I read a veiled threat there, but his gaze was open and sincere. "What are you saying? Either I get on the bus or get thrown under it?"

"It wasn't always like this. Once we had a common goal." Nicholas shook his head with regret. "Now many of our people are drifting away, ignoring or outright defying the principles that have allowed us to survive undetected for centuries."

I stared at his sculpted profile, wondering what he wasn't telling me. He hadn't come all this way to hand me a fruit basket and say welcome to the neighborhood. If his people were offering to protect me, they wanted something in return.

His gaze met mine. "Join us. Pledge to The Nine, and let your voice be added to those who would call for unity once again."

There it was. The price of being left alone didn't actually include being left alone. I shouldered my backpack. "This is my life, and I will not be forced into anything against my will." *Not anymore.*

"It's too late for that," he called to my retreating back.

Jitters

*A*s a kid I'd dreamed someone would show up on our door-step to claim me as the lost princess of some magical realm, but time had ground those fantasies into bitter dust. The need to know where I came from still flickered inside me, but the girl who would have blindly trusted such a messenger was gone.

For all I knew Nicholas could be one of those unscrupulous people he'd warned me about, intent on using me and my strange abilities. His parting shot echoed in my mind as I stalked the main parking lot, seeking a familiar face who could give me a ride back to town.

With the philosophy that beggars can't be choosers, I reluc-tantly accepted a ride from Dr. Hamilton, but regretted it almost instantly when his hand slipped from the gearshift down to my knee. The guy was at least as old as my dad. Someone needed to toss a bucket of ice water on those ridiculously tight pants.

On the rare occasions I purposefully sought out a vision, physical contact wasn't necessary, but it helped. With Dr. Hamilton's hand on my knee, it took only a moment to pluck an event from his past sure to cool him off.

I swiveled toward him as much as my seatbelt allowed and flirtatiously twisted a finger around a lock of my blond hair. "I've always really liked you, Dr. Hamilton."

He lit up like he'd been plugged into an outlet. "Please, call me Jeff. I noticed you the first day you walked into my class."

"I'd love to see where you live," I oozed. "You must have an amazing art collection."

"Oh, well," he hedged, his hand magically sliding off my knee, "that's probably not the best idea."

"Why not?" I blinked with such innocence that somewhere angels wept.

"Well, um, if you must know, I still share a house with my, uh, ex-wife." Liar, liar, tight pants on fire.

There was nothing ex about the angry wife I saw in the past vision. She was fed up with her husband's infidelity. She had threatened him with divorce, reporting him to the school dean, and the removal of a beloved bit of his anatomy if she ever caught him straying again.

"That's okay, I'd love to meet her." I whipped out my phone. "What's her number? I'll let her know we're on our way."

He forced a laugh. "That would be great, but I just remembered a faculty meeting…back at school…that I forgot."

I sighed, disappointed. "I bet she's an amazing woman to have caught a man like you."

Dr. Hamilton looked positively ill. I contemplated whether I should tap into his future for potential heart attacks, but we pulled up in front of my apartment in record time. I'd barely shut the door before his car squealed away.

The Volvo's designated parking spot was empty. Warren must still be reeling from a nightmare come to life, but Scarlett never flinched when things got messy. I'd learned that early on in our friendship.

We'd met as kids when her parents moved in down the street. Her father left within the year, and her mother filled the vacancy with boyfriends and gin. The Wilder house became her sanctuary, and it was inevitable she'd soon figure out there was something different about her new best friend. It happened right before one of my sister's softball games.

At nine I was too young to stay home alone, so my parents would force me to sit through Jordan's games. Scarlett happened to be with us that day when we all piled into my dad's SUV, so at least I'd have company in my misery. We'd just arrived at the park when suddenly a premonition hit. It scared the crap out of me because this time, the victim was my seven-year-old sister.

The accident would happen when it was almost her turn at bat. She would slip out of the dugout to grab a batting helmet tossed in frustration by a girl who'd struck out. It had come to rest a few feet to the side of home plate where her friend Lily was swinging wildly at any pitch in the same zip code.

It all happened so quickly. Lily swung, the bat flew out of her grip, and it rocketed straight at Jordan. The bat hit her square across the face. She hit the dirt so hard a cloud of dust puffed around her prone body. I couldn't tell if she was even breathing.

If Scarlett weren't in the car, I could tell my family what I'd seen. My parents would make some excuse to pull Jordan from the game, and we'd go for ice cream. But Scarlett *was* in the car. I hadn't had a best friend since kindergarten, when I hadn't yet learned how important it was to keep my secrets to myself. I'd told my friend Rena she should come to my house when her daddy started hitting her mom after dinner, and she burst into tears. Rena stopped coming to school after that, and soon after my dad told me they'd moved away.

I couldn't lose Scarlett, but neither could I let my sister get her face bashed in.

My dad pulled into a parking spot, and Jordan hopped out of the car. She'd spotted members of her team and rushed to join them. My heart started to pound. She had to be stopped before she went into the dugout.

"She forgot her bat bag," I blurted, hoping my parents would call her to come back.

"That's okay, I'll get it," my dad said, ever the pushover for his girls.

It was so unfair. I gazed at Scarlett, blissfully unaware for just a few more moments of what I was. The trust and loyalty growing between us would be ruined, and the same look of fear I'd seen on Rena's face would distort Scarlett's features. She glanced at me, puzzled at my frightened expression.

I faced forward, hating my visions, hating that I had no choice, hating myself. Why was this happening to me? My dad pulled the key out of the ignition. My mom gathered her purse.

"Jordan can't play today," I said, my voice barely above a whisper. Both my parents froze. Dad glanced regretfully at Scarlett before asking the question he knew would forever change the way she looked at me. "What's going to happen?"

"Lily is going to accidentally hit Jordan in the face with a bat." I twisted my fingers together until they hurt. "It's bad."

My mom's stricken expression sent them both scrambling out of the car, leaving Scarlett and me alone in the backseat. I kicked the seat in front of me, watching my Converse leave scuff marks on the clean black leather. I waited for her to react with fear, disgust, or maybe both, but what I didn't expect was silence.

I turned to her. "So now you know. I'm a freak, okay?" I almost dared her to agree.

She scratched her nose, seemingly unconcerned. "My mom drinks so much she sometimes forgets to buy food."

I stared at her a few moments before finding my tongue. "You don't care?"

She shrugged. "You don't, like, turn into an ogre at sunset or anything, do you?"

I giggled, flooded with relief. "Nope. Scary visions are pretty much it."

She glanced out the window. "Do you think we can go to the snack bar before we leave?"

Dropping my backpack inside the front door of our empty apartment, I had an uneasy feeling this day would leave another permanent scar.

I texted Scarlett. *Everything ok?*

She immediately texted back: *Warren's a mess. What about pretty boy? Does he need his ass kicked? Cuz I know peeps.*

Probably, I texted, *but first I gotta go to work. Pick up at 10 plz.*

I walked the six blocks to Jitters, the coffeehouse where I worked part-time. A steady stream of students, lonely professionals, and would-be performers, because it was open mic night, would be dropping by. My boss, Al Vanderbeek, stood behind the counter filling various coffee canisters, a chore my often-tardy coworker Cindy was supposed to do.

Al had once lived in San Francisco's Haight Ashbury district, the home of free love, the adopted city of Jack Kerouac, and to hear Al tell it, the last bastion of freedom in America. Jitters had become his own personal battleground in the war against chain-store coffeehouses, mindless conformity, and Republicans. In his late sixties, he still wore his now-gray hair in a low ponytail, and the blue-tinted glasses perched on his nose were in a decidedly John Lennon fashion.

Like Al, Jitters was a throwback to the past. The coffeehouse occupied the ground floor of one of Santa Carla's oldest buildings, a red brick two-story that had once been home to the city's first bank. At one end of its cavernous space a dozen well-used café tables clustered around a tiny stage. Dog-eared posters of classic rock bands such as The Doors and The Beatles were plastered on the wall behind it. The other side of the room looked like we were having a yard sale. Mismatched sofas, chairs, and end tables were strewn about in a haphazard yet comfortable arrangement. Between the two sections, the coffee bar elbowed its way into the action.

"Bloody capitalists," Al muttered, glaring at his phone as he ignored the incoming call. "That Sutton Sinclair won't be satisfied until he steamrolls over every bit of history in this town and turns it into a parking lot."

I'd only lived in Santa Carla a few months, but the name of hotshot developer Sutton Sinclair was often in the news and on signs around town. The city had sprung up around a centralized commercial district with the residential areas located a comfortable distance away. Sinclair was going to change all that by bringing urban housing into the heart of the city's business center, injecting a shot of nightlife into an area that practically rolled up the sidewalks after dark.

"His people aren't taking no for an answer?" I foamed a cappuccino at the next machine over.

Al's eyes blazed with righteousness as he regarded me over the rim of his eyeglasses. "Mark my words: I will chain myself to the front doors before I let him take this building from me."

"I vote for a barricade, like in *Les Miserables*," I said, handing off the drink order. "You know, cute but disgruntled students, lots of flag waving, maybe even a catchy showtune or two."

He snickered. "Sinclair wouldn't know what hit him if we broke into song."

Al started singing *R-E-S-P-E-C-T* under his breath as one of our weeknight regulars stepped up to the counter. Selena was a striking woman who proudly displayed the streaks of gray in her glossy black hair as if she'd earned them the hard way. She lived in jeans and blazers, and always carried a floppy little mutt, Chico, in a tote. The two were inseparable, and she talked about him as if he were human. We kept a glass canister of dog biscuits on the counter, and I offered him his nightly treat.

"You spoil him, Blake," she said, affectionately ruffling the dog's furry head as he crunched his biscuit. Golden brown ears incongruously framed a white face, making it look like he'd been assembled from spare parts. "It's gotten so bad, he sulks if we don't come here right after work."

I set her standing order of a decaf chai latte on the bar. "He goes to work with you?"

"Five days a week." She hoisted her cup in a toast. "It's good to be the boss."

The next customer in line was a young woman who must also have come directly from work, still outfitted in a cheap version of an expensive suit. Everything about her reeked of ambition, from her Hillary Clinton blonde bob to the sleek computer bag slung over her shoulder. Her eyes twitched nervously, but since she ordered a double cappuccino, I put it down to caffeine overload.

I swear we didn't touch. I was always really careful never to come in physical contact when handing off drink orders, but it didn't seem to make a damn bit of difference. The ground shifted beneath me, and I couldn't break the link between us to save my life.

She sat alone at one of the round tables, her laptop open with a Jitters cup alongside. Her clothes were the same, so this premonition would most likely happen tonight. The view jumped to her typing, and I was immensely relieved. Unless she started clobbering customers with her computer, this was going to be a really boring vision. Tonight, boring was good.

Then I read the contents of her email: *I know who you are, and I have proof of your fraud and betrayal. I'm attaching a copy of the document, so you'll know I mean business. Try to find me, and I'll send it to the authorities. I'll contact you soon to arrange payment.*

She hit send.

I snapped back to the moment as little Ms. Blackmailer took her coffee. Grabbing up a bar towel, I made a production of cleaning up a bit of steamed milk until my hands stopped shaking. I'd spent years enduring hit-and-run visions, my life a non-stop series of horror shows chipping away at my sanity until I'd finally learned how to lock down my mind. Yet here they were again, three in one day. I didn't know if I could survive another trip to hell.

The blonde settled in at a table with her computer, a self-satisfied smirk marring her features as she began to type. What she was doing was underhanded and despicable but not necessarily fatal. Maybe Nicholas Thorne was wrong, and my visions weren't destined to grow in darkness and intensity.

Another customer approached the counter, and I forced a smile. It slipped a bit when another terrifying thought whispered in my ear.

What if everything Nicholas had said was true?

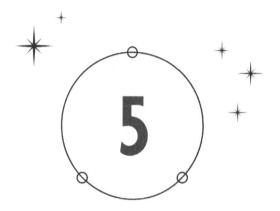

Past and Future

I jerked awake at the sound of the red Mustang crashing once again into the farm truck. For a few heartbeats the stench of burning flesh assaulted my senses, but then I realized it was only the smell of breakfast on the stove.

My toes curled when they met the cold floor, but I didn't mind. With every other surface in the apartment generically whitewashed, the old hardwood floors gave the place some character. Scarlett had almost finished sweeping up the remains of a broken plate when I entered the kitchen.

"Sorry," she said. "I didn't mean to wake you."

I shrugged off her apology and poured a cup of coffee.

She joined me at the kitchen table with her prison-fare breakfast of scrambled egg whites and dry wheat toast. She pushed the plate in my direction. "You want some tasteless, chewy stuff? Or maybe a piece of toasted cardboard?"

"It's hard to resist, but I'll pass," I mumbled into my cup.

She shoveled in a few joyless bites. "I can't stop thinking about yesterday. It's stupid to say now, but I once kind of envied what you can do."

I stared at her. "You're kidding me, right?" I hadn't always been able to keep my visions to myself, and Scarlett had witnessed the resulting social suicide.

She shook her head. "Who doesn't want to have superpowers? But now I get it. That accident was the worst thing I've ever seen."

Not me, but I worked hard to keep the particularly gruesome memories buried. "Have you checked in on Warren this morning?"

She'd stayed with him until it was time to pick me up from work. "Not yet. Poor boy was totally wrecked last night, but he's also really sweet."

"Do you think I did the right thing?" I asked. "About Nicholas?" I'd tossed in bed for hours wondering if maybe I'd been too quick to turn him away. How had Nicholas known what I was and then tracked me down? What would it be like to be around others who understood what it was like to be so different?

She deliberated for a moment. "Doesn't it seem kind of convenient that the minute Pretty Boy shows up, something awful happens?"

The coffee cup froze halfway to my lips. Had Nicholas somehow triggered my loss of control? I didn't see how he could possibly have caused the accident, but she sure was right about the timing.

"It doesn't matter," I decided, taking another sip. "I doubt we'll see him again."

"Good." She pushed the remaining eggs around her plate, her appetite absent for once. "I don't trust him."

I reached for her toast, making a face at its complete lack of flavor. "Don't we have any jam?"

"I hate you, you know," she said without heat as I plucked the blueberry preserves out of the fridge. I had the metabolism of a jackrabbit.

I slathered on the jam and grinned. "Too bad you're stuck with me for life."

All signs of the accident had been cleared away by the time we arrived at school, but a makeshift shrine had sprouted in its place. The side of the road was piled high with cellophane-wrapped flowers, tall prayer candles, and stuffed animals. A line of cars turning into the parking lot snaked slowly past, much like a funeral procession.

Dr. Fisher, my English Lit professor, wore her usual dowdy head-to-toe black for the first class of the day, but for once it was appropriate. Her daily uniform was indicative of her obsession with Sylvia Plath, Virginia Woolf, and death, not necessarily in that order. Curious over how someone could become so enchanted with mortality I'd dipped into her head during the first week of classes. One trip into the nightmare of her childhood was enough to make me go out of my way to be nice to her.

"Did anyone know those poor, unfortunate boys?" Her oversized glasses were attached to a heavy silver chain, their lenses distorting her dull brown eyes to startling proportions as she gazed soulfully out at the class.

We all looked at one another, but no one raised a hand. A grief counselor stepped into the room then, a young woman wearing a shapeless knit dress and Birkenstocks with knee socks. She talked about how we all experienced grief differently, but my thoughts turned inward.

If my guard had been up, I wouldn't have even had that premonition, but now somewhere out there, two families were being ripped apart because I hadn't tried hard enough to save their sons. Had other people died because I'd been so intent on shutting out my visions? What kind of life would I have if I let them all in? How did I learn to live with this? The rest of the morning was spent stewing over questions I couldn't answer.

When at last lunchtime arrived, I took three steps out of a dim classroom and into the bright sunshine when a shadow fell across my path. It was almost a relief to see Nicholas walking beside me, his hands thrust into his pockets. Scarlett's warning not to trust him hovered in the back of my mind, but she wasn't the one whose future was in danger of going up in flames.

"I've made a complete hash of things," he said after a few moments, his voice contrite. "I wouldn't blame you if you never spoke to me again, but I want you to know how very sorry I am about yesterday. Is there any chance we can start over?"

"I don't know. I'm so confused right now," I confessed.

"Then please let me help." He bounded ahead a few steps and turned to face me. "I know what you're feeling, and you don't have to go through it alone."

I stopped in front of him, bombarded by doubt and uncertainty. "Have you ever questioned every choice you've ever made?"

His eyes flickered as if I'd touched a sore spot. "None of this is your fault, you know."

"Isn't it?" Tears blurred my vision. "All I wanted was to go to college, get a boyfriend, and maybe see a few football games, you know?" I knew that sounded pathetic, but it was hard letting go of the dream of starting over when I'd left home. "But now I don't know anymore."

"You can still do all that," he said gently. "Just think of acting on your visions as an extracurricular."

I used the hem of my sweatshirt to blot my face. "If it's all the same to you, I'd prefer the Sierra Club."

His mouth pursed with skepticism. "It's not like you were ever a big joiner."

I pulled up short. My class schedule and very short list of friends was one thing. Knowing the only way I'd ever have joined a club in high school was if you'd held a gun to my head was at a whole different level.

"Have you been spying on me?"

The stiffening of his shoulders told me everything I needed to know. "Blake, let me explain."

"No need," I said, reaching for his hand.

I'd never been to London, but there was no mistaking the landmark Ferris wheel looming over the river Thames, nor the distinctive Gothic buildings lining its banks. I took in the breathtaking view from a spacious rooftop terrace where Nicholas lounged on an elegant sofa wearing a sleek gray coat over a white turtleneck and jeans. Watery afternoon sunshine sparkled on a wall of smoked glass dividing a furnished patio from the rest of the modern building.

The images unspooled seamlessly, confirming whatever I was about to see had already happened. Past visions were fully fleshed out with sounds, colors, and smells. Maybe it was because the past was complete and unchangeable, while the future was still up for grabs.

Across from Nicholas sat the only other people taking in the rarefied air. One was a young woman with a broad face and easy smile who wore her ebony hair curled into a lacquered flip. Next to her lazed a guy with a tangle of dark hair falling over deep-set eyes, the shadow of a beard framing a square jaw.

The ultra-modern surroundings would have been impressive in any circumstance, but one detail nudged it into the surreal:

almost everything within easy reach of the trio floated several feet off the ground. Chairs, throw pillows, glass lanterns, and planters were suspended in midair.

The man held a pad and pen. "The score is, Nicholas: thirteen, Miranda: eleven." He looked to the woman. "Time to step up to the plate, old girl. My weekend at the Paris house is riding on it."

"*Your* weekend?" she snorted, her British accent harsher than either of the guys.

The man grinned. "It's all duty and responsibility whenever I'm there with Nicky. I'm sure you'll be a lot more fun."

"Aren't I always?" She laughed, leaning forward in her seat. A nearby coffee table rose into the air, soon followed by a graceful floor lamp and a leather-covered footstool.

"C'mon, Miranda," the scorekeeper cheered. "Just one more to win."

Nicholas looked askance at his friend. "Whose side are you on, Dev?"

"The fun side, of course," he quipped.

A metallic chattering came from an end table as a silver ashtray tried to free itself from the bonds of gravity. It went on for several seconds until Miranda swore under her breath, finally leaning back in surrender.

"Your turn, Nicholas," Dev said with a complete lack of enthusiasm. "Oh, joy."

With a boyish grin, Nicholas turned his attention to the sofa where his friends reclined. Very slowly, it lifted off the ground, one agonizing inch at a time while Miranda and Dev nervously held on. Nicholas barely breathed, his absorption in the task all-consuming. The sofa was about two feet off the ground when it happened.

"Nicholas."

The voice sliced through the air, carrying an authority that demanded attention. Everything crashed to the ground, including the sofa. Miranda managed to hold on, but Dev sprawled across the elegant travertine floor. Nicholas buried his face in his hands.

"Miranda, Devraj, would you please allow me a word with my son?" Though the speaker's tone was perfectly civil, Dev bolted to his feet and followed Miranda through the tinted glass doors.

Even if he'd never said a word, there was no question it was Nicholas's father. Henry Thorne was as tall as his son, though his shoulders weren't quite as broad. They both shared strongly defined cheekbones, but Henry's features bordered on hawkish. Perhaps if Nicholas's friends had stayed, they would have noticed the slight stoop in the older man's posture, and the glint of worry in his eyes. The elder Thorne may have once been an intimidating man, but time and circumstance had worn away his edge.

Henry dropped a bright red folder, thick with papers, on the nearest table. Nicholas eyed it warily. "What is that?"

Henry pulled up a chair and indicated his son should do the same. "Insurance."

Once Nicholas was seated, he flipped back the cover and stared at the top page. It was a candid, eight-by-ten color photo of me. Despite my surfer girl coloring, the expression on my face was anything but chill. The picture must have been taken while I was still in high school.

Nicholas looked up. "What's going on?"

The older man rested his elbows on the table and steepled his fingers. "Blake Wilder, age eighteen, and now a Class One voyant." Nicholas didn't comment, but his father had his full attention. "What's even more remarkable is that until recently, she lived her entire life isolated in the dusty California farm town where she grew up, and still has no idea who she really is."

I bristled. I knew all too well who, or what, I was.

"How did our sentinels not find her until now?" Nicholas asked.

Henry broke eye contact with his son. "If word had circulated there was a young voyant who was a Class Two by the age of fourteen, she wouldn't have stood a chance."

Nicholas drew back in astonishment. "You knew about her and didn't tell anyone? How could you betray your oath like that?"

"You're nineteen. You're not a child anymore," his father said with a sniff. "You know why."

Nicholas stared at his father a moment before turning his attention to the file. He thumbed through my high school transcripts (mostly As), a photo of me and Scarlett taken at last summer's county fair, and to my amazement, a copy of the psychiatric report from the one and only time my parents had ever brought in a professional to evaluate their odd child. I'd never been allowed to read it, but my mom, a physician herself, dismissed it later by saying she didn't need men who played with ink blots to tell her what she already knew.

"Why are you showing me this?" As if Nicholas hadn't spoken, Henry reached across the table and withdrew my headshot from the file.

"She's grown quite lovely, hasn't she?" Maybe Henry wasn't such a jerk after all.

"She's more than lovely," Nicholas agreed, "but I know you're not here to talk about women."

"Quite right." He looked up from my picture. "I'm here to discuss our future."

Nicholas shifted impatiently in his chair. "Don't you mean your future as chancellor?"

Henry's eyes narrowed. "If you won't think of me, at least think of our people." He leaned back in his chair and glanced at the spectacular view. "Any challenge right now would be a disaster."

"What do you want?"

"This girl," Henry said, holding up my photo, "has moved to Southern California. To Santa Carla to be exact."

Nicholas froze, though the significance of his father's words was lost on me.

"We need to be the first ones to make contact, and I want you to do it," Henry said. He pulled a plane ticket from his jacket pocket. "You leave tomorrow."

A Shared Secret

It was unsettling how easily I'd slipped into his mind. With most people, it was like peering through a window, but with Nicholas, there had been no such barrier. It was like I'd actually been there.

"What did you see?" If he was offended by my poking around, he didn't let it show.

Even Scarlett didn't always pick up on the moments I was in another time zone, but Nicholas was two for two. "How can you tell when I'm having a vision?"

He gripped my hand. "Do you feel that?" He gently squeezed for emphasis.

The same jolt of energy I'd felt the first time we touched skin to skin traveled up my arm and through my body, erasing all other thoughts. I may not have much experience with guys, but this was ridiculous. I started to pull my hand away.

"Wait," he said, not letting go, "do you feel it?"

Every cell in my body hummed with awareness.

"We share a link—all of us do. When you have a vision, it's almost as if the air around you is alive." He still hadn't released my hand, and his face glowed as if he too were savoring our connection.

It felt amazing, and it made me wonder what it would be like if we touched more than hands. Vivid mental images leapt to mind, and his eyes met mine as if he not only sensed my thoughts but shared them as well.

The ringing phone of a passerby recalled me to the moment. I tugged my hand away, rubbing it as if it burned. "That was, ah, interesting."

His lips turned up into a knowing grin. "There are definitely some perks to being one of us."

In that moment, it would be easy to pretend we were simply two people finding common ground, but the questions raised by my vision wouldn't let me forget why we were there.

"What does it mean, that I'm a Class One?" I asked.

A look of wariness passed over his face. "What did you see?"

"You were right. I *can* see into the past." Sticking to the facts, I told him what I'd witnessed. "How did you dig up all that personal stuff on me?" My psych evaluation was privileged information.

He shrugged. "Everyone is investigated and tracked if and when they reach Class Two. We have fleets of scouts known as sentinels whose sole purpose is to find people like you."

I flashed back to the age of fourteen, the year Henry Thorne said I'd hit that milestone. It was my freshman year at the high school from hell, a rambling institution with almost three thousand students in the middle of Central California's farm country. The student body was an uneasy mix of languages and cultures, the kids of migrant farm workers forced to contend with the entitled offspring of the area's wealthy landowners and professionals. It seemed the only thing they could all agree on was their mutual dislike of me.

I couldn't blame them. Each time I entered a crowded class-room I'd stumble my way to a seat, bombarded by images of passion and pain, tragedy and triumph. I probably looked like an escapee from the psych ward by the time school ended each day.

And then came the day that cemented my reputation.

I had been shuffling between classes like always, trying to be invisible, when suddenly and violently, my brain got hi-jacked. It was like being caught in an undertow. Shaking, I slumped against a bank of lockers, squeezing my eyes shut and putting every ounce of strength I had into fighting the invasion. It passed within seconds, but the damage was done. When I opened my eyes, my upgrade to the official school freak was complete.

"Oh my God," I exclaimed. "That was you?"

He flushed slightly. "Your file said you had an unusually strong reaction during your first contact."

I reared back. "Is that what they called it? Do you have any idea what you people did to me?"

"You have to understand your reaction was completely un-expected and caught our investigator totally off guard. A Class Two shouldn't have even known he was there."

I couldn't believe he was asking *me* to understand how dis-turbing it might have been for *them*. I would have said so, but our conversation had to be put on hold as we entered the food court where the lunchtime rush was in full swing.

We got in line behind Scarlett, who waited her turn at Food for Thought, a glass-fronted kiosk with a chalkboard propped out front listing sandwiches and salads. She shot a pointed look at Nicholas before turning her attention back to yet another magazine quiz, this one titled *How To Know If He's The One*. She had the magazine stowed and the lid off her salad by the time we joined her at one of the outdoor tables.

"I've taken three years of fencing and can stop a man's heart with a single thrust," she said to Nicholas, her fork vi-ciously stabbing a cucumber for emphasis.

"Good to know." He gave her the same disarming smile he'd turned on me when we first met, but her eyes narrowed slightly. Smile fading, he said, "We're on the same side here. We both want to keep Blake safe."

She scoffed. "We were doing fine until you showed up."

"He knows." I unwrapped my tuna sandwich. "They've been watching us for years, though apparently I'm some big secret."

"What do you mean, a secret?" she asked, her gaze darting between Nicholas and me.

He took a bite of his turkey sandwich before answering. "My father felt keeping Blake's existence known only to a select few was the best way to avoid others from making contact before she was ready."

"Ready for what?" she demanded before another voice cut in.

"May I join you?" Warren stood behind the empty seat next to Scarlett, a pizza slice and a soda in hand.

"Of course." Scarlett looked at Warren with the expression of sympathy I knew well, the one that said even if your problems couldn't be fixed, she'd be happy to share a pint of Ben & Jerry's while you talked them out. Warren, on the other hand, looked terrible. I couldn't believe the transformation that had taken place in less than twenty-four hours, but the best word to describe him was haunted.

"I didn't think you'd be here today," she said.

Warren slipped into the empty seat. "I didn't want to be alone. Every time I close my eyes, all I see is the way Kevin looked at me before they drove off." He pulled in a shaky breath before turning to me. "Thank you. I don't think my mom could've handled it if something had happened to me."

I glanced at Nicholas, who reached over and gave my hand a reassuring squeeze as if to remind me to focus on the life I'd saved rather than on the ones I couldn't.

"Scarlett said I shouldn't ask too many questions," he continued, his voice thick with emotion. "But how can I pretend you didn't know about the accident when I'm here and they're not? Please, I have to know. Why did you save me?"

Until yesterday, I would have argued there was no why, that life was completely random, get over it. But if what Nicholas said was true, and there was a purpose to my premonitions, then Warren had been spared for a reason. Though what fate had in store for a shaggy-haired skater boy was a mystery to me.

"You're here because you're supposed to be," I said simply. "I wish I had a better answer for you, but there's a lot I'm still figuring out myself. This is Nicholas Thorne, by the way."

Nicholas extended his hand, and Warren did likewise. "Warren Hartman."

"I'm very sorry about your friends," Nicholas said. "I regret not having done more to stop them." At my raised brow, Nicholas sent me a look that let me know I wasn't the only one questioning certain long-held beliefs. "Eventually we'll figure out why you were the one to be saved."

Warren only looked more bewildered, if that was possible. He reached for Scarlett's hand like it would somehow set the world right. I wouldn't have thought twice about it, but the gentle way she regarded him in return spoke volumes. There would be time to contemplate it all later but right now, I had another thought in mind.

"Warren, have you told anyone I warned you before the accident happened?"

He shook his head. "No one would believe it. I'm not even sure *I* believe it."

I breathed a sigh of relief. It might be selfish, but I was relieved my anonymity was still intact. "Then please, this needs to be a secret, just among the four of us."

Tiger Lady

C indy was behind the counter when I walked into Jitters for the evening shift. She was a sweet girl who oddly peppered her sentences with words like "gosh" and "gee whiz." That wouldn't have been so weird if she looked like the girl next door, but her style was more like the girl next door if you lived in a Tim Burton movie.

She wore eyeliner like a ghoul, dressed Goth, and had an encyclopedic knowledge of every horror movie ever made. She'd worked at Jitters since graduating high school a few years before but showed no signs of ambition beyond attending cosplay conventions with her loser boyfriend Todd and his geeky friends.

Al's office was in the former bank vault, and I stowed my purse in a large safety deposit box before pulling an apron from the stack. They all had coffee quotes printed on them, and tonight mine read, *You haven't had enough coffee until you can thread a sewing machine while it's running.*

We got busy fast. Even Al was pressed into service to keep up with demand, and I had little time to think of much else.

I was behind the bar, making change for a customer. All kinds of people came through the place, so it didn't occur to me at first that the woman waiting at the counter was anyone out of the ordinary.

She was tall and thin, with catlike eyes the color of butter-scotch. Thick dreads flowed halfway down her back, and the skimpy silk tunic she wore showed off flawless copper skin. Her most striking feature, however, was a tattoo that began on her neck (God only knew where it ended). It was of a fearsome tiger with claws at her throat, his teeth poised to sink into her jugular, but I was still clueless she might want anything more than a large hot chocolate to ward off the evening chill.

As fast as a striking cobra, her hand shot across the bar and latched onto my wrist. The telltale jolt of energy from another Nine came hard and fast, but it wasn't the seductive warmth I'd felt when Nicholas had taken my hand. I gasped and tried to pull away, but she held fast, a steely grin plastered on her face as she stared me down. Her cold eyes raked over me, and my adrenalin spiked. With our physical connection it would be easy to reach into her mind and see how *she* liked being messed with.

A thick layer of fog shielded her memories, and I only managed to glimpse a few violent and disconnected images before the window into her brain slammed shut. That had never happened before. Ever.

She instantly released me, and we both stared at the other with shock.

"What are you?" Her lilting accent called up images of blue waters and rum drinks, though her expression was anything but tranquil.

I rubbed the half-moons her claws had left on my skin and tried to shrug off my panic. "That's none of your business."

She reached into the back pocket of her skin-tight pants and slapped a business card down on the counter. "Whatever interests the Thornes interests my employer. We'll be expecting your call." She looked me over again before sauntering out the door.

As if someone had momentarily muted the volume, the sounds of the coffeehouse resumed. I inched over to the counter and picked up the business card with my fingernails as if it were contaminated with bubonic plague. The card belonged to real estate magnate Sutton Sinclair. Was it possible that one of the city's most powerful men was also a member of The Nine?

"Blake, are you okay?" Selena and Chico watched me with concern, though in the dog's case it was probably because he thought I might forget his daily treat. I postponed my personal freak out in favor of whipping up her decaf chai latte and tossing the pooch a biscuit.

I continued to go through the motions of waiting on customers until I heard Cindy mutter appreciatively, "Oh my goodness!"

Nicholas had walked in. With his long stride, *GQ* wardrobe, and classic good looks, he *was* kind of hard to miss. He came directly to the counter, and Cindy moved at warp speed to take his order. She leaned over, giving him a spectacular view of the cloud of bats tattooed across her chest.

"See something you like?" she said in a voice that encouraged him to order off menu. Her boyfriend would choke on one of his ridiculous clove cigarettes if he could see her now.

The rush had died down to a pace manageable for one barista, so I whipped off my apron. "I'm taking my break now." I slipped under the bar and dragged Nicholas to an unoccupied corner table and away from my suddenly annoying coworker.

"I'm happy to see you, too," he said with a laugh, dropping into a chair.

"A woman was here," I said, perching on the edge of my own seat. "A tall, scary, tiger tattooed lady who somehow pushed me out of her head."

Nicholas sobered immediately. "What do you mean, pushed you out of her head?"

"I got a few images from her, but that was all." Though now that I thought about it, how had she even known I'd tried to invade her memories? No one had ever detected my presence before. Then I registered his complete lack of surprise. "You know her?"

He nodded. "Her name is Khalia Clarke, and she's a very powerful sentinel. They have the ability to evaluate each person's specific connection but are immune to any of our influences." He leaned forward, his gaze penetrating. "You shouldn't have been able to see into her mind at all."

I pulled the business card she gave me from my back pocket. "She left this."

His expression hardened when he read the card. "She worked for us until about six months ago. Now I see who gave her a better offer." He glanced back up at me. "Sutton Sinclair is slowly chipping away at my father's allies."

"So he's part of The Nine, too?" It was the only logical explanation.

Nicholas nodded. "He's an elementalist, someone who can control earth, water, fire and wind. Most elementalists are more powerful in one element than any other and with Sutton, it's earth."

It made perfect sense, of course. Sinclair had an amazing record of success with his development company, building one huge project after another. I suppose you never had to worry about the soundness of the land you built on when you could shape it any way you wished.

Nicholas had said people would be interested in my skills, but I couldn't imagine what a powerful man like Sinclair could want with me. "Once he hears I'm just a voyant, he'll leave me alone, right?" My fingers drummed anxiously on the table.

Nicholas placed a calming hand across mine. The energy sparked between us, and his breath quickened as if he felt it too. "I wish I could say that was true," he said, "but voyants are the rarest among us."

It took real effort not to be distracted by our connection. I'd spent most of my life avoiding human contact, so even an innocent touch from a troll would probably make me melt from the inside out. Of course, Nicholas was about as far from a troll as you could possibly get.

"How rare?" I asked, hoping my cheeks weren't as flushed as the rest of me.

"You're only the ninth living voyant we know of." He smiled. "Kind of poetic, wouldn't you say?"

I stopped listening after he said there were eight other people like me. Maybe it wasn't a lot as far as he was concerned, but that was eight more than I'd known about thirty seconds ago. "Where are they? Can I meet them? Are any of them close by?"

He laughed at my rapid-fire questions. "Let's see. Two are in Africa, one is in Japan, a couple are in Europe, one in Peru, and one is in New Orleans."

"That's only seven," I pointed out. "Where's number eight?"

His thumb stroked the back of my hand, and I wondered if he was even aware of it. "He was last sighted about three months ago in Australia. He said he'd rather go it alone than enjoy the protection of The Nine."

I'd initially said the same thing, but now I wasn't so sure. "Are there many who refuse, er, membership?"

His face took on a grim expression. "No, but there are a brave few. Those who refuse to pledge are known as Shadow Nines. Their existence can't be called much of a life, though, always looking over their shoulder. Shadows are often targeted by the criminal element among us because they know we won't do anything to help them, and it's not like they can call the police if they're being threatened. What would they say? I'm being forced at gunpoint to read minds or to use my telekinesis to stop a train? An American named Jesse James went down for that last one, by the way." He pointedly met my gaze. "Those people's lives are spent on the run."

My relationship with my sister was already strained. I could only imagine what would happen if someone tried to use her as a bargaining chip to force me to perform on command.

"Let's say I agreed to join The Nine. What then?" I asked.

"Every door would be open to you, starting with access to the other voyants. We've also had centuries of investing and collecting, and our resources are beyond your wildest imagination. Just at Alder House alone we have a collection of art and literature that are unequaled by any museum or library in the world." His face lit up as he warmed to his topic. "Shakespeare wrote several plays about our people never seen by the outside world, and wait til you see what Da Vinci did with the entire top floor at Alder House."

It sounded magical, and to a certain extent it was, but nothing this extraordinary came without a price. "And what would I have to do in return?"

He paused as he considered his words. "Each discipline has certain, ah, obligations. As I've already mentioned, voyants are asked to occasionally use their gift for the purpose we believe it was intended."

If my mom were sitting there, she'd tell me there was no higher calling than to use my ability to save lives. I'd even signed up for a chemistry class in case I decided to follow her into medicine. So then why did I recoil at the idea of letting someone else decide when and where I opened myself up to premonitions if they could help people?

"How do you know when someone needs saving, and how do I find them?" It seemed an impossible conundrum—how would they know who needed saving before I told them?

"They will come to you," he explained. "Call it faith or call it fate."

If what he said was true, Warren forgetting his pen and then sitting down next to me had been no accident.

"Is that what you stopped by to tell me?" I asked, unsure how to feel about being part of some grand cosmic design.

"No, I wanted to make sure you had my number." His eyes flicked to Sinclair's card on the table between us. "Now I'm glad I did."

"You could have texted me." If he had my psych report, he must also have my cell number.

"I could have," he said, his eyes meeting mine again with an intensity that made my heart skip a beat. "But then what other excuse would I have to see you?"

I dropped my gaze, unsure what was happening between us. It had been a long, lonely stretch since my first and only disastrous date last year, so maybe I was reading too much into Nicholas's words. The guy I'd gone out with hadn't had Nicholas's looks, but he'd been smart and funny, and kissing him might have been fun. I'd been determined to avoid ruining it by slipping into the twilight zone, but a momentary lapse of control forced me to witness the humiliating bet he'd made with his friends. Asking out the class freak had been only part of the challenge. Wagers had been made on how far he could take me in the back seat of his car.

I'd been so hurt I lashed out with the most effective weapon at hand. I dove into his past with the single-minded goal of seeking out his most painful memory. I hit pay dirt.

"Your father is right," I'd said, my words dripping venom. "You are a worthless piece of trash who drove your mother away."

It was not my proudest moment. He'd been heartless and cruel, but I'd sunk to his level. His anguish was later apparent whenever we crossed paths at school. It was yet another painful memory I'd hoped to escape with the move to Santa Carla.

"My phone is in my purse," I said. "I'll put your number in as soon as my shift is over."

"I've got a better idea." He crossed the room to retrieve a Sharpie from a cup near the register. When he turned away, Cindy caught my eye and clearly mouthed: *OH. MY. GOSH!*

Back at the table he reached over and slowly rolled up my sleeve. My flesh tingled as he jotted down his number on the delicate skin of my forearm. "Call me, day or night, for anything."

We stared at each other as his words hung in the air. Out of my depth, I pushed back my chair, ending the moment.

"I need to get back to work," I said, avoiding his gaze. We both got to our feet.

"What are you thinking?" He stood close enough for me to take in his clean, subtle scent.

I dared to tilt my face up to his. "I think there's a lot I don't know about your world."

He leaned in slowly, and my lips parted. He lowered his face to mine, but at the last moment, he dropped a kiss on my cheek. "Then allow me to show you," he said before disappearing into the night.

Ashley Norman

I'd arranged my school schedule to have Fridays off, and I used those mornings to get a jumpstart on the weekend's homework and chores. Then when Scarlett got home with the car later in the day, we'd do a grocery run.

She'd left me a pot of coffee and had even brought in the newspaper. I was probably the last person in America under the age of thirty to still subscribe to a daily paper, but I'd picked up the habit from my dad. He always grabbed the obituary pages first, saying the stories of lives well lived were the best modern history lessons a dollar could buy.

I was at the kitchen table doctoring a cup of coffee when I saw her picture. There was no mistaking the perfectly styled blonde hair, the aggressive smile, and the eyes already looking past the photographer to the next item on her to do list. It was little Ms. Blackmailer, the woman who'd sent that vile email while sitting at Jitters two nights ago. Her name was Ashley Norman and according to the headline, she was dead.

"Holy crap," I said, setting my mug down harder than intended.

The story said she'd been killed the day before, struck by a car at the busy downtown intersection of Hope and Carmen. The distraught driver, a middle-age mom taking her son to his violin lesson, claimed the car flew out of control. Witnesses reported they heard the sound of an engine gunning, leading police to suspect the presence of drugs or alcohol, though none were found at the scene.

I dropped the paper, wrapping my suddenly icy fingers around the hot mug. Was it merely coincidence she'd committed extortion one day and was dead the next? Would I have seen her impending doom if her blackmailing scheme hadn't stood in the way? Or was her fate not sealed until she'd hit the send button a few minutes after my premonition?

She'd been in management at the Bank of Santa Carla, the story read, and had been "a valued employee," her boss was quoted as saying. Not exactly the most stirring epitaph. I grabbed a pair of scissors to cut out the article while debating what to do next.

My first reaction was to call Nicholas but being around him confused the hell out of me. His father had sent him with a job in mind, and I was pretty sure it didn't include hooking up with me. Henry Thorne had called me "insurance"; what did that even mean? I grabbed my phone, knowing whom I really needed to call. It picked up after two rings.

"Luke Wilder."

"Dad?"

"Hey, honey." The warmth in his voice flowed through the receiver. I pictured him in his cramped office at Bachman College, a small private school in Central California. He'd have his silver wire-rimmed spectacles perched at the tip of his nose, his salt-and-pepper curls most likely needing a haircut, and his eyes would be brimming with good humor.

"Do you have a minute?" He would say yes even if he had an entire class waiting for a lecture on the most gruesome forms of torture used during the Spanish Inquisition (guaranteed to pack the house).

"You know I always have time for you." This was his attitude toward life in general, and one of the reasons he was the most popular professor in the history department.

"I don't want to worry you, but my premonitions seem to be ramping up. I'm starting to see stuff that's more than just somebody falling off a bike or getting into a fender bender. People are getting hurt." I would ease into the part where I mentioned the hurt was fatal.

"How often has this happened?"

I technically hadn't foreseen Ashley Norman's death. I also hadn't known for sure that Eddie and Kevin would die.

"Well, once maybe, but I've been told it'll happen more and more."

There was complete silence on the other end, but I knew I had his undivided attention. "Who told you this?"

"This is going to sound a little weird," I said, pinching the bridge of my nose, "but I've been contacted by a representative of a whole society of special people—people like me."

"Who?" That one word in his take-no-prisoners voice spoke volumes.

"His name is Nicholas Thorne, he's about my age, and he's from a place in England called Alder House." The last thing I expected to hear was a muttered curse. "You know them, Dad?"

"I, uh, met one of their people at that German conference I went to a few years ago." One of the few perks of his job—besides the low pay, long hours, and ungrateful administrators—were the summer conferences he got to attend.

"But you didn't know their members were, um, different, right?" He would have told me if he did. I waited for him to express surprise at that revelation but was met with silence. That's when I realized he *did* know. "Oh."

"All I wanted was to keep you safe," he rushed to say, his voice begging me to understand and forgive. "These people exist behind walls of secrets and subterfuge, and I was afraid of what would happen if you went looking for them."

My world had suddenly tumbled off its axis. "You knew there were others like me, and you never said anything?" My ability fascinated him, and we had always talked openly about it. "You know how much I suffered thinking I was all alone."

"I know, but every time I tried to dig into their history, phone numbers became disconnected, websites suddenly disappeared," he explained. "I've barely been able to scratch the surface of who they are or what they do, so imagine if they became interested in a special girl like you. Where would I begin looking if you suddenly disappeared?"

I didn't know what to say or how to react. This was still my dad, the man I loved most in the world, yet it was as if a door had slammed on my childhood, and I'd crossed over a dividing line from which there was no return. I'd been telling my parents for months not to worry about me, that I was an adult and could take care of myself. If that was true, I must now view his actions through that same prism of maturity and wisdom I'd so proudly claimed as my right.

"I'm sorry," he said, filling the silence that had overtaken us again. "You have every right to be angry."

I wasn't angry, I realized. He'd made the only decision he could live with, and I would have to do the same. "Promise me something."

"Anything. You know that."

"Stop trying to protect me. From now on, tell me everything you dig up and help me protect myself."

He didn't answer right away. Our relationship was being redefined with one phone call, and it was probably harder for him than for me.

"I promise," he said at last. "Now tell me: what do they want?"

"They want me to pledge to The Nine, whatever that means." A bunch of classmates had recently gone through rush week and were now vowing loyalty to various sororities and fraternities, but somehow I didn't think The Nine would be handing me a sweatshirt and inviting me to a kegger. "But there's something else. I'm afraid I may have seen something that led to a woman's maybe not so accidental death."

He connected the dots pretty fast. "You need to come home. I want both you and Scarlett to get in the car, and I want—"

"Dad! No, I'm not coming home. Running away won't solve anything. You know that. What I want is your help in deciding what to do now."

I heard a few choice words muttered under his breath. Begrudgingly, he asked, "What does this Nicholas character think you should do?"

"I just found out a woman I'd had a vision of supposedly died in an accident, and you're the first one I called." It wouldn't kill me to let him know he was still at the top of my list.

"You got a number for this guy?"

I read the number straight off my arm, though I didn't tell him that. It would take more than one shower to scrub off the Sharpie.

"You know you'll always be my girl, right?"

Instantly the tension leftover from our clash disappeared.

"I know." But now it was time to be my own woman.

"Speaking of girls," he said, his voice taking on a worried note, "would you give your sister a call?"

"Why, because she misses me so much?" Within months of starting high school, Jordan had frozen me out of her life. The only communication we'd had since I left was her texting to ask if I'd packed a certain sweater she coveted. When I said I had, she didn't bother texting back.

"Jordan is kind of touchy these days. Maybe you can find out what's going on."

I laughed. "It's called hormones, Dad."
"If you say so, honey," he said doubtfully. "If you say so."

End of the Innocence

It was still early in the day when the strident buzzer that passed as our doorbell rang. Nicholas stood on my doorstep, his expression tight. "May I come in?"

"That depends," I said. "Why do you look like someone peed in your tea?"

He glanced at the Jitters cup in his hand with distaste. "Thank you for ruining a perfectly decent cup of Earl Grey."

I stepped back and swung the door open wide. "There's still some coffee in the pot if you want, though by now it's probably aged past infancy and entered its troubled teen years."

He shuddered. "I'll never understand Americans' obsession with coffee."

Scarlett and I had carved a living room and dining area out of the rectangular space not taken up by the kitchen at the far end of the apartment but with limited success. I gestured to the seating arrangement made up of two brown easy chairs facing a slip-covered relic of a sofa in faded blue canvas. In between lurked a mahogany coffee table marred with water rings we'd hauled back from a garage sale.

"Your father called," he said, settling into one of the chairs and placing his tea on the table. "He said you had a vision of a woman who's since turned up dead."

"It's more complicated than that." Taking a seat on the sofa, I told him what I'd seen and my theory that Ashley Norman's fate hadn't been sealed until she'd sent her extortion demand.

"Then her loss, while tragic, doesn't affect us." He relaxed. "Your father was remarkably open-minded. He was quite eager to learn more about The Nine, and your potential place within it."

No kidding. He'd probably questioned Nicholas in the guise of a concerned father rather than the informed academic I knew him to be.

"You're not worried he'll tell someone?" They hadn't kept a low profile all these centuries by being careless.

He waved a dismissive hand. "If you don't join us, he'll be dealt with."

"Excuse me?" I half-rose to my feet, alarmed by his ominous words.

Nicholas grinned. "Relax. I only meant his memory of our conversation would be erased by an enchanter, which is completely harmless. What did you think I meant?"

I sank back onto the sofa. "You're not funny, you know."

"I think I'm hilarious," he said, enjoying the moment. He extended a hand, and his cup hopped into it.

I started in surprise. "How long have you been able to do that?" I could only imagine what it would be like to raise a kid who could turn toys into guided missiles.

"Not until I was fifteen. We all come into our abilities at different times, but I have to say, when I discovered I was a telekinetic, it wasn't a moment too soon."

How different my life would have been if I'd been practically an adult when my clairvoyance kicked in.

"My mum always said I would have a special skill," he continued. "I assumed it would be something intuitive like her."

"Intuitive?"

"She was a telepath," he said in an offhand manner, as if people who could read minds were as common as reality show housewives. "She died when I was twelve."

"That's terrible." I couldn't imagine losing a parent at an age when I'd needed them more than ever. "That must have been so hard for you."

He brushed aside my sympathy. "I waited for some sign, something that would tell me what my place was in The Nine, but nothing came. We lived at Alder House among some of the most extraordinary people in existence, yet every time I walked into a room, I could feel their pity. I had to go away to boarding school because only Nines can attend class there."

Despite an outward calm, his memory of the day he'd discovered his ability must have been highly compelling because I could suddenly feel the lure of his mind. I resisted, but electricity danced in the air. He tensed slightly, and I knew he felt it, too.

He sent his cup hopping back to the table and moved to sit next to me on the sofa. Very deliberately he placed his hand across mine. With the switch thrown, I stepped over the threshold.

The boy in the mirror was in the twilight of his youth. His handsome face still retained the soft innocence of childhood, but he had to stoop to reach one of the low hanging sinks as he washed his hands. It was Nicholas at fifteen, and from the row of stalls behind him, he appeared to be in a large boys' bathroom.

An outside door banged open, and half a dozen boys slouched into the room. They all wore the same school uniform as Nicholas: navy blazers, white shirts, and cornflower blue ties. Recent growth spurts made some of them look like they were about to bust a seam or two. They formed a loose ring behind Nicholas.

The biggest kid, a brutish-looking boy with his lip curled in scorn, stepped forward. "What a surprise," he said, his voice laced with sarcasm. "Thorne admiring his girly face in the mirror, again."

Nicholas's expression remained neutral. If he were scared or intimidated, he refused to show it. He turned from the mirror. "I have no beef with you, Stanton."

"That's too damn bad," the other boy snarled. "Cuz we've got one with you. Evans!"

A gangly boy with narrow shoulders and a bad case of acne stepped forward. He quivered with outrage as he faced down Nicholas.

"Julia Martin won't go to the dance with me," he said as if her refusal was an insult of biblical proportions. "Do you know why?"

Nicholas shrugged dismissively. "Because you're a douche?"

Evans flushed an angry shade of red. "Always a smart answer for everything." He glanced at Stanton. "I'll pay you one hundred pounds if you make sure Julia Martin never wants to see Thorne's ugly face again."

"Okay boys, you heard 'im." Stanton grinned maliciously at Nicholas. "Maybe if you're real lucky, we'll let you keep some of your teeth."

Nicholas's chest rose and fell with the shallow breaths of a cornered animal, but that was the only sign of his inner turmoil. The bully came at him with a cocked fist and let it fly. Nicholas was able to block it for the most part, though Stanton's pinkie ring left a small gash on his cheek.

"Hold him!" Stanton ordered, and a couple of boys rushed forward to pin Nicholas's arms.

"Get off of me!" Nicholas cried, and amazingly, Stanton flew across the room to bash into a tiled wall. The boys holding Nicholas captive both stumbled back a few steps as if they'd been shoved.

The bathroom windows began to rattle, the stall doors violently banged open and shut, and one by one the faucet handles along the row of sinks burst skyward as if they were jet propelled. The remaining boys froze in fear as the room came alive around them.

"Leave me alone!" Nicholas yelled. The exit door crashed open as if it had been kicked.

Abandoning their ringleader, the gang of boys fell over each other in their terrified dash to escape. As the door slammed shut behind them, the room quieted until only a few stall doors swung lazily on their hinges.

Nicholas stepped over to where Stanton slumped on the floor. He hunkered down to meet his foe's stunned gaze.

"You and your gang of thugs are no longer running this school," Nicholas said. A teardrop of blood oozed from his cut and slowly made its way down his cheek. "The next time you come near me, you won't be walking away. Do you understand?"

Stanton glared at Nicholas before nodding in agreement.

Nicholas swiped his cheek with the back of his hand. The blood smeared, obscuring what was left of the boy he had been.

I flashed back to the present, and the first thing I noticed was the faint scar on Nicholas's cheek. I half raised my hand to touch the smooth white line before coming to my senses.

"Why did you show me that?" Rarely had I been invited into someone's memories. Even my dad refused to communicate that way and seemed relieved I'd never picked up a stray vision from him.

"I guess," he said, drawing it out as if he weren't quite clear himself, "I wanted you to see it's not easy for anyone. I know you had a rough go of it, but it does get better."

"Did they leave you alone after that?"

He smiled at the memory. "Stanton got expelled for vandalism. His friends pinned the damage to the bathroom on him. I might also have found inventive ways to torture that dirtbag Evans and practice my new skills until I moved back to Alder House and started school there." He made it seem like embracing who you were was the answer to everything.

"If I were to take just one step in the direction you want me to go," I asked, "where would that lead me?"

"Are you free tonight?"

I nodded. I wasn't scheduled to work, and Netflix would survive without me for a night. He stood. "I'll pick you up at eight. Wear a dress."

I shot to my feet. "Wait—where are we going?"

"Someplace that will answer every question you've ever had about who you are." When I hesitated, he stepped closer. "Would you trust me? Just a little?"

I glanced away. "I, um, don't really own like a dress up dress." I lived in jeans, and it's not like I'd ever really needed a date dress.

He smiled. "I've got the company credit card. We can fix that."

Fifteen minutes later we were in Jasmine's Boutique. It was on the same street as Jitters, and it was the first place that came to mind when Nicholas asked where I wanted to shop.

The lone salesgirl eyed us inquisitively, probably trying to figure out what a gorgeous guy like him was doing with a girl in sweats and a ponytail. I stood lost in the middle of the store, not sure where to begin in a place that didn't sell denim.

Nicholas had no such problem. Despite the clerk trotting after him like a besotted puppy, he flipped though several racks before an expression of triumph flashed across his face. He held up a silky dress in a rich shade of sapphire. "This one."

I made a face. "It's so...blue." There'd be no flying under the radar wearing that.

"Trust me." He steered me to the dressing room.

"You say that a lot," I grumbled. The sooner I tried it on, the sooner he'd see we should stick with something a little less dramatic.

Once in the dressing room, I yanked off my pullover, losing my hair tie in the process. The cut of the dress would make wearing a bra impossible, so off that came as well. As I tugged the dress over my head, the salesgirl thrust a pair of silver sandals with sky-high heels through the curtain. There wasn't a mirror in the cubicle, so once I'd buckled on the shoes, I emerged.

The shocked look on the clerk's face made me wonder if I'd put the dress on backwards, but the glow in Nicholas's eyes told a different story. I turned to a triptych of mirrors set up in the dressing area and stared.

The dress was perfection. The bodice hugged what modest curves I had while the rest of the dress skimmed my slender figure. The color brought out the blue in my eyes, and my hair, freed from the elastic, fell in loose waves.

Nicholas came to stand behind me. His heated gaze touched upon every inch of my skin before meeting my eyes in the mirror.

"Blake Wilder, you are beautiful."

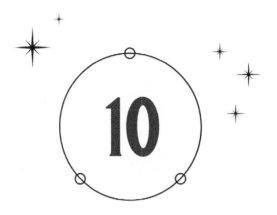

The Lower 8

I wasn't the only one nervously awaiting a knock at the door.

"Warren asked me to dinner," Scarlett said, rushing to add, "to thank me for my help this week." If all Warren wanted was to show his gratitude, he'd have sent flowers.

She wore a black wrap dress, snug to the waist and flared out at the hips. Her beautiful red hair had been pulled off her face, and her eyes sparkled with anticipation. She'd bagged a couple of boys in the drama department last year but had decided sex without love wasn't for her. I wasn't the only one starting over in Santa Carla.

"Don't take this the wrong way," she said, "but are you sure you know what you're doing?"

I had asked myself the same question every time I'd looked in the mirror tonight. The girl in the blue dress appeared worldly and experienced, but I was neither of those things. Maybe she could handle a guy as compelling as Nicholas, or be excited by the evening's mysterious agenda, but the girl in jeans had serious doubts.

"No," I admitted, my quivering voice betraying my fears. "But I've been running from who I am and what I can do my entire life. How will I ever be free if I don't stop and face this?"

I'd spoken to my dad again, and he'd agreed I should learn as much about The Nine as possible, insisting we first activate my phone's tracking app before I went anywhere. He in turn told me Nicholas had given him access to a website specifically intended for parents of unusual kids, though it was very generic and lacked much detail. Keeping it sketchy probably made it easier to suck the memory of it from his brain later, though I didn't mention that to him.

"Have you told Mom about any of this?" I'd asked him.

In Dr. Charlotte Wilder's well-ordered life, everything had a rational, scientific explanation. The house painter who suddenly spoke with a foreign accent was discovered to have a brain tumor. The kid whose skin turned blue turned out to be the victim of a colloidal silver overdose given to him by his off-the-grid parents claiming it was an alternative allergy medication. There were no problems that couldn't be solved, no mysteries not rooted in reality, and she maintained an abnormal chromosome was responsible for my visions. I often wondered how she ended up married to a man who collected and told stories about dead people for a living.

"Oh, you know," he'd hedged. "I'll tell her when we have something to tell."

Growing up, the phrase "Don't tell your mother" had been a constant refrain. I'd once thought we were keeping the day-to-day stuff from her because hearing about my visions would make her angry. It wasn't until I was a teen and overheard a tearful conversation that I understood my dad was protecting her. I'd unthinkingly blurted out the news that a boy she'd recently treated for a broken arm would be back in the next few days with multiple fractures given to him by his stepfather. She would move heaven and earth to help her patients, and it killed her she couldn't stop the horrors of the world from filling my head.

Scarlett's voice recalled me to the moment. "You could have dinner with me and Warren and tell Pretty Boy to take a hike."

The blaring doorbell interrupted our debate. I opened the door, but Warren's eyes darted right past me. The way he looked at Scarlett confirmed my suspicions.

"Wow," he said softly. "I mean, you look great, Scarlett." He spared me a quick glance. "You too, Blake." I wasn't the least bit offended when he immediately returned his admiring gaze to my best friend. "Are you ready?"

She grabbed her purse but then paused in front of me. "Haven't you ever wondered why I've never been bothered by what you can do?"

Of course I had, but to question her friendship seemed like tempting fate, and I was too afraid of what I might hear. As long as we never talked about what being my friend cost her, there wasn't any risk of losing her or the closeness we shared.

"It's because one day I know you will find a way to do something special with it," she said. "No matter what Nicholas tells you, decide for yourself what you want. Don't be the victim, be the hero."

I gave her a watery smile, touched by her faith in me. I glanced at Warren to see what he made of all this, and he shrugged. "Sounds good to me," he said agreeably.

This was Scarlett's first date in ages, and I wasn't going to spoil it by getting all weepy. "Go. Have fun," I ordered, waving them out the door.

Five minutes later the bell buzzed again. I opened the door, and my mouth went dry. Nicholas was dressed in a coal black suit, the kind with a subtle sheen that softly reflected the light. Underneath he wore a pristine white dress shirt, the top few buttons left undone to reveal a smooth expanse of collarbone. By the time I got to his face, he wore a faintly amused expression.

"You, ah, look great," I said, my cheeks pinking at being caught staring.

His appreciative gaze swept over me. "No one will even notice me standing in your shadow tonight." Despite my doubts and reservations, I'd have to be completely braindead not to feel a rush of pleasure at being complimented by an incredibly attractive guy. "Are you ready?" A gleaming black Tesla waited at the curb.

"Nice car," I said, pulling the front door closed behind me.

"It seemed appropriate," he said. "Nikola Tesla was an evanescent, which is someone who can conjure and direct energy."

"Of course he was." I wondered if I'd ever get used to these pronouncements.

The car doors shot open as we neared.

"Aren't you worried about people seeing things move by themselves?" We were alone on the street, but that didn't mean prying eyes weren't watching from behind drawn curtains.

He pulled out his phone and flashed the Tesla app. "Amazing what they can do with electronics these days, don't you think?"

We were headed downtown when I asked, "You promised answers. Isn't it time you told me where we're going?"

He tapped a few icons on the car's touchscreen to adjust the music volume and temperature before answering. "Santa Carla is one of our sanctuary cities. Nines from all over the world know they can come here and find others of our kind."

"Okay," I said, remembering how Henry Thorne had made such a big deal about the town. "But what does that have to do with tonight?"

"If you're going to bring people together, they need a place to meet."

My stomach dropped. "We're going to a place…filled with Nines?" He must have heard the panic in my voice because he grabbed my hand and a wave of calming energy surged through me.

"There are dozens of colleges you could have gone to in California," he said. "What made you choose Santa Carla?"

I blinked at the abrupt shift in topic and answered without thought. "I just knew it was where I wanted to go."

"And why do you think that is?" The harsh glare of oncoming headlights revealed his earnest expression.

Goosebumps prickled. "What are you saying?"

"What I said before. We are all connected, and you feeling compelled to come here wasn't an accident."

It was like a punch in the throat. My big bid for freedom, for control of my life had been an illusion. All I'd done was deliver myself right into the arms of The Nine. We passed through downtown without either of us saying a word.

"Are you okay?" he finally asked.

I shook off the feeling of being dropped into a game where I didn't know the rules and focused on the here and now. "Why did your father call me insurance?"

He flinched at the unexpected question. Welcome to life with a voyant. "Henry is worried about our future. Your presence would help protect the people of The Nine from those who would see our way of life destroyed."

"You call your dad Henry?" My father fondly reminisced about the days when I still called him daddy. He'd shut me down if I ever called him Luke.

"There came a time when it seemed…appropriate."

I wondered what friction had brought them to that point, but mostly I wanted to know if people like Sutton Sinclair really posed such a threat, or if he was simply being used as leverage to suck me in.

"Will people know what I am?" I glanced down at the graceful folds of my skirt. It would definitely be a waste of a fabulous dress if I insisted he turn the car around.

"Any Class One sentinel—" he began before catching my impatient frown. "Khalia must know, and of course she would have told Sinclair, but since Henry kept your evaluation under wraps, I doubt either of them yet knows how strong you are. However, even if you decide you don't want to go through with this, it won't be long before word about a new voyant gets around."

I drew a ragged breath. Revealing my otherness to anybody, even other Nines, went completely against my nature, but wheels had been set in motion that couldn't be stopped.

We entered Santa Carla's industrial section. By day the area was a hive of activity, but by this time on a Friday night it resembled a ghost town. Streetlights were sparse along the two-lane blacktop as we passed manufacturers and warehouses shuttered for the night. We turned onto a particularly lonely stretch of road, which led to what appeared to be an isolated and abandoned warehouse. Not a single light advertised its existence, nor did any sign inform the curious as to its purpose. We drove around the back and discovered a large, badly lit parking lot half-filled with cars. Only people who knew what they were looking for would find this place.

Nicholas turned off the engine. "Are you ready to meet your future?"

The decision to come to Santa Carla may not have been entirely my own, but that didn't mean I would be batted about like a leaf in the wind. Learning to navigate this bizarre new world might be the only way to survive it.

Be the hero. I unbuckled my seat belt. "Let's go."

A single red light burning at the top of a high metal staircase announced the second-story entrance to the windowless building. Nicholas gave a sharp rap on the door, and a small portal opened, just like in an old gangster movie. A pair of dark eyes peered at us before the little window banged shut again, and the front door opened.

A stunning young woman stepped back to admit us. Her slight form was tightly encased in a gold lace dress showcasing her boyish physique. Long black hair hung like a curtain down her back with blunt bangs in front. Her delicate features were dramatically made up, the vibrant palette of colors straight out of an edgy fashion magazine.

"Nicholas," she said, giving him the slightest of bows. "Welcome to The Lower 8."

"Suki," he returned warmly. "I'd like you to meet Blake Wilder, who just moved to Santa Carla. Blake, this is Suki Kim, a friend and former fellow prisoner at Alder House."

Suki laughed at the introduction, revealing teeth as white as pearls. "You are so bad, Nicholas," she mock scolded before turning to me. "Don't listen to a word he says. If Alder House is a prison, it's the best money can buy."

We were in a small antechamber. The only furnishings were a purple velvet loveseat against one wall, while a hostess stand positioned front and center supported a large reservation book. Pounding music bled through the interior walls along with something else that made me feel like I'd just downed a quart of high-octane coffee.

"Who's here tonight?" Nicholas asked, handing over his credit card.

She zipped it through a card reader. "It's still early, but the bar is already hopping. Jessie and Marcus are here, of course, and almost all the tables are booked. How old are you, Blake?"

I was surprised by the non sequitur but answered her honestly.

She pulled a red plastic bracelet out of a shallow drawer in the hostess stand and moved to snap it on my wrist. When her fingers brushed my skin, she jerked her hand back as if it had been burned.

Her wide eyes darted to Nicholas. "Is she a…?"

He nodded.

"Wow," she said, meeting my gaze. "The only other voyant I've met is the regent. I didn't even know another had been found." Her fingers trembled slightly as she fastened my bracelet.

"I was as surprised as you are," Nicholas interjected, which was technically true, but I also knew there was more to the story.

"You're a sentinel?" I asked, shutting down my inquisitive mind. Who knew if Khalia had figured out I'd trespassed where none had gone before, but I wasn't going to risk giving myself away again.

She lifted her chin with pride. "Class One, Alder House trained." At my curious look, she added, "Only those who show the most promise at an early age are educated at Alder House."

"Every gathering place for our people is guarded by a sentinel to insure only Nines are admitted. The Lower 8 is very lucky to have a sentinel of her caliber," Nicholas explained. "You'll understand why once we get inside."

Suki reached into her drawer for another red bracelet and Nicholas grimaced. "I don't need one of those."

"It may be legal for you to drink in England, but in the state of California, you still wear the red badge of the underage," she said primly as she placed it on his wrist. A knock sounded at the front door, commanding her attention. "Enjoy your evening."

Every fiber of my being vibrated with tension. Beyond that inner door was the answer to my prayers, or maybe my worst nightmare; at that moment there was no in between. My life, my happiness, my future hinged on what happened in the next few minutes. The ornately painted words over the interior entrance only added to my confusion: *virtus est potentia multis*.

"What does it say?" I asked.

"The power of the one is the power of the many."

I glanced up at him, bewildered. "Meaning?"

"It'll make sense once you're inside." His hand found the small of my back, the intimate contact a welcome distraction from my internal drama. "Ready?"

For better or worse, there was only one choice to be made. "Ready."

Host with Ghost

We stood at the top of a grand staircase, the kind intended for an elegant movie queen to sweep down. There were at least a hundred people on the ground floor, gathered around the bar or milling about tables scattered throughout the club. As if being forced to make a dramatic entrance wasn't nerve wracking enough, I suddenly understood what had made me so jittery. The collective paranormal energy in the room took my breath away. It crashed over me, and the impact left me trembling.

"Are you okay?" Nicholas had to speak up to be heard over the club music.

Steeling myself against the pull of so many powerful minds, I said, "I can do this." I didn't know which one of us needed to be convinced.

We'd only taken a few steps down the staircase when heads began to turn. I was seized with anxiety. The last time the spotlight shone so brightly had been that long ago day in school, and the faceless mob had taunted me, condemned me. Now the rumble of the crowd grew, and it didn't take a telepath to figure out we were the topic of conversation. Amazingly, I even caught an envious glare or two.

Nicholas reached for my hand, and his seductive energy wrapped me in warmth. "I won't let go."

A premonition flashed through my mind. A couple would hook up tonight and have a private party in the back seat of a sedan. Then another vision pushed its way in, this time from the past. Someone here had found her mother overdosed in a bathtub. A third vision overtook it, this time a grisly accident with a skill saw sometime in the near future.

Enough! I couldn't tell from whose minds the visions had come, but it felt like a YouTube channel without end. I called up every defensive strategy I'd ever learned to block the unfiltered energy rolling over me. The invasion stopped, but I wasn't sure how long I could keep it at bay.

We made it to the bottom of the stairs where a pixie waited. She couldn't have been more than five feet tall and perhaps ninety pounds. Her spikey, jet-black hair played up her elfin features, and her diaphanous dress outlined her lithe form.

"Hi, I'm Layla," she said with an impish grin. "Did you know you have the most amazing aura? It's really bright and complex. You must hear that a lot, huh?"

"Um, hi Layla, I'm Blake," I said, letting out the breath I'd been holding. "I bet you already know Nicholas." She looked pleased as punch at my introduction, and I relaxed enough to smile back.

"Yes, of course. Hello, Nicholas." She gave him a delighted little wave. "Now Marcus and Jessie say you absolutely *must* take the house table. Besides," she added with a conspiratorial wink, "it's the only way you'll be able get some distance from the gawkers."

She breezily linked her arm with mine, and I shot a startled glance at Nicholas, who shrugged with bemusement. As she blazed a trail through the crowd, I stared at the spectacle around me, suddenly understanding the attraction of a Nines-only zone. Everyone here was free to reveal his or her true nature without fear of discovery.

Behind the bar, bottles sailed through the air as drinks were magically mixed. At one table, a man smoothly lit a woman's cigarette from the flame dancing at the end of his finger. At another, a young guy with tattoos running from shoulder to wrist grinned as empty cocktail glasses refilled themselves with frosty liquids.

Layla pulled up short at tattoo guy's table, frowning. "We've had this discussion before, Raymond. Even if you refill the drinks yourself, you still have to pay for them." She didn't wait for his sheepish reply before she pulled me away. "I swear," she huffed, "some of the materialists who come in here have the worst manners."

We arrived at a spacious booth elevated slightly off the main floor, allowing an unencumbered view of the entire club. Of course, that also meant we'd be on display for the curious masses.

"Don't let any of it bother you," Layla said soothingly as if she sensed my apprehension. "There may be huge envy in this room, but that's their problem."

Ordinarily, her words would have jacked my nerves up yet another notch, but strangely, I felt a calmness steal over me, the tension ebbing out of my body.

"Layla's a double empath," Nicholas said as we slid into the booth. "She can read moods as well as influence them."

My mouth dropped open. She was the human version of Prozac.

"Cool, huh?" Layla practically danced with excitement, but I suspected that might be her permanent state of being. "Now what would you like to drink?"

"Whiskey and soda," Nicholas said without hesitation.

"Two mineral waters with lime it is," Layla said with a grin before skipping off.

Now that I was no longer on the verge of a panic attack, I could appreciate how cleverly the building's interior had been converted from its days as a warehouse. A massive bar with graduated rows of spirits anchored one side of the space, while a dance floor and stage filled the other. The walls were painted the soft gold of a ripe pear, and swaths of red fabric softened the cement pillars rising from floor to ceiling. The whole effect was one of casual elegance.

I was curious as to who Marcus and Jessie might be, seeing as I'd been here for all of five minutes and heard them mentioned twice.

"They're partners in The Lower 8," Nicholas said when I asked. "Jessie McCabe is the brains behind the operation, Marcus Sinclair is the money. Or, rather, Marcus's father is the money. I think it's a last ditch attempt by Sutton to mold his son in his own image."

My tension level ratcheted back up. "Sutton Sinclair is one of the owners?"

As if on cue, his vile sentinel Khalia strode down the stairs as if she owned the place. Her cropped, skintight top exposed rock-hard abs, and a short skirt and stilettos showcased legs to die for. I was tempted to slump down in the booth and hope she didn't notice me.

His fingers grazed my bare shoulder. "You're safe with me. I promise."

I met Nicholas's gaze and smiled. "I believe you."

Layla's return interrupted the moment. "Guess who I found?" She set down our drinks. "Blake Wilder, meet Jessie McCabe." She zipped off to deliver the rest of her orders.

The man standing in front of us was one of those guys who sucked the air out of a room with just a smile. In his mid-twenties, he wore his shoulder-length blonde hair brushed neatly behind his ears, framing a face that had a sweet, boy-next-door quality, an image dispelled a moment later by a devilish grin. The navy silk shirt and trousers he wore contrasted with eyes so gray they bordered on silver, and I was amused to see he'd added cowboy boots made from the skin of some unfortunate reptile.

"Ma'am," he drawled in a twang that dripped honey. He touched his fingertips to the brim of an imaginary hat in salute.

"Uh, nice to meet you, Jessie," I breathed, extending my hand in greeting. He grasped it, and I could feel tingling all the way down to, well, just about everywhere. I probably could have stayed that way for a few minutes more if Nicholas hadn't spoken.

"McCabe," he said, in a voice that held little warmth.

"Thorne," Jessie said in a similarly dismissive tone. Without waiting for an invitation, he slid into my side of the booth, his glittering eyes skewering Nicholas. "I just had a most enlightening conversation with my door sentinel."

Nicholas's expression gave nothing away, making him look even more like his imperious father. "And?"

"And you people have stepped on the wrong set of toes," the other man snapped. "I should have been notified a new voyant had been discovered in my city. It was my right to make first contact."

"The chancellor felt I was the best choice, so he sent me." This was another half-truth, but the friction between them appeared well established.

I felt like a bone tossed between two snarling dogs. "Gosh, this is fun," I said in my driest voice. "You guys really know how to have a good time."

Jessie turned to me, humor tugging at his lips. "Beautiful *and* clever. It would have been my honor to be your patron."

My brows raised in query. "My what?"

"Everyone is assigned a patron if and when they reach Class One status," he explained. "Someone to help them understand their ability and obligations to The Nine."

"I've got it covered, McCabe," Nicholas ground out.

"Introducing a newcomer to the ways of The Nine is a privilege given to those who have contributed greatly, in ways social or monetary, to the growth of our organization," Jessie continued as if Nicholas hadn't spoken. "The thing of it is, the first time one of us shares his or her energy with another of our kind is the purest. It will forever add to the strength of the Class One it is given to."

I squirmed at the virginal analogy. Perhaps my thoughts were transparent because Nicholas quickly spoke up in his own defense.

"Blake," he said, "you know why Henry sent me."

Did I? I'd initially thought the chancellor had kept my existence a secret so no one would bother me until I was old enough to take care of myself, but what if that wasn't the only reason?

Layla popped up in front of us like she'd been fired from a cannon. "Nicholas, that table asked if you would be so kind as to join them for a moment." With a nod of her head, she indicated a booth directly across the room before scurrying off again.

His jaw tightened as he surveyed a tableful of people smiling in our direction, one of the men nodding in greeting. He glanced at me in indecision.

Jessie gloated. "I would be delighted to keep Miss Blake company while you run along and kiss tail for your daddy."

Nicholas gave Jessie a hard stare. "Don't you have a floor to go mop or something?"

"I'll be fine," I insisted. "Do whatever you have to do."

He surprised me by reaching over to tuck a stray curl behind my ear. "I won't be long." He shot a long look at Jessie before slipping out of the booth and winding his way across the room.

"I apologize if I caused offense," Jessie said. "It's just that I've worked so hard for everything, while that boy gets it all handed to him on a silver platter." He dropped his head with just the right amount of hangdog despair.

"Despite what you may think," I said, "Nicholas gave you credit as the mastermind behind this place." Jessie brightened immediately, and I felt emboldened to ask, "I hope this isn't a rude question, but what are you a Class One of?"

"I'm a phantomist, at your service, ma'am." I must have stared at him a beat too long, prompting him to explain. "A phantomist is able to tap into the collective energy of departed souls, and depending on how strong he or she is, can communicate with and direct it. A Class One phantomist can also distill the spirits of former Nines, which is the most powerful energy of all."

"You're a *ghost whisperer*?"

He groaned good-naturedly. "I've seen that old TV show, and except for admiring Jennifer Love Hewitt's big, uh, personality, it has absolutely no basis in reality."

I laughed. "But you can speak to people who are, um, no longer here?"

"You can call them dead people," he assured me. "They don't mind."

Layla veered by to wordlessly drop off a Coke, which Jessie gratefully accepted.

The club music shifted into a dramatic tempo, and everyone's attention turned to the stage. Warm applause greeted the appearance of an attractive woman wearing a skimpy version of a ringmaster's costume, complete with fishnet stockings and a black cutaway coat.

With a theatrical wave of her hand, a translucent tiger materialized. He glowed brightly with an interior light as he trotted to one of several pedestals positioned around the stage. She repeated the gesture several more times until she had a collection of magical animals—lions, bears, gazelles, zebras—ready to do her bidding.

"That's Cassandra, an evanescent. She can convert energy to mass," Jessie said as the tiger jumped high over the heads of the audience. "Einstein was an evanescent, too."

I tore my eyes away from the spectacle and stared at Jessie. How many famous people in history had the added advantage of being a Nine? My dad would probably camp out on the doorstep of Alder House once he heard about this.

The tiger suddenly burst into a shower of falling stars, and the audience ooh'd and ahhh'd. My focus stayed on Jessie, determined to learn more about my new world. "When did you first know what you could do?"

"I didn't start hearing spirits talk until I was a teenager." He was matter of fact about something most people would find terrifying. "Of course, at first I thought I was crazier than a dog in a cat factory because there wasn't anyone around to tell me what was happening. I guess being a Nine must have skipped a few generations in my family."

Relief at learning I wasn't the only outlier made me giddy. "Then it's hereditary? Do you think there could be another Nine in my family?"

"Most definitely," he said, chuckling at my enthusiasm. "Ask your grandparents which relative was nuttier than a squirrel turd, and I bet you'll have your answer."

It was tempting to drop everything and text my dad, but I wanted to hear more. "So then what happened?"

"About six months after hearing them talk, I started seeing them, too. The first one was Cedric. He must have been lonely because, man, did that guy talk my ear off. He's the one who told me what I was because he was a Nine in life. He also claims…" Jessie lowered his voice, his smile full of mischief, "that he was a member of British royalty, but I have yet to find any record of it."

Maybe it wasn't so scary after all. "How many other, uh, dead people do you see?"

"I used to have six fulltime spirits, but one of them, Lucinda, seems to have faded away. None of the others know why that happened, but apparently it does from time to time." He sounded as if he were grieving the loss of a friend.

This had to be one of the most startling conversations I'd ever had. "Do you get a vote on who drops in?"

Jessie laughed. "It's not like I'm a country that can be invaded. We feed off each other's energy, and they can do things, discover things I never could on my own." Suddenly he looked distracted, his eyes losing focus for a moment. "Damn those fools." He swiveled to survey the crowded club.

"What is it?"

"Cedric says a couple of Sutton's goons are planning to mess with your boyfriend," he said grimly.

"He's not my boyfriend." I should be more concerned with Nicholas's welfare than my relationship status, but I couldn't help setting the record straight.

"Yes, ma'am," he said with a delighted smile. "I stand corrected."

I blushed and glanced away. I wasn't sure what if anything was happening between Nicholas and me, or even if I wanted it to, but I'd waited all my life for an interesting guy to take notice. Now, maybe there were two.

"Whatever my opinion of Nicholas Thorne might be, I can't send him back to his daddy in pieces," he said with a sigh. "Would you please excuse me for a moment?"

As he slid out of the booth, Layla flagged him down, followed by a guy who looked like he ate iron for breakfast. Dressed all in black, his tight tee shirt with The Lower 8 logo revealed beefy arms and shoulders that could only be the result of long hours at the gym. Despite his appearance as a typical door bouncer, I knew that in this place he was surely anything but. After a few words with his boss, the bouncer vanished into thin air. I wondered if I could ever get used to this.

Jessie worked his way across the room where Nicholas stood casually chatting with an attractive couple. Apparently, the social obligations of the chancellor's son were many. I was amused to see his glass of mineral water had been replaced with an amber liquid over ice.

Two men leaned against a nearby pillar staring intently at him. The glass Nicholas held started to smoke and boil and without the least hesitation, he threw it toward the vacant dance floor where it exploded like a bomb. Several people shrieked, but no one appeared to be injured. The music died, Cassandra's remaining beasts winked out of existence, and all conversation in the club stumbled to a halt.

From out of the blue, one of the troublemakers doubled over with a loud "oof", as if a fist had been driven into his middle, while the other one's feet were suddenly yanked out from underneath him. As they both lay on the floor gasping, the bouncer winked back to visibility. A moment later, both assailants were airborne and floating over the heads of the crowd as they were tossed from the club.

"Sorry for all the commotion, folks," Jessie called out a moment later. "Just needed to show a few over-achievers to the door." He searched the room until his eyes fell on the table of materialists who had earlier conjured up a round of drinks. "Let's just make sure that doesn't include you, Raymond," he said with a smirk, much to the amusement of the crowd. The laughter turned into conversation and within moments, the ambience of the club was restored.

Nicholas reappeared at our table, and this time he had company. "Blake, I'd like you to meet Marcus Sinclair, Jessie's business partner."

The son of the all-powerful Sutton Sinclair was the very picture of a successful club owner. He wore tight jeans, a tailored jacket, and a watch that cost more than my annual tuition. The whiteness of his shirt was in sharp contrast to his deeply tanned skin and thick black hair. His dark eyes flashed over me, confident and welcoming.

"So you're the girl who's got my father in a twist." He grinned. "Well done."

I laughed at the unexpected comment. "I'm guessing it doesn't happen often?"

"Nothing happens in the Sinclair kingdom without Dad's say so." His glance took in both Nicholas and me. "Well, very little that is."

He gestured to a young woman who'd been hovering behind him on the outskirts of the conversation. "Alice, come meet Blake and Nicholas."

The girl who beamed at being singled out was about my age, which was about ten years younger than Marcus, but she lacked his sense of style. Her skirt and blouse were plain and shapeless, and her wavy brown hair overpowered her unremarkable features. Her expression was friendly enough but also distracted; she gawked at people like a tourist intent on memorizing every detail.

Nicholas offered her his hand. "Are you new to Santa Carla?"

"I hadn't planned to stay, but everyone's been real friendly here." She gazed at Marcus like she couldn't believe her luck.

"I just moved here too," I volunteered. "Where are you from?"

"Someplace where she didn't have to deal with people pulling stunts like exploding drinks," Marcus interjected. "Sorry about that, Nicholas."

Layla chose that moment to return to offer another round. Jessie and the bouncer arrived at the same time, the latter intent on having a talk with his bosses. I sat alone in the booth, a swirl of energy and emotions washing over me. The music kicked into overdrive, the driving beat pounding inside my head.

I once again tried to envision my brain locked inside a box, protected by a fortress of energy, but my control was at an end.

A vision slipped past my defenses. Somebody had recently come out to his clueless parents, and it hadn't gone well. Another vision crowded in: a distraught woman cradling her ancient cat while a sad-eyed vet sent the animal peacefully from the world. Then another vision, and another. Each one was another anonymous trip into someone's personal hell until suddenly, a premonition appeared that took hell to the next level.

Outdoor lights stretched over a lonely rooftop parking lot, holding the night at bay. Waist-high safety cables edged the cement pad, offering a protective barrier from the sheer drop to the street many stories below.

A woman set a couple of file boxes on the backseat of the only car in the lot. She straightened, and I had a flash of recognition. It was Selena, the decaf chai latte and dog biscuit customer.

"Don't worry, Chico," she said, loading the dog into the car. "The weekend will be here before you know it."

The premonition jumped and now she stood with her back to the silver Acura, alarm etched across her face. Her dog's paws were pressed against the window.

"You have no business being here," she said, reaching for the door handle. "I told you on the phone. There's nothing more I can do." I turned to see who would soon be confronting her but was met with only darkness.

Selena's fingers were wrenched away from the door handle, and she stared at her hand as if she'd never seen it before. Her whole body jerked like a puppet on strings, and she took a wobbly step away from the vehicle.

"What's happening?" she cried.

The scene skipped forward. She was at the edge of the parking lot, standing at the railing. The stiff evening breeze riffled her dark hair, and her face was streaked with tears. Her hand gripped one of the cables separating her from empty space. Chico clawed at the car window, his nails clicking out a frantic beat.

"How are you doing this?" she sobbed. Her foot stepped onto the first rung of cables, and she screamed. "Please, I don't want to die! Let me go, and I'll do anything you want. I swear!"

The image fast-forwarded to Selena standing on the wrong side of the safety cables with nothing separating her from a fatal fall.

"Please," she whimpered. It was the last thing she said before her body swayed gracefully over the side and disappeared.

Chico unleashed a mournful howl.

I Hear What You're Saying

I had witnessed a murder. Or, at least, one in the making.

I scanned the crowd, but I already knew Selena wasn't there. She'd been too shocked at having her movements controlled by another. Now that I knew about materialists, empaths, and evanescents, it wasn't a big stretch to accept there must be somebody who could possess your body, if not your soul.

It also meant someone in the room was a killer—or soon would be.

As I glanced about the place, I was pulled up short by a woman staring directly at me. Standing at the edge of the crowd, she was elegantly thin with shiny brown hair cut bluntly at her shoulders. Her white silk blouse and flowing navy trousers looked expensive, as did the pearls at her throat. Was she the source of my premonition?

Goodness no. I practically jumped out of my skin. The feminine voice had come from inside my head. *Terribly sorry*, the voice said contritely. *I didn't mean to startle you.*

Nicholas and Marcus were deep in conversation while the wide-eyed Alice gazed contentedly about. Jessie still consulted with his bouncer. No one looked my way.

Um, can you hear me? I thought the words slowly and silently to myself.

Of course. And just think your words naturally, you don't need to go to extremes. The throaty voice was accented with something exotic.

The woman across the room turned away and was occupied with greeting two or three friends with hugs and air kisses.

Is that you? She smiled and nodded at some comment directed at her. Then she turned and gave me a quick wink. She was quite attractive, and I judged her to be in her mid-thirties.

I'm forty-one actually, but holding together rather well, if I do say so myself.

Oh, uh... I stuttered, embarrassed.

Marina Novak, Class One double telepath. I can hear your thoughts as well as send you mine. That was some vision you had there, kiddo.

My brain must have lurched in a dozen different directions because she said, *Calm down! I mean you no harm.*

I took a few deep breaths and did as she asked because other than dashing blindly for the stairs, what other option did I have? There was no place to hide.

Not true, she said. *I will leave you alone if that's what you wish, but I bet you could use a friend. Most people here have never met a voyant, you know.*

She laughed outwardly at some comment, and I wondered how she could have two totally separate conversations at once. She was right, though; despite all the friendly faces that had greeted me, I'd never felt so alone in all my life.

You won't feel like an outsider for long. My life began when I was first contacted, and I suspect yours will, too.

Geez, could I have a single, fleeting thought that she *couldn't* read? A gentle laugh acknowledged that, no, I could not. I got the impression Marina sympathized with my anxiety and fear, which was odd; I'd never felt someone's emotions before.

You're right. I do understand. Our eyes met, and she smiled. *See for yourself.*

Rain pattered lightly on rows of ancient stone houses, the narrow cobblestone street running between them rutted and cracked. The air was spiced with the smell of damp earth and savory cooking, telling me this was a glimpse of Marina's past.

She was a pretty sixteen-year-old wearing a knee-length skirt and fitted jacket as she slipped out her front door. Her schoolbooks were carried in a messenger bag slung across her body. She turned up the street at a brisk pace.

A cluster of old women dressed like crows gossiped at the corner. As Marina neared, they turned as one to glare at the girl.

"*Vjestica!*" muttered one woman. Then she spat on the ground.

"*Vjestica!*" The other women picked up the chant. One pulled out a pack of matches. As soon as she had one lit, she threw it at the girl, though it immediately sputtered out on the wet street.

Marina marched past with her head high, as if she ran this gauntlet often. She had just passed them by when one bent down and picked up a loose stone. With a strength born from fear, she threw the rock at Marina. It struck the girl on the back of the head, and she fell to her knees.

The other women grabbed rocks of their own and descended on their hapless victim. "*Vjestica!*" they chorused. Marina curled into a ball and covered her head as blows rained down on her back.

"Stop!"

The attackers barely paused at the sight of a couple running toward them. The newcomers dashed to Marina's aid. The man stood protectively over her body, his presence enough to interrupt the assault, while his female companion bent over the injured girl.

The ringleader of the mob let loose with a string of curses. She raised her hand to let another missile fly, but she never got the chance. A strong gust of wind suddenly blew her back a few steps, and she collided with her cronies. A windstorm immediately engulfed them all, whipping scarves from their heads and ripping at their clothes, though not a leaf stirred on the nearby trees. They huddled together, shrieking in terror.

Marina was bloodied and dazed, and the woman at her side helped her to her feet.

"Are you okay? Do you speak English?"

Marina's eyes widened when she saw the weather phenomena engulfing her attackers. "How are you doing this?"

"It's Yuri. He's an elementalist. I'm Helen, a sentinel." Helen examined the girl's cuts and bruises. "Let's get you to a doctor."

"Wait," Marina said. "Do you know what I am?"

Helen smiled warmly. "A very special girl."

What is a vjestica? I mentally asked when the crowded nightclub swam back into focus.

A witch. The grown-up Marina took a sip of white wine. *Helen and Yuri took me to Alder House the very next day. I haven't been back to my village in Croatia since.*

And I thought bullying cheerleaders were bad.

I recognized that woman and her dog from your premonition. The way Marina said it made me uneasy. *I've seen her with Sutton Sinclair, though I don't know her name.*

Everywhere I turned, Sutton Sinclair loomed. I'd tossed his business card on my bedside table without a second thought, but now it seemed to mock me.

It's Selena, and she's a customer at Jitters, the coffee place where I work, I thought, *but I don't know how to find her.*

If you can't find the victim, you must find the killer.

I stared at her. *Why me? What do I know about any of this?*

She turned and met my gaze. *It is the sworn duty of a voyant. And because an innocent woman will die if you do nothing.*

I felt movement beside me. "I'm sorry about all the interruptions. Are you all right?" Nicholas regarded me with concern.

I glanced back at Marina, but she was gone, enveloped by the crowd. Instead I saw Jessie eyeing me thoughtfully, most likely hearing Cedric's observations of the past few minutes.

My endurance had come to an end. "Would you mind if we left?"

"Of course not." He slid back out of the booth and helped me to my feet, keeping my hand tucked in his as we headed toward the door. The crowd had doubled since we'd arrived and traversing the room with him was like walking through a party with a rock star. Everyone wanted a word with the chancellor's son.

We'd finally reached the bottom of the grand staircase when a nerdy guy with springy dark curls and a gap-toothed smile plucked at Nicholas's sleeve. As he stopped to acknowledge the man, Jessie appeared at my elbow.

"Don't trust Thorne," he breathed into my ear. At my startled reaction, he said, "His father is on shaky ground, and you don't want to be caught in the middle if that ground shifts."

"Am I supposed to trust you instead?" I asked dryly.

"Hell no." He gave me that wicked grin, and my insides quivered. "But Thorne is a boy when what you need is a man. If you ever need help, you come to me. I swear on my life I will do whatever it takes to keep you safe."

I stared at him, wondering why he would make such a vow, or what could possibly happen that would send me running to him of all people. Before I could ask, Nicholas turned back and met Jessie's hard stare with one of his own. I decided to let it go, for now.

Outside, I gulped in the night air. Laughter floated on a mild breeze as a couple threaded their way past us on their way into the club. We found the car, and Nicholas walked with me around to the passenger side.

"I did it again, didn't I?" he said, letting go of my hand and jamming his hands in his pockets. "I wanted so badly to show you everything that I didn't stop to think if you were ready."

I smiled, which surprised him. It had been the most astonishing night of my life, but I didn't regret having my eyes opened. "I don't think anyone not born into this could ever know what it's like to be in a roomful of Nines until you're actually there."

The moon had risen, giving off just enough light to see Nicholas's relieved expression as he leaned his back against the car. "McCabe was right, though. He should have been the one to make first contact, but I don't really give a damn."

Maybe it would have been easier if Jessie had reached out to me first. You knew where you stood with him within five minutes of making his acquaintance. Unlike Nicholas, Jessie wouldn't have asked for my trust, and had even issued a warning to the contrary.

"What is it between you guys?" I asked.

"The spirits a phantomist attracts are a reflection of his or her personality," he explained, "so in McCabe's case, his phantoms are as ambitious as he is. They gather gossip like apples from a tree, ready to be traded or sold for fun and profit."

"And?" The bad blood between Jessie and Nicholas went deeper than simple disdain.

"I merely pointed that out when the phantomist regent retired last year, and McCabe was drumming up support to replace her."

"What is a regent?"

"The Nine is governed by the chancellor and nine regents, one from each discipline." A satisfied smile touched his lips. "I may have tipped the scales against him, but I have no regrets."

"Do you think his spirits are watching us now?" It was silly, but I searched the stars overhead for a glimpse of ghostly vapor.

"Undoubtedly." He grasped both my hands and gently tugged. I allowed him to draw me into the gap between his knees, giving in to the pull of standing in the moonlight with an attractive guy. His lips curled into a sly smile. "Shall we give them something to talk about?"

My heart danced as he slowly closed the distance between us, giving me every opportunity to turn away, but I wanted this. I felt seen by someone other than my family or Scarlett for the first time in my life. It didn't matter why he'd come to Santa Carla, only that he was there.

The heat of his lips on mine erased all other thoughts. He gently nibbled my lower lip, and a surge of longing sliced through any doubts and fears. The tip of his tongue teased open my mouth as his fingers played along my jaw, and I tasted the lingering smokiness of whatever drink had been in his glass. A flame ignited deep in my soul, and I suddenly hungered for more. I slanted my mouth against his to take him deeper, even daring to explore with my own tongue. His answering shiver provoked a primal thrill.

He finally pulled back, his breath coming as quickly as mine.

"That was my first real kiss," I said when I could finally think straight. The random boys I'd occasionally kissed at the annual county fair didn't count.

I caught a glimpse of Nicholas's grin in the dark. "That was my best kiss." He ran his hands along the bare skin of my arms, feeling the goosebumps. "You must be cold. Let's get you in the car."

"So what happened in there?" he asked when we were both buckled up with the heater blasting. "You kept lighting up like a winning slot machine."

"I couldn't help it," I said, shaking my head. "It was like everyone was an open book waiting to be read, and everything was so vivid." The premonition of Selena was even clearer than the one I'd had of Warren.

I caught my breath at a sudden thought. The second and more detailed vision of Warren's future happened when I was with Nicholas. Then everything I witnessed tonight was in the company of Nines.

"The sign over the door. 'The power of the one is the power of the many'," I recalled, both excited and incredulous. "Were my visions clearer because I was with other Nines?"

He nodded with approval. "I knew you'd figure it out. We are stronger together. What did you see tonight?"

"It was all the usual depressing stuff, until…"

"Until?" He prodded, throwing the car into reverse.

As we left the club behind, I told him about my premonition of a murder disguised as a suicide. "What kind of person can take away your free will?"

"An enchanter." The car raced down the dark road, but he was at ease behind the wheel. "They always seem to go out of their way to find trouble. An enchanter can take control of a person's body and sometimes their mind, though they can often lose theirs in return. Every major cult leader from Charles Manson to Jim Jones to that Heaven's Gate lunatic were enchanters."

No wonder Henry Thorne wanted to keep a lid on what Nines could do. If it got out that there were people who could kill with their thoughts, the Salem witch burnings would look like a neighborhood BBQ in comparison to what would happen.

"Did you recognize any enchanters there tonight?" I asked.

He nodded. "One, but there could have been several that I don't yet know. We can't jump to conclusions."

"Well, I wasn't the only one who saw the premonition." I told him about my telepathic conversation with Marina. "Is she an empath or enchanter, too? She gave off all these warm and fuzzy vibes, but I'm not sure what to think."

He shot me a curious glance. "Marina Novak is a trusted friend and a powerful telepath, but she can't influence your feelings. Why some empath would intervene to convince you of Marina's good intentions is quite odd."

"She said Selena works for Sutton Sinclair," I continued. "It all keeps circling back to him, but I get the impression you and he aren't exactly friends."

"Sinclair only cares about money and power." His clipped tone was tinged with scorn. "As the elementalist regent, he tells our people what they want to hear without considering how dangerous his vision of the future could be. Rumor has it he will soon challenge my father for the position of chancellor."

I hadn't originally connected Henry Thorne's agitation over a potential challenge with the news I'd moved to Santa Carla, but now it seemed clear it was my proximity to his political rival that had bent him out of shape.

"What would happen if Sinclair became chancellor?" I asked.

"For the past five hundred years, all Nines have sworn, under penalty of death, not to enter into organized religion or politics. We learned a hard lesson in the sixteenth century with Henry Tudor." The windows were beginning to fog up, so he tapped a few buttons on the car's screen. "Sinclair believes the pact has outlived its usefulness."

"Wait a second," I said, holding up my hands. "King Henry the Eighth was a Nine?" The oft-married monarch had resented the Pope meddling in his love life, so he'd turned his back on the Vatican and founded the Church of England. It didn't go over well. It cost untold lives and, as my dad occasionally lamented, the destruction of over eight hundred monastic libraries.

"He was an empath," Nicholas confirmed, "which is how he was able to discover and execute anyone with enough hatred and courage to oppose him."

My father always said the only constant in history was human nature. Maybe Henry Thorne was right to fear what could happen if Nines were once again set free to stride the most hallowed halls of power. Sharing my dad's fascination with the past, I could easily have gotten lost in more of The Nine's origin stories, but an innocent life was on the line. I couldn't let Selena die if there was any way to prevent it.

"Do you think Sinclair would be willing to help us find Selena before the killer enchanter does?" I chewed my thumbnail as I considered how the crime appeared to happen on a weekday. "She's probably safe until at least Monday night."

"As long as it's in his best interests to do so," he answered.

"You think he might have something to do with wanting to harm Selena?" I'd been so stunned by how the murder was committed I hadn't gotten round to the question of motive.

"I'll call him," Nicholas promised. "Let's see what he has to say."

I relaxed into my seat as we turned into Rosewood Gardens, the older, slightly rundown neighborhood where I lived. It was a small suburb made up of single-family homes and apartment buildings in the modern design once favored by builders in postwar Southern California. He guided the car to the curb and turned off the engine.

"Tonight was...enlightening," I said, still a bit overwhelmed by the evening's revelations.

He chuckled. "Don't go all diplomatic on me now. What did you really think?"

I smirked. "Would you prefer I'd said bizarre, revealing, shocking, mind blowing, freaking weird—"

His laughter cut me off. "There's the Blake Wilder I've come to know and love."

I tried not to read too much into his offhand comment. "I still have so much to learn. What will I do when you're not here to guide me?"

"Trying to get rid of me already?" Deep shadows made his expression impossible to read, but something vulnerable in his voice caught at my heart.

"Don't you need to get back to your life in England?" I ventured, plucking at my skirt.

He unbuckled his seat belt and leaned toward me. "You tell me. Do I have to return home, or will you change my future?"

"I don't know," I said, his nearness throwing me off balance. "Shall I take a look?"

"I've got a better idea," he murmured, drawing me into another kiss.

The List

There was nothing like murder to keep you up at night. Eddie, Kevin, and the blackmailer Ashley Norman were all beyond my help, but Selena wasn't. I wasn't going to sit on my hands while another person died. I'm sure I slept some, but it was a relief to open my eyes and finally see the morning light. After answering two texts from my dad assuring him I'd survived a night rubbing shoulders with Nines and promising details soon, I made a quick trip to the bathroom. The mirror confirmed my hair was the biggest casualty of my restless night, but I ignored the brush in favor of coffee.

I was on my second cup and almost through the front section of the paper—blissfully free of any mention of Selena's presumed suicide—when my phone rang. It was Nicholas. After the kissing started last night, there'd been no further talk of anything.

"Did you find her?" I blurted, not bothering with a greeting.

"I made two calls this morning," he answered, unphased by my abruptness. "The first was to Sinclair. His company uses a payroll service owned by a woman named Selena Flores. He said he'd have an assistant track her down immediately."

I sighed with relief, though I still had my suspicions about the man. "Did he have any idea why someone would want to hurt her?"

"He said he didn't, but then again, he knew the question was coming." He was silent for a moment. "Marina Novak wasn't the only telepath in the club last night. Word of your premonition is lighting up the message boards."

My breath froze in my chest. It wasn't Nicholas's fault I got blindsided by that premonition, but it wouldn't have been a problem if I hadn't been in a room full of Nines. Of course, then Selena's fate would have been sealed, and a would-be murderer would walk free. As it was, that same person now knew what I'd seen. I forced air into my lungs and focused on remaining calm.

"Blake? You still there?"

"Yeah, I'm here. And the second call?"

"To Suki, the sentinel working the door. If anyone knows who at the club last night has the ability and perhaps the motive to commit such a crime, it would be her. She's agreed to meet us at noon."

Her place was about fifteen minutes from mine, so Nicholas promised to pick me up on the way. I'd just hung up when Scarlett emerged from her room. She was as neat as I was rumpled wearing cuffed jeans, a straw hat, and a basket weave tote she dropped by the front door.

"Off to the hen house, Daisy Mae?" I couldn't help myself.

"An actress is always in character," she quipped, my grumpiness not making a dent in her cheerful mood. "As a matter of fact, Warren and I are going to the farmers market this morning."

"So the date went well?"

"Yes!" As she made breakfast, she told me everything she knew about Warren Hartman, which turned out to be quite a lot. He grew up in San Diego and came to Cal State Santa Carla for their excellent science program, though its proximity to the beach didn't hurt. His parents were divorced, and his dad remarried.

I listened carefully, trying to pick out the one detail that would tell us more about why he'd been destined to live when others hadn't, but it wasn't like he planned to cure cancer or invent a remote control that never got lost in the sofa cushions.

"And what about you?" she asked, sitting down at the table with black coffee and scrambled egg whites. "How was your night?"

Her face lit up when she heard about The Lower 8, Layla the pixie, and Jessie the hot phantomist, but her amusement fled when I got to the part about enchanters and their dangerous abilities.

"What the hell?" She set her mug down so hard the silverware danced. "Did Pretty Boy tell you about these people before he got you mixed up with them?"

I didn't dare tell her just how mixed up I was. I'd never lied to Scarlett before, but my feelings for Nicholas were too new and uncertain to risk being picked apart.

"The important thing is we're doing everything we can to find Selena," I pointed out. "We'll be talking to the door sentinel from last night to see if we can figure out who might want her dead."

She stared at me like I'd lost my mind. "Why? The next thing you know some murderous lunatic will come looking for the person who outed him."

The knock at the door was a welcome interruption because I didn't have any reassurance to offer. Taking a potential killer off the streets was a no-brainer, but joining the hunt almost certainly put me at further risk.

Scarlett climbed to her feet and dumped her dishes in the sink. "Do you know what I like best about Warren? He's normal, just like me."

Ouch.

She opened the door, and Warren called out a greeting. I mumbled something in return. Scarlett retrieved her straw bag before turning to me with a guilty sigh. "I'm sorry. That was a really bitchy thing to say. It's just that I'm scared for you. Promise you'll be careful?"

I did my best to reassure her with an answering smile. Once they were gone, I debated canceling on Nicholas, but my sense of duty won out. Whenever I complained to my mom about her staying too late at the hospital or a medical emergency caused her to miss Sunday dinner, she would say there were those who did and those who watched. There was no question which type I was expected to be.

Next I put a call into my dad, who, as predicted, practically fell off his chair when I told him about the empathic Henry the Eighth. He cut the rest of the conversation short, mumbling something about checking the historical record for all the political rivals who'd died at the hand of the king's extremely busy executioner. I had to smile at his boyish enthusiasm.

As soon as we'd hung up, my phone lit up again. *Good morning, gorgeous*, read the text. *It's Jessie.*

I stared at my phone wondering how Jessie McCabe had gotten my number when another text popped up.

I want you...to have my number.

I laughed out loud. He probably flirted with every female who crossed his path, but I wasn't any more immune to a gorgeous guy than the next girl.

The phone chimed again, this time with a selfie of the phantomist. With pillows propped behind his head and a bare chest on display, he looked like he'd just woken up from a particularly steamy dream. Subtle this guy was not.

I'll be waiting...

I got up from the table without answering, thinking it might be wise to keep him waiting. A man like Jessie was a Ferrari, and I'd only just gotten my learner's permit. I'd planned on taking a long, hot shower before Nicholas picked me up, but as I headed to the bathroom, I knew it had better be an icy cold one.

Suki lived in an especially nice part of Santa Carla. Her condo resided in a row of expensive townhomes leading to the exclusive enclave of Las Brisas Estates. Either being a sentinel at The Lower 8 was fabulously rewarding, or there was family money lurking in the background.

She answered the door barefoot in a tight white tee shirt and jeans. Her shiny black hair hung straight to her waist and even without a stitch of makeup she was gorgeous. Her living room could have come from the pages of a design magazine, right down to the fresh flowers on a spotless glass coffee table. I hovered on the edge of a white sofa, trying my best not to dent the cushions.

"What's happened, Nicholas? Why are you here?" She was not a believer in small talk. Her expression became guarded as she regarded me. "You had a vision, didn't you?"

"I'm afraid so." I was forced to recount the details of the brutal premonition once again.

"Why are you telling me this?" she asked, her face ashen. "You should be calling the Prime Sentinel, or at the very least, Nicholas, your father."

I pursed my lips. What was a Prime Sentinel and why was I only now hearing about this?

"If we can keep it quiet," he responded, "maybe we can avoid a lot of drama."

There was intelligence behind Suki's dark eyes as she quickly analyzed the situation. "What do you want from me?"

"You can tell me who at the club last night would be capable of doing such a thing," he replied.

She shot us both nervous glances. "All right. Wait here."

Crossing into the adjacent kitchen, Suki quickly returned with a list of names but withheld it until we'd been herded to the front door. The picture of Ashley Norman I'd cut from the newspaper was in my pocket, and I withdrew it before she could throw us out. "Do you know this woman?"

For a moment I thought she would refuse to even look at the clipping, but at last she relented. "No. Now I would appreciate it if you didn't mention where you got those names." Before I could promise it would be our secret, the door closed in my face.

"That was weird," I mused.

"I knew she might not want to get involved," he said, leading the way back down a brick pathway dotted with decorative urns, each overflowing with trailing plants. "But the way she acted is not like the Suki I know."

I looked at the list she'd thrust into my hands. Four names were on it, each noted as an enchanter. I showed it to Nicholas.

He frowned as he scanned the names. "Protocol would be to contact the Prime Sentinel and ask him for background on these people."

"What is he, sort of like your sheriff?"

He shot me an amused look. "If by sheriff you mean a Class One sentinel with the absolute authority to do whatever's necessary to enforce our laws and make sure the outside world never learns of us, then yes, he's our sheriff."

"Sounds scary," I surmised.

"And official," he added. "Since no crime has yet been committed, I'd rather see if we can handle it ourselves rather than bringing in the big guns."

I went around to the passenger side. "How do we dig up information on these people without revealing where we got the list? We promised not to drag Suki into it."

"I'll call my father," he said, the car doors once again swinging open by themselves. "He'll appreciate the need for discretion."

We got in the car and buckled up, but Nicholas made no move to put the car in gear. A couple biked past while a teenager glued to her phone trudged by with a golden retriever intent on visiting every well-trimmed tree on the street. He distractedly observed the dog's meandering progress while I waited for him to break the silence.

Finally, he said, "Did I kiss you too soon?"

My brows knit together. "I didn't realize there was a schedule."

His mouth quirked with humor. "What I mean is, everything has come at you so fast. I didn't mean to be one of them."

Now it was my turn to be amused. "It's okay. I think I can keep up."

His gaze was clouded with uncertainty, as if there was something more to say, but whatever it was, it could wait. I wanted him to know this was my choice as well as his, so I reached across the center divider and pulled him into another kiss. His momentary hesitation gave way to a blistering connection that left us both trembling when we paused for breath.

"I told you I could keep up," I murmured.

Plan of Attack

If you want to keep a secret, don't tell a Nine. Those message boards Nicholas had mentioned must get a lot of traffic because news sure traveled fast that there was a new girl in town.

I was at Jitters working the afternoon shift with Olive, a senior at Santa Carla High, a member of the varsity cheerleading squad, and as cute as a box of kittens. Girls like her usually worked at the mall, or at the very least Starbuck's, where the customers all seemed to wear polo shirts and drive BMWs.

It was the slow time between the three o'clock caffeine stampede and the evening rush. Olive chattered on about an upcoming cheer competition as we restocked supplies behind the bar. I listened with half an ear, my mind dwelling on Selena and hoping she and Chico would come walking through the door despite the unlikelihood of seeing them on a weekend.

I picked up the buzz of energy before the guy with the expensive haircut and dark aviators strode in the door. Maybe it was from all my contact with Nicholas or perhaps my visit to

The Lower 8 had awakened some dormant intuition, but I didn't have to touch the guy to know he was a Nine. Wearing the same look of amazement that had first crossed Suki's face when she'd learned what I was, he ordered a blended mocha.

The unique pull of his mind beckoned me to come closer, to take a look at what was inside. I hadn't dared let my guard down at The Lower 8, but my visit had left me wondering if all that focused energy between Nines would make it easier to sort through their memories and not get stuck picking up random visions. An electrical current charged the air between us, so I let it wash over me. I felt his excitement and curiosity at meeting a voyant.

What the hell?

Emotions were not part of the deal. I handed off his drink with a strained smile, wondering if he was a powerful empath who needed to be reined in. I continued to wait on customers, convinced the overly personal connection had been a one-time thing. I would prove it with the next Nine who came in.

My opportunity came in the form of a spry old man. His white hair and lined face pegged him as grandfather material, but the lightness in his step and the evident pleasure he took in his surroundings was that of a much younger man. Energy surrounded him like one of Layla's auras, so I let down my guard.

Hot steam shot across my fingers. "Crap!"

"Are you okay?" Olive glanced over from her place behind the register.

"Fine," I said through clenched teeth, but it wasn't the burn that had me worked up. When that man looked at me, I'd felt hope. What he was hoping for, other than the plain cup of coffee he ordered, I didn't know, but I'd read his state of mind as clearly as if he'd been holding up a sign.

Did this happen to other people in The Nine? Did talents blend and grow, as mine apparently were? I wanted to ask Nicolas about it, but my natural caution told me to keep this to myself for now.

The sky overhead was streaked in pink and gold when my shift ended. Happiness surged through me at seeing Nicholas leaning up against the Tesla, his hands thrust into the pockets of his jacket. The setting sun had chased the warmth from the day, and I hurried to be greeted with a warm kiss. It was made all the sweeter by feeling his pleasure at seeing me, too. Maybe my new empathic tendencies weren't such a big deal after all.

He nuzzled against my neck. "You smell wonderfully edible, like coffee and chocolate."

My body arched against his in response, and he recaptured my lips—until his mouth curled up in a smile. "We have an audience."

Behind me several of the customers occupying Jitters' window tables were grinning at our display. I jumped out of Nicholas's arms like I'd been shocked by a cattle prod, which only amused the onlookers even more.

"C'mon," he said with a laugh. "I have something to show you."

I wrinkled my nose. "The last time you showed me something I ended up at The Lower 8. Not that I minded, but it's kind of been a full day."

He walked with me over to the passenger side. "Unless you're throwing a party for Nines in your apartment, I think you'll be fine."

"My place?" I asked, suddenly uneasy. "I don't know if that's a good idea."

He didn't seem surprised. "Scarlett?"

Nicholas could handle himself with my best friend. I'd seen him in action at The Lower 8 and realized he was a born politician. It was Scarlett's potential reaction to our budding romance that worried me, and the fact I'd kept it from her. She wasn't the kind to take the easy way out of anything, so why was it so hard for me to do the same? I got in the car hoping for the best but expecting the worst.

A large white envelope was on the front seat, and I fingered the heavy, expensive stock. Nicholas's name had been dashed across the front.

"It's from my father," he said as he settled behind the wheel.

Warren and Scarlett were in the kitchen when we walked in, and the smell of tomato and basil seasoned the air. Warren's loopy smile was back as he slowly chopped onions with the attention one would pay to brain surgery. Scarlett, standing at the stove, didn't bother to hide her displeasure at Nicholas' appearance.

"Hey, man." Warren sniffed as tears welled. "Have you ever chopped an onion before? These things are wicked."

"I'm not very good in the kitchen," Nicholas admitted.

"What a surprise," Scarlett sniped under her breath.

"I can only imagine what you must think of me," Nicholas said, tackling her hostility head on. "But I want the same thing you do: Blake's safety and wellbeing."

"Really?" Scarlett used a wooden spoon to aggressively stir a pot of spaghetti sauce. "The last time I checked, I hadn't taken her to a club filled with people who can kill with their thoughts."

Warren, surprisingly, didn't look as thrown by that statement as I would have expected. "It's cool," he said, catching my wide-eyed stare. "Scarlett told me all about it."

A guilty flush stained her cheeks. She had never revealed my secret to anyone, not even her mother, so this spoke volumes about her feelings for Warren. Nicholas looked appalled, like she'd broadcast state secrets on the evening news.

I quickly jumped in before angry words caused damage that couldn't be undone. "I'm glad everything's out in the open. If there's someone out there thinking they can get away with murder, it's better there're no secrets in here, don't you think?"

Nicholas and Scarlett regarded each other in stony silence broken only by the wooden spoon repeatedly smacking against the sides of the pot. She finally put it down and wiped her hands on a dishtowel. "What's with the envelope?"

I'd almost forgotten it was in my hand. I pulled out a chair at our small kitchen table and broke the seal, fanning out a sheaf of papers.

"These are the pictures, bios, and contact information of the four people at the club last night who would be capable of enchanting someone," Nicholas said, joining me at the table. Henry Thorne sure worked fast. There were two men and two women, and all looked like nice, ordinary people.

Scarlett and Warren wandered over. "You think one of them is a murderer?" she asked.

"Not yet, I hope," I said, trying to see past the ink and paper and into their lives.

Warren picked up a headshot of a man in his fifties, the harsh lighting and blue background typical of a DMV photo. "How are you going to figure it out?"

I was still sketchy on the details myself. Even if I could walk up to each person and hold their hand, would I be able to determine with certainty their intent to murder Selena? Would the guilty party even cooperate, and could this put my own life at risk?

"I'm hoping I can get a future reading by being near each one," I said, thinking aloud, "but I'm not positive it will work."

"Why don't you try it on one of us?" Warren had no idea how touchy that suggestion would be to Scarlett. She had few secrets from me, an occupational hazard when you befriended a clairvoyant. Only once had I shared a glimpse of her future that wasn't life or death, and it nearly destroyed our friendship.

I rushed to cover the potentially awkward moment. "Are you volunteering?"

He grasped Scarlett's hand before meeting my gaze. "I couldn't save Eddie and Kevin, but maybe I can help someone else."

It looked like Scarlett had found a guy worthy of her. Relaxing as best I could, my thoughts centered on Warren, seeking out an incident of danger and violence. Almost immediately I was transported to the day of the car accident, experiencing it all over again from his perspective. It was no longer a jumpy, obscure image; now it was fleshed out with smells, colors, and emotions. I pulled out of it with a gasp.

"What? What happened?" he asked.

"It was the day of the accident," I said with a grimace.

His eyes welled with tears, but he brushed them away. He plunked down at the table. "Try again," he insisted.

Nicholas nodded in encouragement, but this time I put my hand across Warren's before sending my thoughts out into the days ahead. As it had been with Nicholas, the connection was almost instant, and I jumped into his future.

He was with Scarlett. They strolled through a quiet night along the familiar streets of our neighborhood. A cold spell must be coming because they were bundled up.

The next moment revealed two men lurking in the shadows. One was dark and unshaven, the other with light skin and greasy brown hair. Both were dressed in clothing that had seen better days, the dark-skinned man wearing a dingy green army jacket with oily stains on the sleeves. My heart raced in dread.

The vision flashed to Scarlett, her back against a car while Warren hunkered defensively in front of her. The one in green had a knife, slicing the air with it while his accomplice grinned.

Please, Warren, just toss him your wallet, I thought frantically.

Then the most bizarre thing happened. One moment the attacker menaced Warren with a knife. The next, the sleeve of the man's army jacket sparked and glowed. He stared at it, dumb-founded, before dropping the knife as the light intensified.

The image skipped again, and all I saw were the faces of Warren and Scarlett, illuminated by a bright, flickering light. They both looked horrified by whatever they witnessed. Then Scarlett grabbed Warren's hand, and they ran like hell.

I shook my head in disbelief, unable to make sense of what I'd seen.

"You and Scarlett need to be careful when you walk at night," I finally said, "or you're going to get mugged."

"That's it?" He sounded disappointed.

"Well, it's a really scary mugging," I said defensively, wondering if he'd still find my vision lacking if I told him his attacker appeared to burst into flames, just like the red Mustang. Future visions could be frustratingly vague, but that one was just plain freaky.

"The important thing," Nicholas said, "is that you were able to call up a specific future event. You've proven you can do it at will." Yes, I had, but for true clarity, I would have to physically touch each person. So much for discretion.

Scarlett and Warren drifted back to the kitchen while Nicholas and I thumbed through the rest of Henry Thorne's report. The oldest potential suspect, Reginald Costas, was a fifty-five-year-old salesman at the local Mercedes Benz dealership. It made me wonder if the high number of luxury cars in town was the result of a booming local economy or the influence of one Mr. Costas. He was single, had a fondness for Cuban cigars, and was a regular at The Lower 8.

I recognized the youngest one on the list from her photo. Flashing it at Nicholas, I said, "This was the girl with Marcus Sinclair last night, the one who just moved here."

Nicholas retrieved the short report that accompanied the picture. "Alice Ferndale, age nineteen, from Filton, Oregon, population five thousand. No recorded family connection to The Nine, nothing remarkable in her history, became a Class Two enchanter at age seventeen. Graduated high school last year and now works at a fast-food restaurant." He studied her senior yearbook picture, which showed Alice staring off into the distance as if her future was just in the next room. "I wonder what she's doing here?"

She was like a million other kids from small towns across the country, including my own. Maybe she'd decided if adventure was unlikely to find her at the drive-up window, she'd go looking for it instead.

We moved on to the other woman on the list. Samantha Gibson was a pretty suburban housewife of thirty-five. Nicholas picked up a posed studio portrait of her and her smiling husband, Dr. Harold Gibson, along with their three shining young children. With her trim designer suit and perfectly manicured nails, I couldn't imagine her putting snail bait in her garden let alone taking down another human being.

The final suspect was Tristan Murrieta, age twenty-eight, who looked nothing like his name might suggest. His parents must have been hoping for a dashing heartthrob of a son when they christened him with such a classically heroic name. What they got instead was a thin-shouldered guy whose pallor indicated his interests were limited to the great indoors. He also looked familiar.

Holding up the picture that showed him with a strained, gap-toothed smile, I asked, "Do you know him?"

"I spoke to him just as were leaving the club last night." His gaze met mine. "He's an accountant, and he works for Sutton Sinclair."

That was the connection. He and Selena both worked for Sinclair, and maybe she'd discovered he'd been stealing from his employer. People had killed for less.

I zeroed in again on his photo. "We have to stop him before he kills Selena Flores."

The Doctor's Wife

It was Sunday, and I had the morning shift at Jitters. If I wasn't convinced Selena was safe at least until tomorrow night, I would have called in sick and spent the entire day hunting down the four enchanters, even if it did mean leaving Al to pick up the slack. He'd been great about giving me time off to go home for the holidays, and I didn't want to abuse his good nature.

My parents called as I got dressed.

"Your sister got suspended from school," my dad said with a heavy sigh.

That was impossible. Jordan was the perfect kid. She made top grades with seemingly little effort, was president of the junior class, and was so popular the cheerleading squad had recruited her in freshman year.

"What did she do? Get a B+?" I asked with sarcasm.

"This is serious," my mom piped up. Dad's phone was on speaker, and I could hear her moving about in the kitchen. "She got into a fight."

Whoa, go Jordan. Maybe if I'd had the guts to take a swing at my first bully, life in high school would have been bearable.

"What happened?"

"She won't talk about it," Dad said.

My mom moved closer to the phone. "She's changed a lot since you left."

Sundays for Mom started at the gym, so she'd be in yoga pants with her blonde hair caught up in a ponytail. I'd inherited her lean frame and coloring, while my sister had my dad's height and dark hair.

"Maybe you can find out what's going on?" she ventured. "When you're home for Thanksgiving?"

I'd be the last person on earth she'd confide in. However, I got the feeling they wanted the full story of my sister's fall from grace and weren't particular about how they got it.

"I will *talk* to her." I knew they were worried about Jordan but spying voyantly on her felt disloyal.

There was a click. "Blake," my mom said, the clarity telling me we were no longer on speaker. The household noises continued, and I could chart her progress from the kitchen to unlocking the sliding glass doors leading to the back patio. The scrape of wrought iron chair legs on brick told me she'd taken a seat at the outdoor table.

"It must be nice out," I said for something to say. We were as close as any other mother and daughter, but her long hours at work meant my dad was the one who managed our lives. Any news I shared with him would make its way to her and vice versa. She only tracked me down when there was a problem.

She heaved a sigh. "I'm sorry."

It took a few moments to process that. "Um, for what?"

"I sometimes wonder if the reason I spend so much time helping other people is because I couldn't help you," she confessed.

I stared at my phone, wondering where this was coming from. "I'm not sick, Mom."

"Oh God, of course not," she rushed to say. "It's just I know how hard it was for you, and maybe if I'd been home more..." She paused. "How can I help your sister if I'm not around for her either?"

We both sat with that for a minute while I debated how to respond. Having her in the kitchen baking cookies every afternoon when I got home from school wouldn't have changed anything. In fact, part of what I loved about her was her fierceness, whether it be advocating for her patients or protecting Scarlett from her troubled mother. Maybe guilt came with parenthood, but there was no reason for me to make it worse.

"You're doing great, Mom," I finally said. "If you'd been one of those helicopter parents, I'm sure I'd have gone to college in a different country just to get away."

She laughed. "So you're saying I haven't scarred you for life?"

"Let's not go overboard here," I joked, earning another laugh. "But Mom, whatever's going on with Jordan isn't going to change just because you cut back your hours at work."

The crows who regularly picked through our lawn for bugs and worms cackled as she absorbed my words. "It's not the same without you here," she said at last. "I can't wait for you to come home."

"I miss you, too," I said, "but right now I've got to go deal some caffeine. My junkies are waiting."

"Lovely job description," she said dryly before we ended the call.

I carefully composed a text to Jordan while walking to work. Then I rewrote it a dozen times until it could have been written by a monosyllabic stranger. It was the only way there'd be any chance of getting a response.

U good? I asked.

After a minute or two, I tucked my phone in my pocket. A text came in just as I reached the front door of Jitters.

No, she responded. I stared at the word for a minute before taking the plunge. *Want to talk?*

NO instantly popped up on my screen. I sighed. There'd be nothing more from her, but I wanted to give her something to think about. *Those morons at school are clueless...the world they live in isn't what it seems.* For a moment I considered how different things might be if Nines were no longer hidden, as Sutton Sinclair wanted. Those jerks would think twice before coming after *my* sister.

A knock on the coffeehouse window brought me to attention. Despite being a few minutes early, Cindy's harried expression urged me to grab an apron (appropriately, *Coffee: The Vodka of Morning)* and leap into action.

It was a busy day, so time sped by until Nicholas stood by the door waiting for me to clock out. I suggested we start our quest tracking down the most obvious suspect, Tristan Murrieta, but Nicholas had news.

"I called Murrieta's supervisor to get his work schedule," he said. "I figured it would be safer to confront him in front of witnesses. She told me he called her at home last night to say his grandmother had died, and he had to go overseas for the funeral."

"That's mighty convenient." On one hand, it was a relief to think he'd heard about my vision and bolted because I didn't believe any grandmother would die such a timely death. On the other, what if it was just a ruse to stay under the radar for a few days while he continued with whatever he had planned?

"We still need to talk to the other three enchanters," Nicholas said. "It would be foolish to overlook all the possibilities."

"Fine," I groused. So despite it being, in my opinion, a waste of time, we were headed back to Suki's neck of the woods. Samantha Gibson lived in the neighboring Las Brisas Estates, the poshest part of Santa Carla.

A pretentious archway spanning the entire street welcomed us to a neighborhood where each home was grander and more beautiful than the last. Pristine luxury cars dotted the occasional driveway, and artfully designed gardens spilled onto emerald lawns. Growing up, I'd mowed the front yard every Saturday, but I bet the people here had platoons of gardeners to keep every leaf in its proper place.

I recognized the kids from their picture as we pulled up to the curb. The oldest one, a boy of seven or eight, kicked a soccer ball around the wide front lawn. Behind him a younger girl idled in a red swing suspended from the branch of a giant sycamore. Mrs. Gibson herself sat on the front steps watching her youngest daughter doodle with sidewalk chalk.

I'd realized earlier I didn't need an elaborate excuse in order to approach our possible suspects. I would just stick out my hand and introduce myself. Who would refuse to shake hands with a nice girl like me? I put a smile on my face as I got out of the car.

It didn't go quite as planned. Mrs. Gibson stood at our approach, a wary look on her face. She looked as tidy as her home with her trim figure sheathed in matching pants and hoodie in coffee-colored velour just a few shades darker than her skin. Her hair and makeup were beautifully done, just waiting for Dr. Gibson to come home and admire over a perfectly cooked Sunday roast.

"Children, go inside. Tyson, take care of your sisters." The boy started to protest, but his mother simply glanced in his direction before he moved to do her bidding. All three kids practically marched into the house, giving me another glimpse of how useful it might be to be an enchanter, especially as a parent.

She zeroed in on Nicholas. "What can I do for you, Mr. Thorne?"

"You recognize me. I'm flattered." I knew him well enough by now to know he was falling back on manners to cover the awkward moment.

She wasn't buying it. "My husband will be home soon, and all he knows is that I'm a very persuasive person. Tell me what you want."

I stepped forward, extending my hand. "Hello, Mrs. Gibson, my name is Blake Wilder. I asked Nicholas to bring me here to meet you."

She stood her ground and refused to take the bait.

My smile fading, I dropped my hand and decided to go with a version of the truth. "I am a voyant, Mrs. Gibson, and I saw something at Lower 8 Friday night that may lead to the Prime Sentinel coming to question everyone who was there." I didn't know if that was true, but it sounded good.

The shift in her manner was subtle but unmistakable. She was suddenly uncertain, obviously less than thrilled with the idea of more visitors she would have to explain to her unsuspecting husband. "You can't involve me in this. My husband wouldn't understand. He thought I was at a baby shower Friday night."

"We won't have to," Nicholas said, stepping forward. "Please allow Blake to take your hand so we can put this all behind us."

She stared at me a moment before giving a barely perceptible nod.

As we drove out of the wealthy enclave, it occurred to me that the premonition I'd had of Samantha Gibson would have a much longer shelf life than the usual few days or weeks. In fact, the vision of Mrs. Gibson wouldn't come to pass until spring.

Poor Dr. Gibson was ignorant of quite a lot that concerned his wife. She had managed to conceal her enchanting abilities. She had covered the tracks of her ongoing affair with a really hot yoga instructor. And soon she would have to contend with an unplanned pregnancy.

The vision of her future included a frantic search of her calendar while a pregnancy test lay discarded on the bathroom counter. A cheery pink + glowed in the stick's little window. I could understand her panic. The yoga instructor looked like my idea of a Nordic god: blonde, fair-skinned, with a nose and chin so finely chiseled they would do a sculptor proud. Dr. Gibson had soft, fleshy features and a deep, dark complexion. It was going to be a rocky nine months for the unfaithful wife. Her future, however, did not include murder.

"Why didn't you warn her?" Nicholas asked after I told him what I'd seen.

His question startled me. "Until you showed up, I never told anyone what I saw." Talking about it only led to trouble.

"You don't have to be afraid to share your knowledge with other Nines, nor protect those in extreme danger, like Warren was on the day of the accident." He shot me an encouraging smile. "You're not alone anymore."

"Is that how The Nine works? One big happy family?" I let a slight edge seep into my voice.

A flush crept up his neck. "As I said when we first met, our people were once united. Everything we did was for the common good. How will we ever come together again if someone doesn't lead the way?" He was right, of course, and I admired his ideals, but that wasn't the only consideration.

"I won't stand by and let people die if I have the power to save them, but anything else would be changing the future." I'd chased my tail around that conundrum many times. What if I had warned Mrs. Gibson, and she'd avoided the pregnancy? Who was I to interfere in whether or not that child was born?

Something else concerned me. "Do you suppose that since I forced that connection, the usual timeline for events was thrown off?" I'd purposely sought out the most emotional event in her future, most likely leaping over minor problems such as burning dinner or arguing over bedtimes with her kids.

"I would suggest abandoning what you know," Nicholas counseled. "I think you'll get a better understanding of your potential if you open yourself to all possibilities."

I translated that to mean he was as clueless as me.

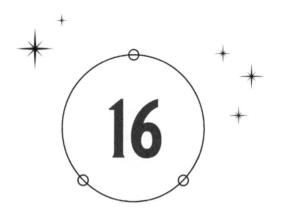

Car Shopping

We started in the direction of the strip of automotive dealers located off the freeway to look up Reginald Costas. Nicholas had set his phone on the wireless charging pad in the car's center console, and it rang before we'd barely cleared Las Brisas.

"It's your dad, I think," I said. The screen identified the caller as HENRY.

Without a moment's thought, Nicholas said, "Let it go to voice mail."

I had met Nicholas because of Henry Thorne. I had gone to The Lower 8 and seen a murderous premonition because of Henry Thorne. I was now approaching potential murder suspects because of one Henry Thorne. For a guy I didn't know, he sure was making a big impact on my life. I hit ACCEPT on the phone.

"Nicholas?" Henry's patrician voice filtered through the car's speakers.

Nicholas shot me a startled glance. "Uh, yes?"

"Sinclair just rang. Why didn't you tell me the Flores woman hadn't been located yet?"

"I…I didn't know myself," Nicholas confessed.

My stomach dropped. Where was she? Maybe Selena had somehow gotten wind her life was in danger and made a run for it. It could also be that even though she hadn't been scraped off Main Street, Tristan Murrieta had indeed learned of my premonition and had simply changed his plan of attack.

"It's not as important as the Wilder girl, who Sinclair seems to know almost as much about as we do already," Henry griped.

I held my breath to see if Nicholas would announce my presence in the car, but he remained silent. As much as I wanted to have a few words with the leader of The Nine, perhaps I'd learn more if I kept my mouth shut.

Henry continued. "He even intimated that she could tip the scales enough to force a challenge between us."

I sat up straight in my seat as another piece of the puzzle fell into place. Nicholas shot me a nervous glance as he said, "Everyone in the world knows you two would like nothing better than to watch the other go down in flames."

"Then you know what's at stake," Henry reminded him. "If Sutton has his way and reveals our people to the world, the consequences will be disastrous for both sides."

"Yes, sir. I understand, but I have to go," he said abruptly, ending the call.

I stared out the window for a minute, the passing scenery a blur as my mind whirled. Selena was still missing, Henry Thorne seemed to think I was a rook on his personal chessboard, and the relationship between Nicholas and Henry contained all the warmth and affection of a rabid pack of squirrels, yet all I could focus on was to wonder how far a son would go to help his father stay in power.

I took a deep breath. "Is that why you kissed me? To make sure I joined Team Thorne?"

"No!" he shot back. "No," he said again more calmly. "I kissed you because I wanted to."

The vice around my chest eased. Part of me wanted to pretend nothing else mattered, but if I'd learned anything about The Nine, it was they hadn't survived centuries of wars and upheaval playing by someone else's rules.

We were nearing the freeway when I asked, "What happens if there's a challenge?"

His lips pressed together as if he were reluctant to speak. "Keep in mind that our society was founded six hundred years ago, and the laws we live by have changed little since then."

"So what? Will your father and Mr. Sinclair joust or fight with swords or something?" I smiled at the image of two rich old guys in their tailored suits charging each other with broadswords.

"Not exactly, but a challenger must come with enough allies to stand against the sitting chancellor and his people."

I quickly understood he was talking about more than a collision of egos. "A battle? What is wrong with you people? Haven't you ever heard of voting?"

It was his turn to smile mockingly. "I've witnessed some of your elections in America. Sometimes I think a battle might be less bloody."

I tipped my head; he had a point. "What does this have to do with me?"

His expression sobered. "Right or wrong, some abilities are more valued by us than others. Whoever comes to the table with a powerful young voyant at his side would be seen as a legitimate contender."

"Or her," I automatically corrected. At his questioning glance I added, "What if the challenger is a woman?"

"That would be a first," he admitted.

"What a surprise," I murmured. Their traditions weren't the only thing that needed updating.

We arrived at the Mercedes Benz dealership. It was easy to find, occupying the biggest parcel of land in the center of the "Mile of Cars" as proclaimed by a banner strung across the entrance. The sky was darkening, but the lot was lit up like the surface of the sun.

Nicholas pulled up to the curb and turned to me, his expression solemn. "I believe in what The Nine stands for, and that the old ways are still the best for protecting our people. Sutton's idea of throwing out tradition and turning us into some sort of global power is dangerous. If we lose our humanity, we'll lose sight of what we've been trying to do for centuries."

"And that is?"

"To remember why we've been given such gifts, and to use them wisely." He believed in the nobility of The Nine; I could feel sincerity rolling off him in waves.

"Thank you for being honest with me," I said.

The car doors popped open, bringing the subject to a close. We strolled onto the lot as if we were privileged young buyers in possession of our parents' credit card. A tall young man with a thatch of red hair and freckles spotted us and practically galloped across the lot to stake his claim. I shot Nicholas a look of exasperation but was instantly sorry. The heavy door of a silver sedan abruptly swung open right into the salesman's path. It nailed the poor guy, who clutched his nether regions before slowly sinking to the ground.

"What? You wanted me to do something, so I did something," Nicholas said at my pained look. I hoped we found Mr. Costas before we had to maim the entire sales staff.

We walked toward a glass rotunda at the center of the lot. Gleaming sports cars and convertibles were arranged like a metallic still life within. No sooner had we walked in the door than we saw Mr. Costas engaged in earnest conversation with a man who appeared to be hanging on the salesman's every word, another satisfied buyer in the making.

Within a few minutes he called over an associate to lead his customer to a room for the contract signing. He'd picked up on our watchful presence and walked directly over.

The enchanter's face was open and friendly, seemingly unaware of our identities or our unique connection. Sporting a tangle of short, curly hair liberally sprinkled with gray, and a nose a size too large for his broad face, he confidently strode straight up to me.

"I am a lucky man," he proclaimed. "My job actually requires me to walk up to beautiful women and introduce myself. I'm Reggie Costas." And he held out his hand.

Nicholas glanced at me, and I shook my head. Costas was innocent. In fact, the biggest event coming into the confirmed bachelor's life would be a woman. He who had loved many women but not enough to marry any of them would be bowled over at an age when most men were putting their kids through college. He would meet her when she came into the dealership to buy herself a fiftieth birthday present. I saw a lot of laughter and joy coming into his life, and I was happy for him.

"We're sorry to bother you. I think it's a case of mistaken identity. We'll let you get back to your customer," Nicholas said, easing his way toward the door. I quickly followed suit.

"Wait! That's it?" Confusion was clearly written across the salesman's face.

Impulsively, I dashed over and kissed him on the cheek. His eyes lit up with delight. "What was that for, beautiful lady?"

For a change I had seen love instead of hate, joy instead of death. "For luck," I said, "and the promise of many more kisses to come."

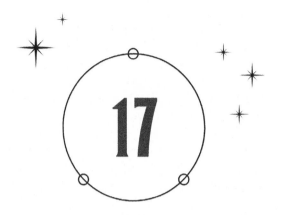

Invitations

I worked the Monday night shift with the fading hope Selena would drop in. School that day had limped by, with an occasional text from Nicholas updating me on his fruitless search for Alice Ferndale and Tristan Murrieta. As the clock ticked well past the dinner hour, my nerves were strung as tightly as the laces on one of Cindy's leather corsets. Every time the front door opened, I jumped.

The flow of customers had slowed to the point where Cindy had time to list all the ways to die if you were a teenager stranded at a deserted campground and being stalked by a homicidal maniac. She'd spent part of the weekend in Los Angeles watching a marathon of horror movies with her boyfriend.

After a particularly brutal description of death by power tools, I asked, "How can you watch that stuff? Doesn't it give you nightmares?"

She gave the question serious consideration while frothing a double dose of foam for a waiting customer. "Gosh, I guess I'm just relieved when it's over. Like I survived even though the prom queen didn't."

I could relate. My visions were beginning to feel like that.

We were cranking out a large order for a group of women all toting the same book when a few of them tittered at the same moment my skin tingled with energy. Jessie McCabe had sauntered in the door. Blue jeans hugged his long legs, a black pullover had been pushed up to reveal a couple of tats on the corded muscles of his forearms, and his blonde hair hung loose about his shoulders. He smiled wickedly at his admirers, actually causing a few middle-aged women to blush, before claiming a table. When all the lattes and cappuccinos had been served, I ducked under the bar and made my way over.

"I've been waiting for you," he drawled as I neared, his slow smile making it clear he didn't mean only at this particular moment. His eyes danced. "Has your question been answered yet?"

He'd texted me a few more times since sending the provocative selfie, but I hadn't responded to any of them. "I don't recall asking one."

He lowered his voice, encouraging me to take the other chair at the café table. "You have to be wondering if you'd be better off if you'd met me first."

Of course I'd thought about it. Jessie wouldn't have gotten under my skin the way Nicholas had. I wouldn't have abandoned my natural caution and made decisions I might still come to regret. I wouldn't have been asked to care about a noble institution under attack, but only how to take advantage of the resulting upheaval. I also wouldn't have kissed him—or if I had it wouldn't have touched my heart.

I didn't say any of this to him. Instead I said, "You tell me."

"I would have given you time," he said, his manner serious for once. "Being a patron is an honor not to be taken lightly. We have a duty to teach and protect, and the bonds of loyalty and friendship the pair often forms are one of the hallmarks of The

Nine. The Thornes have slighted both of us." As if realizing this wasn't the time or place to take this further, his lazy smile returned.

For a group who loved their traditions, Henry Thorne had stomped all over a time-honored custom when he'd sent his son to Santa Carla. Nicholas had descended like a whirlwind, and for the most part I hadn't questioned the pace. Now I understood why Jessie had barely restrained his fury with Nicholas on the night we'd come to The Lower 8.

"Is that what you came here to tell me?" I asked.

He nonchalantly arched a brow. "Do I need a reason to visit the most beautiful voyant in town?"

"I'm the only voyant in town," I blandly pointed out.

"True, but I thought maybe you could use a friend."

I narrowed my gaze at him. "Why do I get the feeling you never do anything without a reason?"

A smile tugged at his lips. "Because you're not a fool. However, that doesn't mean I can't feel protective of a girl who deserves better than to have Thorne as her patron, for however long he sticks around."

I suspected Jessie wasn't a fool either and had deliberately reminded me my time with Nicholas had an expiration date. Nicholas had yet to talk about the life waiting for him in England, but it had to be the reason he kept a certain distance between us. Maybe he thought keeping it light would make it easier to say goodbye when the time came, but it didn't stop me from wanting to do something to break down the walls he seemed to live behind.

"What makes you think Nicholas is leaving any time soon?" I asked, just to push back a bit.

He shoved a lock of hair off his face as he considered the question. "If you were just a girl and he were just a boy, maybe things would be different, but you know that's not how things work in our world."

"Then tell me how it does work," I said with an edge of frustration. "You said I should come to you if I ever needed help, but why would you say that? What do you think's going to happen?"

Two couples came in the front door, followed by a pair of women. The movie theatre around the corner must have just let out, and Cindy caught my eye. Jessie picked up on the signal and got to his feet before extending a hand to me. I hesitated, not needing a reminder of the effect his touch had on me.

He smiled knowingly, and I lifted my chin at the unspoken challenge. Against my better judgement I accepted the invitation. The moment we touched, raw energy flashed between us like dry kindling touched by flame. I barely knew the guy and wasn't even sure I liked him, making it all the more unsettling. When we stood face to face, I tried to reclaim my hand, but his fingers tightened on mine.

"Let me go," I said breathlessly.

"It's not me you need to be afraid of," he said gently, releasing his grip.

I took a step back, putting some distance between us. "Then will you answer my questions?"

"Come to the club anytime, and I'm all yours." It wasn't exactly the answer I wanted, but with a line forming at the counter there wasn't time for more. "Until next time," he said, turning toward the door.

I joined Cindy behind the counter as she ogled the departing phantomist. "Was that your boyfriend and if not, can I have him?"

"What about Todd?" I asked.

"Todd is a boy." She tipped her head toward the door. "That one is a man."

We had a steady stream of customers after that, which gave me very little time to think about Jessie. It only slowed when we were close to locking up for the night.

I was busy cleaning the cappuccino machines when someone called my name. I turned to find Marcus Sinclair, who had exchanged his smooth nightclub-owner persona for the vaguely professional L.L.Bean man. He wore khakis and a navy polo with the Sinclair Development Corp logo sewn onto the shirt's front pocket. Oddly, I hadn't picked up that hum of energy I now felt with other Nines.

I practically leapt across the bar. "Did you guys find Selena Flores?"

He released a heavy sigh and shook his head. "I'm sorry."

Tears threatened, and I closed my eyes.

"Hey, we haven't given up yet," he said, breaking into my misery. "We don't know that she's not off recovering from some lost weekend." He didn't sound like he believed it any more than I did.

He cleared his throat. "I'm actually here on family business. My dad wants to meet you."

Of course he did. It wasn't enough that people around me were dying or disappearing, or that I'd outed myself to the entire preternatural world. Now I had to deal with another powerful man used to getting what he wanted, including a pet sentinel who was barely housebroken. I fumbled about for an excuse to get out of it.

"Between work and school, I'm really stretched for time," I said weakly.

"My father is an important man. He can be a good friend to have. On the other hand…" He didn't have to finish. Making an enemy of Sutton Sinclair would not be in anyone's best interest.

"All right," I reluctantly agreed. "I can clear my schedule tomorrow afternoon. Where would he like to meet?"

Marcus gave me the address of the giant construction project underway downtown. "He's always on site. Give your name at the gate, and you'll be taken right to his office. I like your apron, by the way."

The one I wore tonight said *My Blood Type is French Roast.*

Cindy flipped the sign on the front door from open to closed, so I ventured a question. "Marcus, can I ask what your connection to The Nine is?"

If we hadn't been standing face to face, I might have missed the sudden tightness in his jaw. "I'm just a lowly sentinel, can't you tell? I can barely get in the door of my own club." He tacked on a laugh, but it was just for show.

Maybe that answered the question of why he didn't register on my frequency, and why Sutton had bought Marcus a stake in The Lower 8. If you couldn't earn respect with your abilities, perhaps buying it was the next best thing.

As if he could read my thoughts, Marcus nodded and strode out the door.

Cindy, who'd been watching us while wiping down tables, came up to the counter and tossed down her towel. "Gee whiz, Blake, is there a hot guy in town you *don't* know?"

I was getting ready for bed when Scarlett got home from another date with Warren. She bolted the door but didn't turn when I padded up behind her.

"Scarlett?"

She expelled a breath and pivoted to face me.

"Scarlett! What happened to you?" Her hand shot to her mouth, covering the evidence, but not before I got a good look at her cracked and swollen lips. Fury swept through me. "Did Warren hurt you?"

"No! It's not what you think." She lowered her hand. "I don't know what happened. Warren and I were kissing..." Her face split into a grin before she winced at the pain.

"And?" No mere lip lock would leave her looking like she'd been punched in the face.

"I don't know! We were kissing, and all of a sudden it felt like my lips were on fire. I splashed cold water on them but look at me. How can I go to school looking like this?"

I'd been ready to challenge her story, but then I remembered the premonition of the combustible mugger. What was it about this guy and fire?

"Did Warren get burned?" I asked.

"No, which makes this doubly weird." Her bemusement turned to fear. "Oh my God! Do you think I'm allergic to him?"

I didn't want to make light of her concern, but I didn't think allergies were to blame. "No, I don't think so."

We kept ice packs in the freezer, so we retreated to the kitchen. I wrapped one in a thin dishtowel and wondered if there could possibly be something extraordinary about Warren. He didn't vibrate with energy, but then neither did Marcus. Could that be the reason destiny had singled him out?

I handed her the ice pack. "You really like him, don't you?"

Her face lit up. "He could be the one."

She was ready to fall in love, but what if the guy she'd been waiting for wasn't who she thought he was?

Sutton Sinclair

I guided the trusty old Volvo onto the wide strip of dirt reserved for construction crew parking. More than a dozen heavy pickup trucks were nuzzled up to the eight-foot chain link fence surrounding the building site. A green tarp had been affixed to it, making it impossible to glimpse what was happening on the other side. I turned off the engine and sat for a moment.

I wasn't exactly nervous about meeting Sutton Sinclair, but there was a certain amount of apprehension. The whole clash-of-the-titans thing he had going with Henry Thorne bothered me less than how Sinclair's name popped up every time something bad happened. Could he be involved in the death of Ashley Norman or Selena's disappearance? Was there a connection between the two? Ms. Norman had worked for the Bank of Santa Carla, and surely they had bankrolled some of Sinclair's construction loans. As for Selena, hopefully a bit of voyancy would reveal what he knew of her fate.

I followed the fence to the street entrance where a man with a deep tan and a handlebar mustache stood guard. He wore a white hard hat and an orange neon vest over jeans and heavy work boots. I'd dressed conservatively in black denim, a matching tee shirt, and a trim jacket. Still, from the way his eyes raked over me, I probably could have come with a bag over my head and made this guy's day.

"I'm Blake Wilder, here to see Sutton Sinclair," I said briskly, hoping to covey I meant business.

Those must have been the magic words because he immediately dropped the shit-eating grin and reached for the walkie-talkie hanging from his belt. Within a minute of broadcasting his request for an escort, another man in a hard hat, this time in shirtsleeves with a tie, emerged from behind the gates.

"Ms. Wilder," he said from behind black-rimmed glasses that gave him a scholarly air despite his thirty-something years. He buzzed with the energy unique to a Nine. "I'm Kurt Miller, Mr. Sinclair's assistant." He didn't offer to shake hands, and I noticed several fingers on his right hand were bandaged. "Won't you come with me please?"

I had read about the ambitious plans for Sinclair's latest project but didn't really appreciate the scope of it until I stepped inside the gate. I stood at the precipice of a yawning canyon in the earth so deep it could probably swallow the Titanic with room to spare. Men and machines moved industriously among the metal bars and cement pillars erected for the underground parking of the giant building to come. The walls of the pit were shored up with lumber and braces, but knowing Sutton's capabilities, it was probably just for show.

The assistant led the way along a covered catwalk running the perimeter of the giant hole. Curious about the type of people Sutton Sinclair employed, I practiced my newfound empathic skill but quickly retreated at the mixture of anger and frustration brewing within the man. Maybe he was the guy who did Sutton's dirty work, and he was somehow involved in Selena's disappearance. If she'd put up a fight, it would explain his injured hand.

As much as I didn't want to witness yet another brutal scene that couldn't be erased from memory, Selena needed my help. I pretended to stumble in order to grab Kurt's arm and then plunged into his mind.

I had to work to keep a smirk off my face. Kurt Miller was no killer. He was, however, deluded if he thought he could best Khalia. Apparently, adding the prickly sentinel to Sinclair's staff had incited the assistant's jealously, and he spent his free time dreaming up ways to sabotage her. The vision of him casually dropping a large magnet next to her cell phone had ended with his fingers cracking in the vise of her fist.

The construction offices were three identical trailers set on blocks running end to end. A telephone pole driven into the ground behind them carried heavy power cables to each unit. The door in the center trailer swung open, and Marcus emerged.

"Hey, Blake, glad you could make it." His rueful smile acknowledged he'd left me little choice in the matter. He wore another polo shirt with the company logo on the front pocket, this time in red.

"You work for your dad and run the club, too?"

"I think his goal is to keep me so busy I'll stay out of trouble, but I've never found that a very effective deterrent," he said with a throaty laugh.

"By the way," I said, "I'm hoping to meet up with your friend from the club, Alice Ferndale. Do you know how I can reach her?" Nicholas had called her folks in Oregon to inquire about her current job or address, but they weren't even aware she'd left the state.

Marcus looked puzzled, and then he smiled in sudden recollection. "The girl from the other night? That was the first time I'd met her."

"Really? I thought maybe you knew her better than that."

He shot me an amused glance. "I meet a lot of girls at the club who I get to know intimately within a few hours. It doesn't mean I know much more than their first names."

My face colored, and he grinned in delight. "You really don't get out much, do you?"

"You have no idea," I muttered.

He let me off easy. "Well, I've got to run, but good luck in there."

I followed Kurt through the door Marcus had just exited. The interior space had been divided unevenly in two. The front (and smaller) portion was the domain of an efficient-looking woman wearing a headset nestled into her artificially red hair. She typed ferociously on a desktop computer, nodding at us without missing a keystroke. Kurt strode past her to a closed door, giving it a quick rap before opening it.

The great man sat at his desk. Agitated voices came through the speaker of a desk phone, but he waved us in anyway. He was a big man in every way, from still-powerful shoulders straining at the seams of his monogrammed dress shirt, to beefy hands crisscrossed with ancient scars. His hair was quite gray, almost white, and razed into bristles. A large pair of silver-rimmed glasses shielded his eyes, and despite being diminished by folds of aging skin, they were clear and piercing.

A seating arrangement of modular chairs surrounding a low table took up the front half of his office. Khalia had draped herself across one of the seats in an insolent pose, no easy feat considering the leather pants fitting her like a second skin. Her eyes flicked over me with disinterest before returning to checking the stock market on her phone. She might as well have a sign around her neck declaring that despite being on Sinclair's payroll, no one was the boss of her.

"Stop making excuses, and give me solutions," Sinclair snarled into the phone, his voice deep and gravelly. "You call me back in one hour with how we're going to head off this labor strike, or don't bother calling back at all." He clicked off the speakerphone with a decisive punch of his finger.

He visibly switched gears when he spotted me, dialing back the ruthless developer in favor of genial host. "Blake, how wonderful to meet you at last," he said, rising to his feet. I extended my hand, but he only glanced at it and grinned. "You remember Khalia? Please, let's all grab a chair."

The extraordinary energy in the small space set my teeth on edge, but the boost it provided would make prying into Sinclair's past a cinch, even without physical contact. Years of practicing self-control helped me stroll blithely past Khalia and claim one of the other chairs as if I hadn't a thought in my head.

"I wish I'd been at Lower 8 the night you dropped by," Sinclair said as he settled into his seat. "Maybe if I'd known about your vision of Selena sooner…" He glanced away, as if the subject was too close to home.

"Have you heard from her?" I asked. My hope was fading.

"No, and I can't imagine why anyone would want to harm a sweet gal like her."

"Me either." At his puzzled glance, I added, "She and Chico are regulars at the coffeehouse where I work."

He nodded distractedly before offering me coffee or water, but I passed. I wanted to keep this uncomfortable meeting as brief as possible.

He surprised me. "Do you like being a waitress?"

"I'm a student who works as a *barista* to make ends meet." I didn't like being on the defensive, so I added, "I would think you of all people would respect ambition and hard work."

He chuckled, as if I'd said something cute.

"She thinks you're patronizing her," Kurt said.

I sent a startled glance in the assistant's direction.

"Kurt is an empath," Sinclair said in an offhand way, as if having my emotions announced out loud wasn't completely offensive. "It's his job to read people for me."

Part of me wanted to make a very rude gesture toward the empath and say, "Read this, Kurt," but I restrained myself.

"So tell me," I said instead, "why do I need to be read?"

"Good, I prefer directness myself." He leaned forward in his chair. "Blake, how would you like to make ten, maybe twenty times what you earn at that coffee shop?"

Maybe I should have expected this, but the thought of rubbing shoulders with Kurt and Khalia on a daily basis sent a shudder running through me. "You want to offer me a job?"

"Don't act so surprised," he said with a gruff laugh. "Surely Nicholas Thorne told you there would be others who would find your skills most useful and be willing to pay for your services." His keen eyes continued to probe. "Or perhaps he didn't."

"Look," I said, holding up my hands to signal we needed to slow down, "up until recently, I was just a girl minding my own business who occasionally saw things out of the ordinary. I don't know what it is you think you know about me, but you've got the wrong idea."

He rubbed his chin in thought. "I'll tell you what I think. I think you're one of the most powerful voyants we've seen in years."

"No, sir," I said, pretending to act flattered at being overestimated.

"She's lying," Kurt cheerfully volunteered.

I glared at the empath. "Now that's just plain rude!"

Sinclair chuckled like an indulgent father. "Now, Blake, I thought we agreed to be direct."

He probably wouldn't try to stop me if I got up and left, but neither did I think that would be the end of it if I did.

"All right, Mr. Sinclair, here's the deal. I appreciate the offer, but I have no interest in being kept on a leash and trotted out for company." I shot a meaningful glance at Kurt, who scowled in return. Khalia merely looked bored by the whole thing, making me wonder what her role there might be. "If I change my mind, you'll be the first to know, but in the meantime, I think I'm ready to leave." I rose from the sofa, my posture ramrod straight.

"Okay, okay," he said in an irritated tone, waving me back to my seat. I didn't think he had by any means given up, but there would be no further discussion about it today. "I admire your spirit. If any of my kids had even half your backbone, I wouldn't need so much help running this damn company."

"Marcus is not your only son?" I asked more to smooth over the tension than any real interest.

"God, no. It seems every wife I had wanted a kid or two. But Marcus is just like his mother: weak. He spends my money like a drunken sailor. If he doesn't make a go of the club, I wash my hands of the boy."

It was a bitterly personal observation, and his emotions spiked. It was as good a time as any to slip into his head in search of Selena and Ashley Norman.

Khalia immediately glanced up from her phone. "What are you doing?"

I instantly pulled back, and Sinclair regarded me smugly. "Has no one yet explained to you the shielding power of sentinels?"

"No," I said, embarrassed at being caught.

"Why did you think I was here?" Khalia's snippy tone made it clear her low opinion of me hadn't changed.

"It's good that you're strong," Sinclair said, seemingly unoffended at my thwarted invasion. "You'll need to be in the days to come."

Was that a threat or a warning? "I don't understand."

"No, you wouldn't," he conceded. "I keep forgetting how new you are to all this. Are you aware of the history of The Nine?"

I nodded. "Nicholas has been filling me in a bit. He said it exists to protect its members."

Sinclair folded his hands across his still-firm middle. "From *what*?"

"From each other?" I shot Khalia a pointed look, provoking a mocking grin in return.

Sinclair snorted in derision. "All Henry Thorne wants is to condemn us to another generation of mediocrity. Change never comes easily, but I assure you, it will come."

I leaned forward in my chair. "What does that mean, exactly?"

After baiting the hook, his eyes glinted with satisfaction at my bite.

"It means a world without war because there'd be telepaths and empaths in every government to stop conflicts before they started. A world without hunger because voyants such as yourself would warn us of coming events that would otherwise lead to crop or livestock devastation. A world without want because materialists could provide for those in need. The list goes on."

On the surface, the picture he painted of a future without suffering was ideal, and seemed to fit with The Nine's original vision of using our gifts for the benefit of mankind. The problem was I'd seen too much of human nature to believe this utopia would ever come about without strings attached.

"What do you get out of all this?" I asked.

A self-satisfied smile crept onto his face. "Someone must lead this world, don't you agree?" It appeared becoming chancellor was merely a stepping-stone to higher ambitions, but what would happen to anyone who rebelled at the idea of being ruled by paranormal overlords? Giving anyone as much power as Sinclair sought would only recreate King Henry on a global scale.

He hadn't wasted any time. In the course of ten minutes, he'd offered me a high-paying job and the chance to take my place in a new world order. Then, because I couldn't resist pushing a few buttons, I said, "So, Kurt, how do we feel about all of this?"

"You are anxious, a bit suspicious, but most of all, you're intrigued." His vaguely taunting tone made it sound like he'd uncovered some dirty little secret.

Technology had brought Nines together as never before. Communication and coordination on a massive scale was now possible. Could we be united for the common good without it turning into a power grab?

An intriguing idea, indeed.

I didn't need an escort back to the front gates, but Sinclair muttered something about safety, so Kurt dogged my heels. Surprisingly, I'd actually taken a liking to the big man with his no-holds-barred approach to every aspect of his life. He might be calculating and self-serving, but at least you knew where you stood with him. I couldn't say the same for his petty empath.

Kurt had quickly hidden a scowl when Sutton offered me a job, and despite turning it down, his earlier anger at Khalia had shifted to antagonism towards me. I hated walking to the gate with him behind me. I decided to keep an eye on him in my own way, seeking the next compelling event in his future. If he planned to mess with me somehow, I wanted to see it coming.

There was nothing there. It was like walking into an empty room with the lights turned off. I didn't understand; was he able to block me somehow? I turned to look at him, to see if he was laughing at my attempt to pry into his head, when suddenly an enormous darkness blotted out the sun. Pure instinct sent me diving for the catwalk.

I would never forget the sound. Along with the smashing of wood and the wrenching of metal, the wet crunch of Kurt being crushed by tons of steel went straight to my gut. I stayed glued to the dirty wooden boards as the steel girder swung back the way it came, an errant pendulum continuing on its path. Shouts exploded from the pit. The catwalk vibrated with the impact of running feet, but I wasn't moving until someone peeled me off the walkway.

The first one to reach me was Sinclair. "Blake! Are you injured?"

I lifted my head and saw the section of catwalk I'd just crossed completely destroyed. "What happened?"

He pointed to an enormous crane with a massive steel beam still swinging at the end of its cable. "It had no business being anywhere near here. The operator is one of my best men." He shook his head. "This makes no sense."

He kept an arm around me as he led me back to his office, shielding me from what remained of Kurt.

"Why would anyone want to kill your empath?" I asked, a sob catching in my throat.

"Killing Kurt was probably an accident. I think the target was you."

A Reluctant Agreement

Night had fallen by the time the authorities were satisfied with my version of events. Nicholas managed to skirt the barricade of police, journalists, and the coroner to find me hiding in Sinclair's office. He pulled me into an embrace, and I nestled my cheek against his shoulder.

"Are you all right?" He stroked my hair.

"I don't know," I sniffled.

"You should have told me," he said. "I would have come with you."

I lifted my eyes to his, the hint of censure in his voice stiffening my spine. "This was something I had to do on my own."

Moving to Santa Carla had started a chain reaction. It had caused Henry Thorne to send his son running to my side, resulting in Sutton Sinclair attempting to bring me into his orbit. As I sorted out what I knew about The Nine and how I fit into it, I'd wanted to hear what the big man had to say unfiltered.

Khalia strode into the room and locked eyes with Nicholas.

"Good to see you again, Khalia," he said stiffly. "Interesting choice you've made here."

She sniffed as if he'd read too much into her career change. "Sinclair offered me health insurance and stock options."

Her boss chose that moment to walk in the door, weariness etched on his face. A cynical smile appeared when he spied me in Nicholas's arms, but he settled into the big black chair behind his desk without comment. He appeared more intimidating and less approachable than when we'd first gathered around the coffee table, and I wondered if that was for Nicholas' benefit.

"This wasn't an accident," he announced with certainty. "Ralph's been on my crew for twenty years. He said it was as if someone else was controlling his hands, forcing him to move the levers the way he did. I believe him."

I did too. I'd seen it done to Selena, and it could also explain Ashley Norman's supposed accident. We still had two enchanters unaccounted for.

"When was the last time you saw Tristan Murrieta, who's currently in your employ?" Nicholas asked, his thoughts running along the same lines as mine.

Sinclair looked blankly at Khalia.

"The skinny enchanter," she reminded him. "The one who scuttles away like a crab whenever I walk by." Her lips curled in satisfaction at intimidating yet another lesser being.

"You think he did this?" Sinclair asked.

"It's a possibility," Nicholas said. "He told his supervisor he had to leave town for a funeral, but I have my doubts."

Sinclair picked up his phone and punched a few buttons. "Find Tristan Murrieta," he growled to whomever answered. He hung up and considered Nicholas for a long moment. "It's time we put our differences aside." Then he turned to me. "Are you hungry?"

"Sutton is offering you his protection," Nicholas said as we drove to The Lower 8. We'd left my car behind at the building site.

"How positively Victorian of him," I muttered.

"By the three of us sitting down in public together," he continued, ignoring my gibe, "Sutton is sending a message that should anyone try to harm you, they will have more than just the Thornes to deal with."

"What about Kurt? Are you so sure he wasn't the target?" I had a hard time wrapping my head around the idea someone wanted me dead.

"He was in the wrong place at the wrong time." The Tesla zoomed down one of the narrow roads of the warehouse district. "Your ability will get men like Sinclair to fight for you, but it will also put you in danger."

"Well that's fucking peachy," I growled, staring out into the darkness.

A skittish Suki manned the door. Like the visit to her condo, we couldn't move fast enough to suit her. She was a sentinel and believed herself immune to my clairvoyance, so it couldn't be my talents that had her in a twist. I would have said something about it to Nicholas, but the familiar rush of intense energy washed over me when we entered the main club. I put all my focus into resisting the pull of so many minds.

I gawked at the room's transformation. The elegant nightclub was now a 1920s-era speakeasy, complete with a small orchestra. The waitresses swirled around in mini flapper dresses, and orbs of light were magically suspended overhead, casting a warm glow over the dancing couples.

"Nicholas, what happened to the room? And what's up with those lights?" They looked like tiny stars pulsing with energy.

He followed my gaze but didn't act as if they were anything out of the ordinary. "I'm sure McCabe has a materialist and an evanescent on staff."

We were at the bottom of the staircase, and I almost missed the last step. Jessie appeared, reaching out a steadying hand. He looked tense and relieved, somehow both at the same time.

"Sutton Sinclair called," he said, scanning my face. "Are you all right?"

The number of men fussing over me had increased yet again. In keeping with the evening's theme, he wore a vest and trousers of blue pinstripe with his hair tucked beneath a rakish fedora. A gold watch chain dangled at his waist.

"I'm better," I said. "Kurt Miller wasn't so lucky."

He pinned Nicholas with a hard look. "Is this your idea of being a patron?"

"I don't need a babysitter," I shot back, not liking the damsel in distress role everyone wanted to cast me in.

Jessie's jaw unclenched as he made a visible effort to take it down a notch. "Of course not," he said before glaring at Nicholas again. "This kind of offense cannot be overlooked."

"I'll discuss it with Sinclair over dinner," he responded, turning his back on Jessie to make clear the invitation didn't include him.

As if she'd been waiting in the wings, Layla popped up. The pixie had morphed into a prohibition-era vamp. She wore a gauzy black sheath with layers of pearls looped around her neck. Her lips, painted a vivid scarlet, were smiling, but with an edge that hadn't been there on my last visit. She also had no concept of personal space. I tried not to shrink back as her lovely brown eyes peered questioningly into mine.

"That's odd. Your aura is dimmer than before. It's almost like..." She shrugged off whatever she'd been about to say and pulled me away from Nicholas and Jessie. "Everyone here is just a mess of suspicion and nerves tonight. It's exhausting."

She settled me into a booth while Nicholas trailed slowly behind, stopping briefly here and there to have a word. Just as the novelty of our arrival began to wear off, Sinclair and Khalia entered. Once again, the attention meter went off the charts when Sinclair took the seat opposite Nicholas in our booth. Khalia peeled away to grab a stool at the bar but kept a watchful eye on her employer. Drinks delivered and baskets of sliders ordered, Layla skipped off.

Sinclair knocked back half a scotch and soda before remarking, "The Prime Sentinel will have to be called."

"Yes," Nicholas said, contemplating his glass of mineral water through narrowed eyes. "A Nine is dead. We have no other choice."

"Won't the police investigate?" I asked.

"They will be looking into an accident, not a homicide," Sinclair said, shaking the ice loose in his glass. "The Prime will come to enforce the laws put in place centuries ago, which don't always mesh with modern thinking. I do happen to agree with this one, however."

I glanced at Nicholas for an explanation.

He obliged. "Six hundred years ago, we didn't have the technology to bring our people together. We'd hear about a witch hunt or a miracle, and sentinels went out hoping to find one of us." He paused to take a sip of his drink. "We were few, and justice was swift. If a Nine took another Nine's life, they would forfeit their own. Kind of biblical, you know."

My eyes widened in comprehension. "Are you saying the Prime Sentinel is an *executioner*?" I could see about five things wrong with this picture, including a lack of evidence. When the law, or in this case a ruthless sentinel, caught up with the rogue enchanter, how could they be positive he'd caused Kurt's death?

"It's not quite that absolute," Nicholas assured me. "There will be a trial conducted by the nine regents, and if the guilty party has any accomplices, that will come out too."

The idea that the enchanter who'd murdered Kurt Miller might not be working alone made my blood run cold. "And if he's found guilty, what then?"

"The punishment will fit the crime," Sinclair cut in, his sandpaper voice made rougher by the liquor. "But it's been decades since The Nine has been faced with such a dilemma."

"Her name was Lindy Keisel," Marcus said. I'd been so intent on the story I hadn't noticed his arrival. He slid into the booth next to his father. "And she was an incredibly talented voyant, much like you." His voice was laced with irony. It surely hadn't escaped his notice how effortlessly I had won his father's approval. "She was responsible for over three hundred of our people's deaths, or so the story goes."

I gasped. "How did she get so far?"

"Oh, the man she worked for went a whole lot farther," Marcus added cryptically. "It was 1945, you see, and she aligned herself with the wrong side."

"She worked for *Hitler*?" I'd heard stories that one of history's greatest villains had been obsessed with the occult, but I never dreamed it was based on truth. "What became of her?"

"The war had just ended, and a tribunal of the six surviving regents was convened," Nicholas said, picking up the thread of the story. "Fortunately, both the voyant regent and the telepathic regent were still alive, so it wasn't hard to produce evidence. She was sentenced to death."

Layla stopped by to deliver dinner, and the topic changed to the pending police investigation. I picked at one of the mini cheeseburgers but discovered I didn't have much of an appetite. I excused myself to go to the ladies room, and the unabashed stares let me know I was once again the main topic of conversation. Some things never changed.

Jessie stood by the bar on my return trip, looking rather thoughtful. No doubt Cedric or one of his other spirits had reported back every detail of what had gone down at our table. The cuffs of his white collared button-down were turned up, and my eyes dropped to the ink on his forearms. An amused snort escaped me when I spied an image of Casper the Friendly Ghost peeking out from beneath one of his scrunched up sleeves.

His brows drew together in mock outrage. "Are you laughing at the questionable life choices made by a teenager?"

"God, no," I said with a grin. "I'm looking forward to making a few of them myself."

His eyes glinted with devilish humor. "Then I'm just in time to help lead you astray."

"Humph," I said. "What happened to Mr. I Should Have Been Your Patron?"

"Right here whenever you need me." He leaned in closer and added softly, "All you ever have to do is call."

I'd already learned no conversation, no thought, no vision could remain private when surrounded by so many extraordinary people, so I chose to take his comment at face value.

"I'll keep that in mind," I said neutrally.

Back at the table, I found Nicholas, Marcus, and Sinclair debating how best to keep me safe until the murderer was apprehended. They were so caught up in making plans I wondered if they'd even noticed I'd returned. I didn't mean to be ungrateful, but they acted as if they had the authority to make decisions for me. It wasn't until Khalia's name came up that I realized I'd better pay closer attention to where this conversation was headed.

"What about Khalia?" I asked, suddenly alert.

"You need a bodyguard who can't be tapped," Nicholas said. "She's a Class One, and probably one of the few people you'd be totally safe around."

Sinclair put in his two cents, of course. "She knows how to handle herself."

"That's not necessary." It was a toss up over whether spending time with Khalia or being left vulnerable to a killer was worse. "Whoever killed Kurt is probably a hundred miles away by now."

"Do you want to live another day?" asked Nicholas.

"Do you think Kurt enjoyed meeting with that steel girder?" asked Sinclair.

"Do you really think you'll survive on your own?" asked Marcus.

I glanced over to where Khalia sat at the bar, sipping from a bottle of water. She met my gaze and scowled.

"Fine," I snapped, tossing my napkin on the table. "I will accept Khalia's protection, and just hope she doesn't sell me out if she thinks she can get a better offer, but that's it. From here on out I plan to take my time and learn what it means to be a part of The Nine. Whatever happens then will be my choice. *I* decide. *Me.*"

I glared at the three men to make sure they'd heard me. Nicholas at least had the grace to look chagrinned, but Sutton absently polished off his scotch as if my little declaration was only of passing interest. Marcus didn't meet my gaze, instead contemplating the ice in his empty glass with a rather forlorn expression. It made me wonder if he knew all too well what it was to be steamrolled by his father. I slid out of the booth, and Nicholas made to follow.

"Hold on," he said. "I'll drive you back to your car."

"Stay and finish your dinner," I said, fed up with high-handed men for the night. I needed space to think. "I'm calling an Uber."

I stalked to the stairs where Jessie waited. He leaned against the banister with his arms loosely folded, a delighted grin lighting up his face.

"Oh, shut up," I snapped, mounting the stairs.

His laughter followed me all the way out the door.

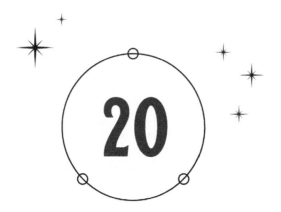

The Bodyguard

There wasn't enough coffee in the world to prepare me for what stood outside my front door the next morning. Khalia seethed with displeasure, her hands balled into fists as if she were spoiling for a fight. For a change, I'd worn a short dress with a cardigan and boots, so without a word, I hiked up my skirt and climbed into the hulking black Escalade at the curb. She slammed the door with a bone-cracking crunch.

We drove in total silence. She could have driven us over the Mexican border, and I wouldn't have dared say a word. Instead I admired her outfit, which was a complete departure from her usual bodyguard chic. She wore a knee-length plaid skirt with a sweater vest pulled over a white oxford. I bet she'd Googled *American schoolgirl clothes*, and that was the result.

I followed in her wake as we marched across campus. Her clothes earned her a few double takes, but she still managed to pull it off with confidence to burn. She hunkered down outside American history while the class discussed the tragic story of

Benedict Arnold, the Revolutionary War general who most likely won the war for the Americans before defecting to the British. The professor said Arnold betrayed his countrymen because he was repeatedly passed over for military promotions and not fully recognized for his contribution to the war effort.

That got me wondering what was behind the betrayal of the rogue enchanter. Was it the standard crime of passion motivated by greed, ego, hatred, or revenge? Or could it be something more complex, like a quest for power?

When I finally exited the class Khalia's perpetual scowl was gone, and instead she appeared deep in thought. I wasn't sure which expression was more unsettling.

"Why is it you study your war with the English?" she asked as we walked across campus.

"I think if you want to understand who you are and where you're headed, it's important to know where you've been."

"Bah!" She dismissed me instantly. "It's only important to know who you are today. The rest doesn't matter."

"It matters," I politely disagreed. "All the decisions you've made in your life have brought you to this moment and made you who you are." For better or worse, I wanted to add.

Her eyes narrowed. "And what is that, I ask you?" Her eyes flicked over me with disgust. "I am stuck wearing stupid clothes and watching over a helpless, ignorant girl."

I decided to ignore the barbs in favor of establishing common ground in case we were doomed to be in each other's company for a while.

"Where did you begin?" I asked. "I mean, where were you born?"

She didn't answer right away, probably wondering why she was having a personal conversation with a life form so clearly beneath her. "Jamaica. My people also fought the English."

I resisted the impulse to point out that maybe we weren't so different, and instead indicated we'd reached the door leading to Chem 101. "Do you want to come in?"

"I'd rather eat ground glass."

Warren sat in the same seat as always, and I claimed the one next to him. His wide-eyed glance told me we were both thinking about how much things had changed in such a short time.

He leaned in. "Are you meeting Scarlett for lunch?"

"Nah, I'm brown-bagging it in the library. I've got to know my Caravaggios from my Cortonas for an exam in Art History."

"Just don't get caught with any food in there," he warned. "The head librarian will kill you." With Khalia as my lunch date, I'd like to see her try.

There was a text from Nicholas waiting for me when I walked out of class. *Have you been sold to the highest bidder yet?*

Haha, I texted back, willing to meet him halfway. *You're still stuck with me.*

The way I like it, he texted back, and I smiled.

On the way to the library we passed Basics, which in addition to tea and coffee served pre-packaged food. Khalia had come to school empty-handed, so I stopped at the reflecting pool.

"I'm sure I'll be fine if you want to grab a sandwich or something for lunch," I said.

She put her hands on her hips. "Did you say that to Kurt Miller, too?"

I opened my mouth to say something snappy about the lack of steel girders in the area when a wave of malevolence cut through me like an arctic breeze. It hadn't come from Khalia; her interior emotions were shielded from me, and besides, it wasn't like she didn't have them on full blast at any given moment. A quick scan of the handful of students dotting the surrounding benches revealed mostly stress and boredom, though one guy tapping fiercely on his phone screen was a stewing volcano of anger. He must have been the source of the random outburst.

Her eyes narrowed. "What is it?"

I shook my head. This ability was too new to trust and too uncertain to share.

The school library was a thing of beauty. The ceilings soared, the staircases gracefully reached toward the heavens, and the extensive use of glass, both in skylights and picture windows, promised clarity of light unmatched by anything with a switch. Usually peace permeated my heart and mind as soon as I crossed the threshold, but something was off today. Of course, being near Khalia could unsettle anyone.

"Are we going to stand here like witless fools, or do you think we can sit someplace a little less exposed?" Khalia flicked a wrist toward the far end of the room where a collection of workstations was efficiently arranged. I sent up a silent prayer to please let Kurt Miller's murderer be found before I forgot to be grateful for her protection.

Most of the dozen or so tables were taken, but I snagged one and tossed down my bag. Khalia slunk away, probably to terrify some unsuspecting librarian. Shaking off my agitation I tried to focus on the masters of the Baroque period, sneaking bites of a peanut butter and jelly sandwich here and there.

I was lingering over a series of Rembrandt's greatest hits when suddenly every hair on the back of my neck prickled with the same icy caress as before. Someone seething with hostility was here. The darkness reached out for me like a restless, hungry animal, and before I could call out to Khalia, I was consumed.

I stood on a busy downtown street corner as crowds of office workers rushed by. The smell of exhaust fumes mixed with the yeasty aroma of a nearby bakery was a sign this was a glimpse of the past.

The people zipping by were all strangers, and the buildings and storefronts were equally unfamiliar. Then I glanced at the street signs, and a cold shiver of recognition rippled through me. It was the corner of Hope and Carmen, the scene of Ashley Norman's violent demise.

My whole body turned cold as I understood whoever had witnessed Ms. Norman's death had followed me into the library.

I searched for the banker's blonde bob among the many sensible hairstyles worn by the nine-to-fivers. My chest tightened each time the traffic lights changed, wondering if this was the moment when a body and car collided.

There she was, suddenly, standing on the opposite side of the intersection, her eyes glued to her phone. Traffic slowed. The light would change in seconds, telling a distracted woman it was safe to dash to her next meeting. Time had run out.

The walk sign popped on, and she stepped off the curb.

The middle-aged woman at the wheel of a massive black SUV looked horrified as her car shot forward. Someone on the sidewalk screamed, another pedestrian flung himself out of the way, but Ashley Norman barely looked up from her phone.

Her body flew through the air, landing just inches from my feet. Even without knowing the outcome in advance, there was no doubt she was dead. Blood trickled from her mouth, her eyes open and vacant.

People gathered around the body. One Good Samaritan checked her wrist for a nonexistent pulse while hushed voices asked, "What happened?" and "Who is she?" I tore my gaze away from the late Ashley Norman to search the crowd for the gap-toothed enchanter Tristan Murrieta.

Among the people who huddled frightened, saddened, or relieved that sudden death had spared them that day, my eye caught on a girl who looked rather pleased. Dressed all in black with her hair swept back in a high ponytail, she appeared quite different from the mousy person I'd met at The Lower 8, but there's no question the girl with the satisfied smile was Alice Ferndale.

Standing dead center in the middle of the library when I snapped out of my vision, she glared at me like I'd kicked her dog. She was dressed once again in head-to-toe black, right down to her Converse high-tops. Bright red lipstick, her only makeup, struck a jarring note as if she were a kid who'd found her way into her mom's makeup drawer. Other than that, she was a dark wraith in a sea of color.

My hands started to tingle, and I watched in horror as they twitched of their own volition. I looked about frantically for Khalia, who leaned against a bookshelf completely absorbed in *The Wall Street Journal*.

"Khalia!" As her head whipped around, the tingling in my hands ceased. Alice's face twisted in anger or perhaps frustration as she realized I wasn't as vulnerable as I'd initially appeared. However, neither was she.

Khalia threw the newspaper down and rushed her, but a passing student, a guy carrying his laptop, suddenly lunged at my bodyguard. The computer caught her square in the face, and down she went in a heap of plaid. Her attacker dropped the makeshift weapon as if it were on fire and backed away in shock.

Alice turned her attention to another student, a guy working at the table next to mine. He was at least six feet tall, well built, and had on a Cal State Santa Carla varsity jacket with the name Vasquez embroidered on the front. He lurched to his feet.

Vasquez wore an expression of stunned amazement as his arms raised a sturdy chair over his head. I dove under a table as the chair came crashing down, yelping at the friction burns on my bare legs, but my sanctuary was short-lived. The table went flying.

I scrambled to my feet, intent on running straight at Alice. We were well matched physically, so maybe I'd stand a fighting chance. I'd bolted a few steps when a book came rocketing out of nowhere. It missed my head by inches, and then another flew by followed by a metal desk lamp. Then something solid and incredibly painful slammed into my knee, and I went down hard. The crown jewel of the geology department display, a small chunk from an asteroid, lay at my feet. That answered the question of why my knee throbbed so painfully.

A cute girl with shiny black hair and a Mickey Mouse sweatshirt advanced. She held a large geode from the library's mineral display. I struggled to my feet, dizzy with pain.

"What is happening?" she cried, raising the rock to strike. In a desperate move, I grit my teeth against the agony and dove at her legs. She toppled over, and I tumbled with her. She barely resisted when I straddled her. I snatched up the rock and reared up to strike but faltered at the sight of her terrified face; she was simply an innocent bystander Alice had used and already discarded.

"Look out!" the girl screamed, but there was no time to react. Something unyielding wrapped tightly around my neck and yanked. I dropped the geode and clawed at my throat as the pressure intensified.

The enchanter stood a few feet away, her attention focused on finishing me off. She didn't notice Khalia staggering up from behind, her face a bloody mess, but her eyes burning with fury. My champion grabbed the girl's ponytail with one hand before smashing a fist into Alice's face with the other. The enchanter collapsed to the ground.

The grip on my throat eased. Gasping, I reached up to yank the garrote from my neck and discovered a man's leather belt.

Vasquez swayed behind me, staring at his hands with uncomprehending shock.

Alice was back on her feet, dodging Khalia while pulling others into her fight. A beefy young woman in braids came up behind my bodyguard, swinging a backpack overhead like a mace. Khalia ducked as the backpack arced toward her head, only to pop up and drive her foot into the woman's midsection. She apparently didn't share my reluctance about injuring innocents.

I picked up the discarded geode and struggled to my feet. Khalia caught sight of me, even as a security guard rushed her with a short wooden flagpole he spun like a staff. She grabbed her car keys from her skirt pocket and flung them at me.

"Go!"

The keys hit my chest and dropped to the floor. I stared at them, still in a daze from my near strangulation. A flash of movement caught my eye. Alice rocketed towards me. Khalia was still busy battling the guard. I was on my own.

It was pure instinct that caused me to throw the geode, and pure luck that it hit its mark. Alice's hands flew to her injured eye as she stumbled blindly, and despite dodging a short wooden flagpole wielded by the security guard, Khalia yelled, "Get out of here before you really piss me off!"

Snatching up the car keys before Alice had a chance to recover, the idea I might actually live through this bloomed in my brain. Still, I was reluctant to leave Khalia to fight my battles, but fear of facing her wrath if I ignored her command spurred me through the emergency exit. The blaring alarm followed me all the way to the parking lot.

The Escalade fairly flew back to town. Tears rolled down my cheeks and every breath was torture, but I needed to get to safety before giving in to the pain. I'd left everything behind, including my phone and house keys, and had no idea where Nicholas was staying. Then I recalled a certain vow that had been made to me, one that for some reason I believed would be honored.

I drove straight to The Lower 8.

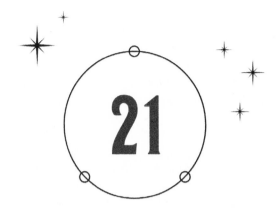

Bitches Need Stitches

Jessie answered the summons at The Lower 8's service entrance. He took one look at my tear-stained face and immediately scooped me up in arms that were like iron bands, carrying me through the busy kitchen and hollering for Layla as he went. Touching him fired up all kinds of empathic energy, and the feelings of shock, concern, and protectiveness I picked up from him momentarily took my mind off the pain. When we reached his office, he gently settled me on a black leather sofa. A gasp from the door announced the pixie's arrival.

"Ice, Aleve, and gin," he barked.

"No," I countered in a cracked whisper. "Khalia. School. Library. Alice. Ferndale." Each word felt like liquid fire being poured over my vocal cords.

Jessie tersely issued further orders but like a runner pushed past her limits, I closed my eyes and let go. I must have slept a few minutes because I awoke to gentle hands placing something cold on my injured leg. Layla gave me an apologetic smile as she carefully packed my knee in ice. We could both see how swollen and bruised my leg had become.

"Can you swallow?" Jessie held up a glass of what looked like cloudy water. "It's a big dose of anti-inflammatories and pain killers stirred into a frosty glass of gin." At my raised eyebrow, he added, "What? Gin is a wonderful muscle relaxant. It's just what the doctor ordered."

In all the years my mother had practiced medicine, I never once recalled her prescribing a shot of alcohol. However, there was a first time for everything, so I took a tiny sip, letting the liquid trickle down my burning throat. By the time I'd managed to drink it all, I knew I would never voluntarily drink the vile stuff again. On the plus side, delicious warmth spread through my body, and I didn't mind the pain quite so much.

I croaked, "Where's Khalia?"

"She's on her way," Jessie said in that lovely Texas drawl, which I swear was getting sexier by the minute.

"And Alice?" I asked.

Jessie and Layla exchanged a dark look. "She kept Khalia busy long enough to slip away."

Inexplicably, I started to giggle.

Layla smiled at me knowingly. "Blake, have you ever had a drink before?"

"Nope," I confessed. "Mustn't let down our guard, must we?" I blinked up into Jessie's handsome face. "But you like me just the way I am, don't you?"

"I like you plenty, Miss Blake," he grinned, "and when you're not all banged up, I'd like to show you just how much. But let's get you better first, shall we?"

"But I feel better already," I said, though my voice still sounded like it belonged to a frog. "Tell him, Layla."

"Oh, she's all kinds of better, Jessie," she said with amusement.

Jessie covered me with a fleece blanket and placed a rolled-up sweatshirt scented with his wonderfully musky cologne under my head. He knelt so that his face was a few inches from mine, his warm fingers stroking the hair back from my face. "Rest now, darlin'. I promise no harm will come to you here."

"I know," I said, feeling his fury that someone had dared to hurt me. Floating along in a haze, I closed my eyes and drifted away.

I awoke to hushed voices but couldn't yet summon the energy to open my eyes. A subtle shift revealed the pain in my knee had been reduced to a dull throb. My throat still burned, but now it was partially from thirst. I took an exploratory swallow and found it tolerable.

"The Prime Sentinel will be here any minute, but it's up to us to keep it contained until he arrives." Nicholas was stressed and angry.

"I've sent our two best enchanters to the school," Jessie snapped, irritated to be reminded of what was at stake. "Two more are erasing memories at the police station as we speak."

"Ow!" Khalia exclaimed. "Watch what you're doing, you bloody butcher."

I cracked open an eyelid. Jessie and Nicholas were squared off on opposite sides of the small office, while Khalia had claimed Jessie's desk chair. A man in green scrubs leaned over her, redirecting a bright task light before returning to the thankless job of stitching up her lower lip. There wouldn't be much he could do for her blackening eyes, but her crooked nose would need setting. Guilt and gratitude, in equal measure, rushed through me.

"I don't understand why Alice would openly attack Blake," Nicholas said, his arms tightly crossed. "She had to know we'd identify her."

"Attack the princess, is it? And yet I am the one with a needle in my face," Khalia complained.

"Maybe she's working for someone else, protecting them from Blake's particular skill," Jessie mused.

I moved to sit up, drawing all eyes. Nicholas crossed the room in a few long strides and wrapped an arm around me while I adjusted to being vertical.

"Easy there. How do you feel?" His voice was soft and low, excluding the others.

"I'll be fine," I rasped, "but I could use some water." Nicholas kissed the top of my head before rising and slipping out to the adjacent kitchen.

I caught my bodyguard's eye. "I owe you my life, Khalia. Thank you."

Her gaze softened, as if my actions in the library had won a small measure of respect, but she quickly shook it off. "I wasn't saving your skinny ass," she huffed indignantly, like I'd accused her of being kind to children and small animals. She gestured toward her damaged face. "I was trying to kill the bitch who did this to me."

Nicholas returned with my water and took a place on the sofa. "I'm sorry to say your throat will have a band of bruises around it for a while."

"Thank God it's almost turtleneck season," I lamely joked, imagining what my boss would say if I showed up looking like an escapee from the gallows. "Oh no! What time is it?" I was probably late for my afternoon shift. "I've got to get to work!"

"Great idea, princess," Khalia said in a dry tone. "Let's go someplace where there's knives and boiling liquids because today wasn't enough fun."

The nurse snipped the thread from the final lip suture and started rolling gauze in anticipation of realigning Khalia's nose.

"She's right," Nicholas said. "You can't go anywhere until Alice is apprehended. Here." He handed me my backpack, which had been propped out of sight beside the sofa. "Khalia brought it."

I gratefully rifled through it, finding everything where it was supposed to be, including the pepper spray my dad always insisted I carry. Until Alice was apprehended, I'd be keeping it a lot closer than the bottom of my backpack.

My phone had fifteen missed calls: one from Al, probably wondering why I was late for work, and the rest from Scarlett.

I called Jitters first. "Whoa, Blake, you sound awful," Al said when I got him on the phone. "Don't you worry, we've got it covered. Stay home and rest."

Scarlett picked up on the first ring. "Thank God, Blake, I've been scared out of my mind! There are all these wild rumors flying around school, the police have closed down the library, and you weren't answering your phone. Where are you?"

In as few words as possible, I told her about Alice's attack. "Don't go home, Scarlett. She got away and may come looking for me there."

"I'm at Warren's, but make sure you tell Nicholas he's doing a super job of keeping you safe." Her relief at finding me in one piece instantly morphed into sarcasm and anger.

The office was so quiet everyone heard Scarlett's side of the conversation. Nicholas stiffened while Jessie sent me a knowing glance.

"SON OF A BITCH!" Khalia screamed as the nurse wrenched her nose into its proper position, and we all jumped. The attendant used the gauze tubes to staunch the flow of blood, and I felt a bit lightheaded.

"What the hell is going on there?" Scarlett yelled in my ear.

"I need to call you back." I ended the call and slumped back on the sofa.

The office door banged open. Layla, who never seemed to stand still, literally bounced in the doorway, her enthusiasm barely contained.

"He's here," she announced breathlessly as a wave of heady excitement washed over me.

Jessie looked as if he too were riding Layla's emotional high. "I'm delighted for you, but can you reign it in some?"

"Oops! Sorry." She sheepishly took a step back before her eyes widened at Khalia's schoolgirl outfit. "What on earth are you wearing, Khalia?"

The bodyguard shot her a frosty glare.

"What's going on?" I asked.

"Please tell him we'll be right there," Jessie said.

Nicholas reached out a hand to help me up.

"Where are we going?" I asked. "*Who* is here?"

From the doorway, Layla chirped, "Akim Silver, the Prime Sentinel."

Akim Silver

Only three people were on the main floor of the club at that time of day: a curvy bartender overseeing bottles of beer rocketing unassisted from case to cooler; a thin, sharply dressed man rifling through papers on a clipboard; and a stranger sitting alone at one of the tables.

Khalia had struggled to her feet as we'd filed out of Jessie's office, so there were five of us coming to meet Akim Silver. As we wound our way past tables and chairs, the man with the clipboard placed his hand firmly against one of the room's supporting pillars. Within seconds leafy vines began growing from the base of the column and winding skyward. I sent a wide-eyed look at Jessie.

"That's Gustav, our materialist," he said. "Tonight is blue lagoon night."

A self-possessed man stood at our approach. Akim Silver called to mind a battle-scarred lion, from his tawny mane and golden skin to a once-beautiful face turned striking by a broken nose and scarred cheek. His monochromatic clothes in shades of gray were loose enough to offer freedom of movement but did nothing to disguise the fit and muscular man within.

Nicholas made brief introductions. Silver's eyes flicked over the bruises on my neck and leg before settling on Khalia, who drooped like a thirsty flower.

"Miss Clarke," he said, his voice deep and melodic. "We owe you a debt of gratitude today. Your selfless act does honor and credit to all sentinels." Khalia straightened, her eyes gleaming with pride at the strangely anachronistic speech. "It is time to stand down and tend to your injuries. Your charge will be watched over in your absence."

She nodded stoically, but there was no mistaking the relief that crossed her battered face as she withdrew.

Silver pulled out a chair for me, which I gingerly accepted. Jessie and Nicholas claimed the seats on either side of me, while Layla hovered nearby as if she expected a summons at any moment. She wasn't disappointed.

"Miss Rivera," Silver said. "Would it be possible to get something to eat while I speak to Miss Wilder?"

She seemed pleased to have something to do while still maintaining her proximity to the table and immediately zipped off to do his bidding.

"You seem to inspire a loyal following, Miss Wilder," Silver said, observing how I was now flanked by a telekinetic and a phantomist. "I had rather interesting phone calls from both Chancellor Thorne and Mr. Sutton Sinclair regarding you. They feel your safety must be assured at all costs."

I stared at him, embarrassed and uncomfortable at all the attention. "I don't think anyone is safe as long as Alice Ferndale is on the loose."

"Agreed. Part of my purpose here is to bring her and Mr. Tristan Murrieta in for questioning." He glanced at Nicholas. "The chancellor conveyed your concerns about Mr. Murrieta's abrupt departure from Santa Carla."

"You think they're working together?" I asked.

"Until they are both found, nothing is off the table," he said. "Mr. Kurt Miller deserves justice."

His wasn't the only murder, something Silver probably wasn't aware of.

"Mr. Silver," I said formally, getting the impression no one called him by his first name and lived. "Alice killed a woman named Ashley Norman. I saw it."

"Jesus, Mary, and Joseph," Jessie swore under his breath.

"Not quite, Mr. McCabe," Silver said, "but it points to motive as to why she is trying to silence Miss Wilder. I'm sure she is afraid of having a witness to further crimes of hers."

Layla returned with another server. They both carted enormous trays of food.

"I wasn't sure what you'd like," she said to the Prime as she laid out what looked like every dish on the menu. Fortunately, the club fare was limited to burgers, salads, and chicken wings.

Jessie looked bemused. "Is there any food left in the kitchen, Layla?"

She shot him a look of impatience. "Mr. Silver is our guest. I want him to feel welcome." She beamed at Silver as she backed away.

Nicholas picked up where we'd left off. "Alice may continue in her attempts to silence Blake."

"A sentinel will be assigned to her at all times until Miss Ferndale and Mr. Murrieta are located." Silver picked up the short stack of dinner plates Layla had set on the table, passing one to me.

"I find courage is best summoned on a full stomach. Shall we eat, Miss Wilder?"

I pulled Layla aside as I limped back from the ladies' room. She must have sensed the jumble of emotions swirling inside my head because she said, "Hell's bells, Blake, it's not that bad."

Immediately, a feeling of calm invaded my senses. She was better than a yoga class and a cup of hot chocolate combined.

"Better?" she asked.

I nodded. "You like Mr. Silver, don't you?"

She grinned mischievously. "Is it that obvious?"

I let out a small laugh. "What is it about him you like so much?"

A dreamy look stole over her face. "You mean besides the fact he's absolutely gorgeous, incredibly mysterious, and could probably take down every other guy in this place single-handed?"

I'd never measured a guy's attractiveness by whether he could fight off the other cavemen, but to each her own.

"It's what's rolling off of him emotionally," she said.

She probably could have gotten lost in a fantasy if I hadn't nudged her to continue. "What are you getting from him?"

She sighed with contentment. "Absolutely nothing. Being around a sentinel is always relaxing, but with Mr. Silver, it's like he's not even there."

I thanked her for the emotional reprieve and trudged back to the table, admiring Gustav's transformation of the club as I went. The room had morphed into an exotic grotto too fantastic to exist in nature. Colorful flowers dripped from vines snaking all the way up the pillars, while ferns and leafy fronds grew in abundance along the walls. The stage had been converted into a lovely stone waterfall feeding into the dance floor lagoon.

Marcus had joined the party in my absence, and he stood at my approach, wincing as he took in my bruises. "I'm so sorry, Blake. I can't help feeling responsible for welcoming Alice into the club. I can't imagine what drove her to come after you today."

"Me either, but Khalia saved my life." If someone had told me this morning I'd actually be grateful for the Jamaican lunatic, I would have thought they'd gone off their meds. "I also owe your dad big time for sending her."

His eyes grew distant at the mention of his father. I didn't know Marcus well, but I understood how he might resent being dominated by the force of nature named Sutton Sinclair. I wondered if the rest of their family hid the steak knives at holiday gatherings.

"Miss Wilder," Silver said with a touch of impatience, and I retook my chair. During the meal we'd guessed at Alice's possible motives, and the likely connections between Ashley Norman, Selena Flores, and Kurt Miller. Now it looked like things were about to turn personal.

"You have seen firsthand what an enchanter can do," he said. "So I hope you will understand why I now need access to your visions and whereabouts."

Wary alertness chased away my exhaustion. "What do you mean?"

"Only if you agree, Blake," Nicholas interjected, sending a warning glance in Silver's direction. "If you give Mr. Silver permission, he will be able to form a temporary mental bond with you that will allow him to see your visions as you have them."

"I thought sentinels were immune from all of us," I said, stalling.

"That is our natural state, yes, but Class Ones and even some Class Twos can lower their defenses," Silver explained. "When that happens, we can share thoughts, visions, and more."

A feeling of queasy violation swept through me. Was I supposed to invite the Prime Sentinel into my head?

"This is for your protection, Miss Wilder," he said, his words stopping me when I would have refused.

"I've heard that before." I couldn't help but cut a glance at Nicholas.

"I understand your hesitation." The Prime Sentinel rose and turned my chair around before pulling another to face it. "Please sit. I would like to show you something. Afterwards, if you don't agree to my plan, I won't ask again."

I hobbled to my chair. When we were both seated facing one another, I asked, "Now what?"

"Take my hand, Miss Wilder."

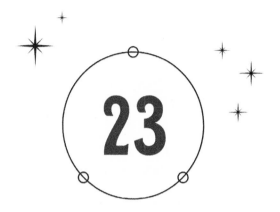

A Painful Past

Bells chimed, calliope music blared, and the wonderful, sickly sweet smell of fried sugar wafted through the air. Groups of high-spirited teenagers raced by while young couples held hands as they strolled. We were on the midway of a carnival on a warm summer night, the variety of languages being spoken the only indication this trip to the past was taking place in a foreign land.

A collection of older boys loitered near a ride called The Octopus, checking out the girls strutting past. At the center of the pack was a handsome seventeen-year-old who had yet to suffer a broken nose or a scarred cheek—there was no mistaking the face of Akim Silver.

Next to him was a boy far younger than the others. He had the same honeyed locks as Silver, though he looked barely out of grade school. He shifted impatiently as the rest of the group flirted with several girls who'd stopped to talk.

One girl in particular eyed Silver. She was all long legs and dark curls, her short flirty skirt and tight tee shirt guaranteed to capture a boy's attention.

"Hey, Akim," she drawled.

"Hi, Sofia." He grinned. "You look really pretty tonight."

"C'mon, Akim," the younger boy butted in. "Dad said you were supposed to take me on some rides. I want to go on the Octopus."

The ride was so named for the metallic beast with the goofy smile at the center of all the excitement. The cars at the end of each of its tentacles rose high into the air as the ride twirled. Shrieks from excited riders carried over the heads of the crowd.

"Rides are for kids, Rafe," Akim said, not taking his eyes off the girl.

The boy jutted out his lower lip. "That's not what you said last year."

The older boy dug a small wad of cash out of his pocket and shoved it at his brother. "Here. Go find some of your friends."

"Dad said I shouldn't go alone. He said you need to go with me."

A flash of impatience crossed Akim's face. "Give me a sec," he said to the girl as he pulled his brother out of earshot. "Look Rafe, you're old enough to control your thoughts. I can't follow you around shielding you forever."

"But what about all these people?" his brother protested. "What if something bad happens again?"

"You've been an evanescent for a whole year now. Don't let your thoughts get away from you, and you'll be fine." Akim turned away, ignoring the fear and uncertainty in his brother's eyes.

Rafe trudged away while Akim returned to Sofia's side. They talked about nothing in particular, but the way their bodies leaned toward each other spoke volumes. So focused were they on each other it took a few moments for the anxiety of the crowd to penetrate.

Akim looked to one of his friends, who stared at the Octopus. "What's going on?"

"The ride," he said, his voice tight with concern. "Look how fast it's going."

The Octopus had indeed picked up speed. Centrifugal force flung the cars into a horizontal pitch, and the riders' screams became laced with terror.

"Rafe!" Akim pushed past horrified bystanders and leapt the metal barricade surrounding the ride. He reached it just as one of the cars detached and sailed over the heads of the horrified crowd. The sudden shift in weight caused the metal octopus to teeter, and everyone panicked.

Akim closed his eyes in intense concentration as the ride wobbled on its foundation. People ran in every direction, climbing over one another in their bid to escape. Metal supports groaned as the machinery began to tear itself apart. It spun once, twice more before it became apparent the ride was slowing. A few more rotations, and the ride ground to a stop.

Sobs and cries for help came from cars still suspended high in the air. A few tentacles had dropped to half-mast, and people climbed down to safety.

"Akim!" The cry came from one of the cars close to the ground, and he raced to help his brother. He gathered the sobbing boy into his arms.

"I only wanted it to go faster," Rafe wailed. "I didn't mean for that to happen."

"Quiet," Akim said, dazed but with enough presence of mind to silence his brother. It didn't matter; those nearby were too overwhelmed to listen to the traumatized ramblings of a boy. The bright music in the background was at odds with the sight of shocked survivors stumbling over the wreckage.

"Am I in trouble?" Rafe asked.

"No," Akim said, a haunted look in his eyes. "I am."

Silver's expression gave nothing away, but his eyes couldn't disguise the sorrow of recalling the painful memory.

"What happened to Rafe?" I asked, my heart in my throat. "Was everyone okay?"

He shook his head. "That night in Tel Aviv altered the destiny of many, my brother included. The bright, inquisitive boy he'd been disappeared overnight." He released my hand.

"I'm really sorry," I said, at a loss for words. "I didn't realize an evanescent could do all that."

"Rafe is more than an evanescent. That night we discovered he was a multi, which is a Nine who has more than one talent. In Rafe's case, he is also telekinetic."

I swayed in my chair, and Jessie gripped my elbow to steady me. Is that what was happening to me? It wasn't enough I was assaulted by terrible visions, but now I would always feel people's horrific pain and suffering, too? What would happen when the people of The Nine discovered my new talent?

"Are you okay, Blake?" Jessie murmured close to my ear.

I glanced at him, hoping my panic didn't show. "I'm still a bit woozy from everything, that's all." Turning back to Silver I asked, "Are there a lot of multies?"

He shook his head. "It's not terribly common, though I too am a multi."

"It's usually limited to two skills," Nicholas added, "but sometimes it can go to three, like with Da Vinci, Michelangelo, and David Blaine."

I paused to absorb that stunning pronouncement before asking, "What's your other skill, Mr. Silver?"

"I am partially empathic. I know when someone is being untruthful." His gaze held mine, and I wondered if he'd picked up on the lie I'd just told the phantomist.

I drew a deep breath and did my best to keep my features arranged in a placid expression. "I appreciate you sharing all this, Mr. Silver, but what does any of it have to do with me?"

"I am trusting you with my greatest shame and biggest sorrow." His unblinking gaze met my own. "As you can trust me with yours."

I considered him a moment. "Let's say I give you a front row seat to my visions. How long will our, uh, bond last?"

"Not long," he assured me. "For a few days, three at most, I will be able to see your visions and know where to find you, but unless we renew our bond, our connection will fade. On my honor, anything I witness will remain strictly between us."

I glanced at Nicholas, whose poker face didn't quite conceal a measure of apprehension, and Jessie, whose playful smile came off almost like a dare. Marcus appeared lost in thought.

"All right, Mr. Silver," I conceded, though I wasn't at all sure this was the right decision. "What happens now?"

He turned to our companions. "You may not want to be present for this."

"Wait, what?" I shot a panicked look at Nicholas. "What are you going to do?"

Silver fought back a smile. In spite of what Layla said about his serene interior, I seemed to bring out a variety of reactions in the man. "Nothing inappropriate, I assure you. In order to form a link, I will need you to open up your mind to the energy that surrounds us. I simply gave the gentlemen here the option of keeping you from prying into their minds while you do so."

Jessie tipped his chair back. "This ain't my first rodeo. She can look all she wants."

Nicholas glanced at Jessie before nodding in agreement, but Marcus rose to his feet. "I think it best to protect the innocent," he said with a wink in my direction before heading out the door.

"Very well." Silver squared his body to face me. "Lean back and close your eyes. It would also be helpful if you relaxed." I did as he asked, taking deep, meditative breaths in an effort to slow my hammering heart. "Now simply allow a vision to come to you."

I couldn't help it. Despite my yearning to feel closer to Nicholas, he remained a stranger to me. He kissed me passionately but made no move to press it further. There were moments when he dropped his guard, but it felt like it happened on his terms. He shared his memories, but only when it suited his needs. With all of my will, I directed the energy rolling off me to seek out his past with a single goal in mind.

I didn't give a damn what Mr. Silver thought.

A party of young and beautiful people decorated the furniture of a sleek high-rise apartment, laughter and music cutting through the pall of cigarette smoke. Behind them a wall of windows revealed the London skyline at night along with a solitary figure leaning against the balcony railing.

"You're missing all the fun." A girl, dressed like she didn't need help from salesgirls at the mall, eased next to Nicholas. She wore a strapless cocktail dress of burgundy velvet, her thick auburn hair curling over delicate shoulders.

Nicholas contemplated the view. Clouds obscured the moon, but the city glowed like a carpet of stars. "Watching Reynolds and Bates play yet another round of Never Have I Ever got old a long time ago."

She pursed her lips. "It's that girl, isn't it?" Her voice had an Irish lilt to it.

"It's the girl, it's Henry, it's the way everyone looks at me like I should be thrilled to be the scion." He let out an exasperated sigh. "Now I'm even starting to hear Henry's words come out of my mouth."

"You are nothing like your father." She turned her back to the railing and faced him. "Don't go to California. Let them send somebody else." She put her hand on his arm. "Stay with me." The hungry way she looked at him made my stomach clench.

He shook his head. "You know I can't do that, Julia. This is a dangerous time for our people, and we can't let a girl like her slip through our fingers. I'll do whatever I must to bring her to our side."

"I've seen her picture. She's quite pretty." She studied his face as if seeking reassurance she had nothing to worry about. "I can forgive whatever you need to do get the girl on our side just as long as you come back to me."

For the first time he smiled. Encouraged, she moved into his arms.

"There were so many times when I was lost and alone, and you were the only one there for me," he said. "I owe you my life."

She offered her lips up to be kissed, and he didn't disappoint her. They clung to each other as the moon broke free of the clouds.

Somewhere in the back of my mind I think I knew: Nicholas was too good to be true. This girl waited for him, and he was doing whatever he needed to get back to her. To compound my pain, I slowly became aware of another presence. It was hard to pin down at first, like a whiff of something tantalizing on the breeze. The energy grew in intensity until I could almost taste the sweetness of it, and then I knew.

Akim Silver had entered my vision just in time to see Nicholas break my heart.

The Real Warren Hartman

It all made so much sense. I wasn't special, or beautiful, or even particularly smart, it seemed. Nicholas had but one purpose in coming to Santa Carla, and I'd made it so easy for him. I'm sure it wouldn't have been long before I'd signed my name on the dotted line, or sworn a blood oath, or done whatever the hell Henry Thorne needed to hold onto power. Scarlett had been right all along. I never should have trusted him.

"Are you all right, Miss Wilder?" Silver's eyes met mine, but his were free of judgment.

"I'm exhausted, I hurt everywhere, and this has been completely overwhelming," I truthfully confessed, tears brimming. Afraid I'd dissolve into a puddle if I sat there much longer, I said, "Can I go home now?"

"Of course." Everyone at the table stood, and Nicholas fished his car keys out of his pocket. Jessie looked like he was about to object when Silver intervened. "I will be driving Miss Wilder home. Until we have Ms. Ferndale in custody and have

located Mr. Murrieta, the only people around her will be sentinels." He glanced at Nicholas. "That includes you, Mr. Thorne."

I turned my back on both Nicholas and Jessie and hobbled
to the door. Silver escorted me to a sporty BMW parked right
outside. Night had fallen, and he kept his eyes on the dark road
ahead as we drove, letting me weep in peace. Without ever asking for my address, we arrived at Rosewood Gardens.

A man skulked in front of my building. "That's Mr. David,
the sentinel who will be watching over you tonight," Silver informed me. "He will know instantly should any enchanter step
foot within a city block of here."

With an unshaven chin and the stub of a cigarette wedged
between his lips, the guy looked like a thug. His wavy black hair
was carelessly groomed, and years of wear had pilled the wool
of his peacoat. He faded back into the shadows as Silver escorted me to the door.

Scarlett hadn't come home yet. I should have called her, but
as we entered the unlit apartment, the need to stop thinking and
feeling overwhelmed me. Ignoring my companion, I stumbled to
my bed and collapsed, barely taking time to rip off my boots before my head hit the pillow. Oblivion beckoned.

The crackle of a fire punctuated with the call of sirens made me
burrow deeper into my pillow. It took a few moments to realize I
hadn't wandered into some neighbor's memories or been buried
deep in a dream. I bolted upright and gaped at the flickering
light playing across my bedroom wall. The fire was right outside
my window.

I whipped back the curtains. Warren stood in the yard with
his arm around Scarlett as the entire company of Fire Station 29
poured out of their truck. It was definitely overkill.

The flames engulfing the anemic pear tree in our front yard were barely enough for a barbeque, but it must have been a slow night down at the station. Within a minute or two, they'd extinguished the blaze and left a smoking twig in its place.

A few nosy neighbors in bathrobes milled about on the sidewalk as Warren shook hands with several of the firemen. I limped to the front door and opened it for Scarlett, who rushed to embrace me. Her face crumpled when she caught sight of the bruises on my throat. The painkillers and gin had worn off, and it hurt like hell. "Are you okay?"

"I'll live," I murmured, both of us now in tears.

"This time, maybe," she said. "But I'm scared."

Warren burst through the door. "I don't get it! What happened to that tree?"

Scarlett's troubled gaze met mine. "We were kissing goodnight, and the tree kind of exploded." Better the tree than her lips.

I dried my eyes and said, "Warren, would you mind holding my hand for a minute?"

He glanced quizzically at Scarlett, who gave a nod, so he complied without a word. At first, I felt nothing, no connection of any kind. Then, so slight as to be almost undetectable, I felt the telltale pulse of the living energy that beat so strongly within both Nicholas and me. There was no question: Warren was a late-blooming elementalist.

"Why don't we all sit down?" I hoped what I had to say wouldn't be unwelcome news for Warren, but Scarlett looked at me with dawning horror. She knew where this was headed.

"What's going on, Blake?" Warren asked with trepidation. "Scarlett?"

"It's all right, Warren," she assured him, her voice thick with apprehension.

He was about to start down the same rocky path I traveled, so I tried to be gentle. "I think I know why you were saved the day of the accident." I told him everything I knew about The Nine, and my suspicion he was a budding fire elementalist.

"Whoa," he breathed when I finally stopped talking. "Do you think I can control this, maybe light up only the stuff I want to?" Scarlett's lips had only just healed.

"Why don't we find out?" Our small apartment was filled with too many things that could catch fire, so I grabbed a cast iron soup pot, and we headed out to the front yard. The street was quiet, the firefighters and gawkers having moved on or gone to bed, but I spied the glow of a burning cigarette coming from the shadows of the oleander hedges lining the property. Mr. David seemed content to stay where he was.

I removed the lid and tossed a handful of dried leaves into the pot, careful to place the lid right next to the potential inferno. "Now Warren," I said, my voice hushed to avoid alerting the neighbors, "direct your energy toward the leaves in the pot."

He looked distinctly uncomfortable. Scarlett slid her arm through his, giving him an encouraging squeeze. "It's okay. No one's judging you."

He gave a resolved nod and then waved his hand with a flourish like a magician producing a rabbit out of his hat. "Fire!" Nothing happened.

I started to giggle. I couldn't help it, and Scarlett caught the wave of hilarity. I tried to stop, but then a glimpse of Warren's indignant expression sent me over the edge. Maybe it was because I'd reached the point where if I didn't laugh, I'd howl, but it was wonderful to explode in silliness.

"Maybe," I gasped, when I could finally catch a breath, "maybe you should do less David Copperfield, and more of a smoldering glare." That sent Scarlett into another fit of hysteria. I could only imagine Mr. David thinking we were all a bunch of whack jobs.

"Yeah, I can do that," he said, squaring his shoulders with resolve, choosing to ignore the laughter from the cheap seats.

"Wait," I said, linking hands with him. "The power of the one is the power of the many."

He narrowed his gaze at the iron pot and stared at it like it was in serious trouble. And then it happened. The leaves burst into flame, not a huge explosion, but a nice, cheery little fire. Warren's mouth gaped open in shock.

"Not bad," I said, dropping his hand.

"I did it," he cried in amazement. "Oh my God! I did it!" He grinned, as proud and astonished as if he'd caught a bullet in his teeth.

"Welcome to the club," I said, meeting his high five. "Now you'll have to come with me to The Lower 8." I smiled at Scarlett, whose expression was strained. The silly humor of a minute ago had drained away.

The fire burned out, and I extinguished the embers with the pot's tight-fitting lid. Warren was exhilarated, recalling moment by moment what was going through his mind as he conjured up the fire. Scarlett listened indulgently as I let myself back into the apartment.

As I brushed my teeth and examined my bruises in the mirror, I thought how Scarlett, always the more rational and levelheaded one, was evidently questioning whether there was a place for another one like me in her life. I hoped there was. She deserved someone who adored her, and I could tell in the few times I'd seen them together that Warren thought himself a lucky guy.

At least one of us deserved to be happy.

Body Count

"Alice Ferndale is dead." Mr. Silver stood on my doorstep, the late morning sun at his back.

I swung the door open wide and retreated to the coffee pot. My throat was tender, and my knee looked like a bruised grapefruit, so I'd rolled over when the alarm went off and blown off my morning classes. The doorbell had summoned me directly from bed. I distractedly filled a mug before remembering my manners. "Want a cup?"

He waved off my offer. I added the usual splash of cream and wondered how I could be so unmoved by someone's death. At the very least I should be relieved the threat to my own safety had been removed, and maybe also saddened that such a young life had been corrupted to the point where we might feel justified to see it end. But mostly, I just felt numb.

"Probably the more interesting detail is where she was found," Silver said, watching as I rooted around in the kitchen cupboard until I found the Advil. I plunked down at the kitchen table, and he took the seat across from me. "Her body was discovered by the cleaning crew this morning at The Lower 8. She appears to have fallen down the stairs inside the club and broken her neck."

I was stunned. What had Alice been doing at the club after hours? Had she really been murdered there? Or had someone staged her death to cast suspicion on either Jessie or Marcus? As far as motive, if Alice had been in league with someone like Tristan Murrieta, being branded a fugitive had probably made her accomplice pretty jumpy. There was no better way of keeping her partner's identity a secret than by silencing her before she could open her mouth.

"What about security cameras at the club?" Assuming there wasn't a paranormal talent that erased camera footage, they might provide a lead.

"We don't allow them at any gathering place for our people. The risk of a hacker gaining access to the identities of a substantial number of Nines could be devastating for us," he explained. "And while there aren't any signs of forced entry at the club, it also seems that half the people who work there have keys."

I mulled that over while battling with the child safety cap on the Advil. After a minute he plucked the bottle from my hand, instantly popped the lid, and shook out three tablets for me.

"Thank you," I murmured, swallowing them down automatically while distracted by another thought. "Alice had recently come to Santa Carla, just like me. I get that it's a sanctuary city, but there's more to it, isn't there?"

His eyes glinted with approval. "If your plan is to overthrow the leadership of The Nine, you will need to know who is sympathetic to your cause. It's no accident Sutton Sinclair was the one who funded The Lower 8 and installed his son as an informant. More of our people are showing up there every week." It was another confirmation of why Henry plotted to get to me first.

"What about Selena Flores? How could she just disappear into thin air?" The woman and her dog still hadn't been found.

His expression softened with regret. "If you were planning to kill someone, but your plans were broadcast to a wide circle of people, what would you do?"

I'd asked myself the same question already. "I'd change my plans. You think Alice already got to her another way, don't you?"

"It's a possibility we need to consider, but it doesn't mean we'll stop looking." He pushed back his chair. "With Miss Ferndale dead and a confirmed sighting of Mr. Murrieta at a funeral in Spain, I've relieved your sentinel guard of his duty. You should be safe for now. My ability to see your visions is fading, so don't hesitate to call if you see or hear anything." He handed me a beautifully embossed card simply listing his name and a telephone number. "I will be here a bit longer looking into Miss Ferndale's death."

Once he was gone, I ignored all responsibility and did stuff that usually made me feel better, like taking a bath and painting my nails. It didn't help. Selena was still missing, Alice's killer might very well get away with murder, and now that I was safe, Nicholas would probably rush back to London to be with the girl he loved.

No one had ever gotten to me the way Nicholas had, and I alternated between tears and wanting to punch him in the face. He would be thrilled to learn he'd accomplished his mission, namely that I would agree to become a member of The Nine and back the current leadership. I wouldn't have survived the last few days if it weren't for them. Of course, it hadn't escaped my notice that those were also some of the same people trying to kill me, but for the first time in my life I felt a sense of belonging.

Nicholas rang twice, but I ignored both calls. Different scenarios of our pending confrontation played out in my head. Would he tell me it was all some big misunderstanding, that the other girl was ancient history? Or maybe he would admit he'd led me on, but I should understand the end justified the means.

Scarlett came home after her last class. She took one look at my nails—Violet Death—and plunked down next to me on the sofa. "What happened?"

After ten minutes of sobbing out the news of Alice Ferndale's death and everything that had happened between Nicholas and me, she was able to piece it together. "I knew he couldn't be trusted."

I sniffled and reached for another tissue. "That's not very helpful."

She smiled ruefully. "Sorry. And I'm sorry he turned out to be such a douchebag, but the way he looked at you, like you were a golden ticket to the chocolate factory, bugged the shit out of me." Had he really looked at me that way? What else had I missed?

"I'm an idiot."

"No, you just didn't look too far past the pretty face. I get it." She picked up my hand and admired the artwork. "At least your nails look great."

"Thanks. What do I do now?"

"Anything you want," she said. "Since the moment Nicholas showed up, you let him set the pace. He pushed you into revealing your existence to all those people before you had a chance to think about it, and it almost got you killed."

I rested my head on her shoulder. "That's not exactly a genie I can put back in the bottle."

"No, but now that you're out and proud, why don't you discover what it means? Instead of them using you, why don't you figure out how to play the game?"

What did that look like? Who, if anyone, could I turn to for straight answers? I lifted my head. "What if it gets me in more trouble?"

She gave me a level look. "The show goes on whether you quit the play or not."

Spoken like a true actress. I took a deep breath and nodded. If I wanted to go looking for answers and trouble, probably in equal measure, I knew exactly where to start.

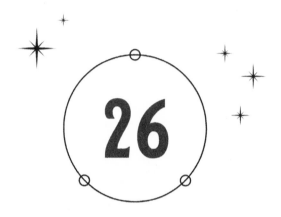

Jessie's Girl

It was late afternoon when I rang the bell at The Lower 8's service entrance. I'd worn loose-fitting jeans to mask my misshapen knee, but nothing could stop my insides from curling at the memory of when I'd stood there last. There was even a bloody fingerprint marring the door's white paint, which I pointed out to Layla when she let me in.

"That must be from Khalia," she said, wrinkling her nose. "Come on in. We're short-staffed today, so Jessie's in the club doing Suki's side work."

"Is Suki sick?" I limped along behind her as we threaded our way past the busy prep cooks. Their heads turned as one as she pranced by in cute Daisy Dukes, a cropped gingham top, and cowboy boots.

She paused at the swinging door leading into the main club. "She left a voice mail this morning saying she was quitting. Can you believe it? No notice, no nothing, and now we're scrambling to find a door sentinel for tonight." She made a face. "All this comes on top of that dead enchanter nobody seems to know much about."

I already knew about Alice, of course, but the news about Suki bothered me. The friendly girl I'd met the first night at Lower 8 had all but disappeared the minute she'd heard about my vision of Selena's murder, and now she'd quit her job?

"Khalia sometimes fills in, but she deserves a few days off. I'd *love* to call Mr. Silver," Layla said, practically licking her lips, "but it would be like putting a lion at the door and pretending he was a house cat."

"What about Marcus?" I asked.

Her mouth turned down. "Don't get me wrong, I like the guy, but calling him a Class Three sentinel is being kind."

She pushed her way into the club, a layer of sawdust on the floor muffling our steps. The lagoon from last night was gone, replaced with pool tables and a mechanical bull. Stacking cases of beer on the bar, Jessie looked in his element wearing tight jeans, a broken-in cowboy hat, and his snakeskin boots. He glanced up with a smile as soon as I entered; Cedric or one of his other spirits must have told him I was in the building.

"I didn't expect to see you so soon," he said, sauntering over. Despite my bruised heart, his animal grace and devilish smile made me feel a little better. He cupped my chin and gently tilted my head to one side as he inspected the bruises on my neck, a flash of anger crossing his face. "If the one who did this weren't already dead, I'd see to it myself."

I got the impression that wasn't an idle threat. The frontier justice of The Nine would take some getting used to.

"Jessie, I'm going to reach out to a few more sentinels for tonight," Layla said as she headed back toward the kitchen. She glanced my way. "Should I find you an evanescent?"

I looked at her blankly, but Jessie answered for me. "Yeah, give Betty a call." He put an arm around my waist and directed me to the nearest barstool. "Come, sit." I sat down with relief, and he leaned against the bar.

"I didn't know if you'd be opening tonight," I said, alluding to the discovery of Alice's body not far from where we sat.

"It's always best when these kinds of things are handled within The Nine, and Mr. Silver gave us the go ahead." He glanced in the direction of the staircase. "The safe was untouched, and nothing was taken. I can't figure out what she was doing here, and with Suki making herself scarce, it'll be hard to figure out if Alice arrived alone when she first came to the club, or if she had company." He shrugged, dismissing the mystery for now. "Now what can I do you for, darlin'?"

His words recalled why I had come, and tears welled.

He gently brushed away a tear with his thumb. "It's like that, is it?"

"You were right about Nicholas. He's all about doing his duty for king and country." I took a deep breath and smiled through the pain. "I mean, I get it. He's just doing his job, right?"

His mouth tightened into a narrow line. "If you start making excuses for that little shit, I swear Cedric will come haunt you tonight." He sounded as if he were only half-joking.

Jessie's complete lack of surprise sent an icy chill down my spine. "You knew about his girlfriend, didn't you?" I hung my head. "Oh geez, does everyone know?"

There was sympathy in his gaze. "He's been tight with Julia Martin for years." He ducked behind the bar and began transferring beers into the cooler, giving me time to absorb his words.

It was humiliating, but I resolved to be done with tears. Nicholas would soon vanish back to London, probably never to be seen again, so maybe Jessie and Layla would help me tackle the new world of The Nine. In turn, I would introduce Warren to his new reality and hope that Scarlett could find room in her heart to love us both. Hell, maybe I'd even take that job with Sutton Sinclair.

"What does Cedric look like?" I asked, doggedly changing the subject.

Jessie doffed his hat and considered me a moment. "Let's try something. I'm going to remember the first time I saw Cedric, and you try to watch. How's that sound?"

"Really?" This could be fun. I grasped his hand to strengthen our connection, and his fingers curled intimately around mine.

"Come to me, darlin'." He gave my hand a squeeze.

Three or four large Tupperware bowls were opened and set in front of a teenaged Jessie. He hadn't yet filled out into the muscular man he would become, but the same blonde hair was pushed carelessly off his boyishly handsome face. With a fork in hand, he eagerly dove into the containers of food as he sat alone at a table in a pretty farmhouse kitchen, the rough planks of the walls painted a warm shade of green. An overhead light softly illuminated what looked to be a midnight raid on the refrigerator.

"That was a wasted opportunity." The complaint came in the form of a clipped English accent, though the speaker was nowhere to be seen.

Jessie picked up a piece of fried chicken. "You're just mad you didn't get to see some action."

"My dear boy," the voice said with a sniff. "I know women, and there was a reason your date left her bloomers home tonight."

Jessie snickered. "Bloomers?"

"You know, a lady's unmentionables, though I must say, that trollop was no lady."

"Trollop?" Jessie asked. "What century are you from again?"

"From a century where one knew what to do with a lass who was ready and willing," he huffed. "Why, there was the night after a successful stag hunt with the king when we were near a most charming village. A group of local girls came to Portney's country home to help serve dinner, a great honor for them, you know…"

As the voice droned on, a flicker of light materialized in the chair across from Jessie. He set down his half-eaten chicken leg and watched in fascination as the glow expanded and solidified into the ghostly form of a man. As the image came into focus, the details became clear. His rounded body was clothed in a rich velvet doublet, a stiff lace collar framing his face. A tidy mustache and goatee in the same shade of chestnut as his sculpted curls were lost amongst chubby cheeks and a double chin. He fluffed his lace cuffs as he concluded recalling the enthusiasm of one country girl in particular.

"Cedric!" Jessie exclaimed. "I can see you!"

The ghost was pleasantly surprised. "So soon? Oh, this is a delightful turn of events."

"You knew this was going to happen?"

Cedric breezily waved a hand. "Of course. Did you think I would waste my time on some second-rate phantomist?"

An older woman in a ratty pink bathrobe entered the kitchen. Her blonde hair and slender face was a feminine version of Jessie's. She placed a gentle hand on Jessie's shoulder. "Are you talking to yourself again?"

Jessie glanced at Cedric, who complacently smoothed his already perfectly groomed mustache.

"You don't see anything unusual, Mom?"

She gave him a tired smile. "I see a boy who's going to eat us out of house and home, and who probably hasn't finished his homework. What do you see?"

"Pretty much the same thing." He smiled up at her. "I'll be up in a few minutes."

She kissed the top of his head. "See that you are."

A happy smile of remembrance lit Jessie's face when I refocused on it a few seconds later.

"Your mom doesn't know you're a phantomist?"

He shook his head. "My folks are church-going, heaven-and-hell kind of people. The last thing I wanted was to wake up to a priest standing over my bed with a cross shouting 'Devil, be gone!'"

"Quite understandable," I said with a wry smile. "Is Cedric here now?"

"Right there." Jessie nodded to the next bar stool over.

"Nice seeing you, Cedric," I said to the thin air. The silence hung for a moment as I gathered my nerve to say what was really on my mind. Jessie crossed his arms and waited for me to spit it out.

It came out in a rush. "Listen, Jessie, I know you would have been my patron if Nicholas hadn't shown up. Do you think we can start over? Would you and Cedric help me now?"

A grin split his face. "It would be an honor. I'll alert the regents you're under my protection now, and may I say you've made a very wise decision."

I should have realized with these people that asking Jessie for help would turn into some form of declaration. "What does that mean, under your protection?"

He rested his arms on the bar. "It means Thorne is out of the picture. When you pledge to The Nine, it will be with me by your side."

That sounded safe enough for the moment. Before I could ask any more questions, the kitchen door flew open. Layla marched into the room followed by an elderly woman whose figure strained the seams of her pink leggings. Her steel-gray hair floated wildly about her head, and she carried a ratty straw handbag.

"Dorothy Berzman will be our door sentinel for the next few days," Layla called to Jessie with satisfaction. "And Betty's here. Betty, this is Blake Wilder, the new voyant you may have heard about."

Betty cackled. "Oh my, who hasn't heard about her?"

I stiffened, and Jessie immediately leaned over the bar to stare down the old woman. "Blake is under my protection now," he fairly growled. "Is that clear?"

She clamped her mouth shut and nodded mutely. Even Layla looked sufficiently impressed. I ignored the flutter of apprehension about the archaic notion of needing protection and stayed silent.

"My apologies, Jessie, I didn't realize," Betty said meekly, using a gnarled finger to push her oversized eyeglasses back in place. "Layla said you needed me?"

His amicable smile back in place, he nodded. "Blake took some abuse at the hands of an enchanter—her throat, and one of her knees. I'd be obliged if you could help."

"Of course." She scurried forward with hands outstretched. I tried not to shrink away as she reached for my throat, but her touch was surprisingly gentle. Heat immediately emanated from her fingertips, and within a minute the lingering pain and soreness was gone.

I swallowed without any tenderness. "That's amazing."

"Energy's energy, matter's matter," she grinned, as if that explained everything. "Which knee, hon?"

I carefully rolled up my pants leg to expose the injured knee. She made a disgusted sound in the back of her throat when she saw the streaks of black and blue. "Baseball bat?"

I shook my head. "Asteroid."

She shot me a quizzical look before shrugging it off. "I had a cousin whose man was fond of drinkin' and swinging a bat, God rest her soul," she said with a sigh. "Let's prop your leg on a barstool. If I bend down, I may never get up again." She patted the same barstool where Cedric sat.

I grimaced. "Let's use the one on the other side, okay?"

Layla came forward to help, holding my leg steady as the evanescent wrapped her hands around my knee. This time I anticipated the heat and the almost instant relief it brought.

"What happened to your cousin?" I asked as energy radiated through my bones.

"Cancer," she tsked. "Such a shame."

"She, uh, didn't die a violent death?"

Betty's eyebrows took flight. "Now why on earth would you think that?"

A snort of muffled laughter came from Layla's direction. She must be used to the old woman's disjointed patter.

"Um, no reason," I mumbled.

Within a minute the pain had subsided, and I could almost see the swelling recede. There didn't seem to be any change in the nasty coloring, but jeans would hide the bruises until they faded.

I rolled down my pant leg and hopped off the stool with no problem. "Wow, what a difference. What do I owe you?" My mom always complained how hard it was to collect after a patient felt better, so I was obligated to offer.

Betty waved her hand to shoo away any suggestion of payment. "Someday I'll need a favor, and I'll collect then. How's that sound?"

I wasn't sure what I could ever do for the old evanescent, but the promise seemed harmless enough. "That's fine."

Marcus chose that moment to burst through the kitchen door and head straight behind the bar. He tossed down his car keys and grabbed a bottle of premium bourbon from one of the top shelves, pouring a hearty shot. As if noticing his audience for the first time, he mockingly raised his glass in our direction before slugging it down. That's when I noticed his clothes looked like he'd slept in them, though the bags under his eyes testified to the lack of any sleep whatsoever. Emotion poured off him in waves, but I had no interest in taking a look at what had put him in such a state.

"Drinking the profits, Marcus?" Jessie's tone made it clear it wasn't the first time. Layla scowled before heading off to wipe down tables.

"Why, yes I am, Jessie," he answered belligerently. "Someone has to pay for shutting down the site while the police investigate Kurt's death and poke through every goddam decision Sinclair Development has ever made, and apparently, it's me."

He threw back another shot. "It doesn't seem to matter that I'm barely allowed through the front gates. My father just needs a whipping boy for everything that's gone wrong."

He reached for the bottle again, but Jessie beat him to it. "Enough," he said. "The only power Sutton has over you is what you give him."

"Now why didn't I think of that?" Marcus smacked his head like his partner had shared a divine revelation. "Now give me another God-damned drink."

Jessie returned the bottle to its proper place with a definitive thunk. "What you really need is a shot of get the fuck over it." Jessie snatched up Marcus's keys. "Betty was just leaving. Maybe if you ask nicely, she'll give you a ride home."

The evanescent had stood openmouthed during the entire exchange, but now she nodded so vigorously her jowls wobbled.

The bluster suddenly drained out of Marcus as if someone had pulled a plug. His face crumpled for a moment, but then he mastered his emotions. "You're right. It's time to go home." He glanced at the old lady. "I probably shouldn't be driving. Can I catch a ride?"

"Of course. My little Subaru may not be as grand as what you're used to, but she'll do the job." She latched onto Marcus's arm as they crossed back to the kitchen, though I wasn't sure if it was for his benefit or hers.

"That was interesting," I said as the door swung closed behind them.

Jessie shrugged. "Marcus is a good guy. He just needs someone to call him out occasionally."

"I've got to go too." I retrieved my purse.

He quickly came around the bar and stood in front of me. There was a certain expectation in the way he looked at me, and I wondered if this shift had something to do with our new arrangement.

He slowly raised a hand to caress the band of bruises on my throat, and his touch made my breath catch. The energy between us flared once again, but I had no intention of giving into it anytime soon. There were still so many questions that needed answering, and I was done letting my emotions complicate everything.

"Will you come back later?" he asked, his fingertips dropping to skim along my collarbone. "It's Urban Cowboy night."

"I'll be back soon, but not tonight. I still have so much to learn about The Nine."

"That's not all I can teach you," he said, his face inches from mine.

I smiled and stepped away. "That's all I need. For now."

I Want You to Want Me

I whipped the Volvo into its covered parking spot and flicked off the headlights. It was a relief to climb from the car without pain, and I almost skipped around to the front of the apartment building just because I could.

I didn't see Nicholas sitting in the darkness of my front steps until I was on top of him. He reached out for me as I stumbled, but I pushed him away as soon as I regained my footing.

"Tell me what I've done," he said, his voice hurt and detached. "Scarlett just slammed the door in my face, and now I hear you went to see McCabe. Why?"

What right did he have to feel wounded? And how did he find out about my visit to The Lower 8 so fast? I held onto my righteous anger. "Does Julia Martin know how hard you've been working to get back to her?"

His face turned to stone.

"I didn't think so." I rushed up the steps to the front door.

"So that's it? You're going to run off without letting me explain?" He remained at the bottom of the stairs, making no move to stop me. Whatever happened next would be up to me.

What could he possibly say that I'd want to hear? Could I even trust anything he said? Knowing it was probably a mistake in the making, I turned and faced him. The porch light was on, so while I stood in a spotlight, he was beyond its reach.

"I'm listening," I said begrudgingly.

"I'm ending it with Julia."

I hated the way hope bloomed in my chest. "Why?"

The last few crickets of autumn chirped half-heartedly from the oleanders, and he turned to listen for a moment. "It's been over for a long time," he said, sadness evident in his voice, "but neither of us wanted to admit it. Now there's a reason to let go."

"What's the reason?" I demanded to know.

"Isn't it obvious?"

"No! Nothing's ever obvious with you," I said, my anger bubbling up in full force. "Is there something happening between us? Do you even like me? Or am I just imagining this whole thing?"

One moment he was in the shadows, the next his body had mine pinned to the front door, his mouth hard on mine. No thought went into my response; I reacted purely out of need and instinct. My tongue tangled with his, and there was deep satisfaction in feeling him tremble in reply.

"I want you to know me," he whispered against my lips, "but I don't know how."

I couldn't believe this was happening, that he would choose a girl who'd barely shaken the farm dust off her shoes over a sophisticated beauty like Julia Martin.

"Tell me the truth then," I said. "Why did your father really send you?"

He released me then, turning to reclaim his seat on the cement steps. After a moment, I sat down beside him. We faced the row of bungalows across the street. Most of the cracker box houses showed signs of life, from a TV flickering through a window to the glimpse of a woman doing the dinner dishes. They were normal people going about their normal lives, blissfully unaware that a powerful and secretive world existed right outside their door.

"We need you," he said after a few moments. "By now you must know keeping our people safe is the right thing to do."

"I do." I agreed the world wasn't ready to learn of the existence of such extraordinarily gifted people, as perhaps Sutton Sinclair had in mind, but The Nine's slavish devotion to their past made me uneasy, too. I'd heard enough stories from my dad to know that traditions mostly served those in power.

"Then pledge to us and announce your support for the chancellor."

That warning bell, the same one that rang when Jessie offered me his protection, went off. "Why? What difference does it make?"

A barking dog broke the peace for a moment before someone opened a side door and called him in. When silence reigned once again, he said, "Sometimes the old ways are still the best. If traditions were abandoned, there wouldn't be a Prime to keep the Alice Ferndales of the world in check. If Sutton has his way, there will be no loyalty, no incentive to protect one another. We mustn't let that happen. By aligning yourself with us, you swear fealty to Henry and his leadership of The Nine."

"Fealty?" What century was this? My dad would fall off his chair if he knew the days of feudal lords weren't over; they'd just traded armor for business suits. "Is that what Jessie wants from me, too?"

He scoffed. "McCabe is bargaining for position and power, like always. Having you in his stable could take him all the way to a regents' seat."

"Stable?" I burst out. "First I'm a serf, and now I'm a horse?" I jumped to my feet, as did Nicholas. "It doesn't really matter who I am or what I want, does it? All you people care about is adding another soldier to your cause."

"You know that's not true," he protested. "I came here with a mission, you knew that, but everything's different now. I'm different now. It was so much easier not to feel anything after Mum died, but you're so bloody alive it almost hurts, and it doesn't scare me anymore. Don't let them take this away from us."

I listened to his plea with half an ear as my thoughts took a dangerous turn. What if everything I'd been through since Nicholas's arrival had been a setup? Frighten the wits out of the naïve voyant, and she'll do whatever she's told in order to stay safe—even join forces with her tormenters. It made perfect sense.

My body coiled with outrage, my hands curled into fists. "Was this all a ruse? Was Alice a pawn in your scheme? Did you sacrifice Kurt Miller to get to me?"

He drew back. "How can you even think that?"

I couldn't back down now. I had to know the truth, no matter how much it hurt. "You would say anything, do anything, maybe even tell me you loved me if it got you what you wanted, wouldn't you?"

He stared at me as if I were a stranger, and I flinched at a stab of pain, his pain. "Everything I've done is for the benefit of our people, but it doesn't mean my feelings for you aren't real. If you can't see that, then you're not the person I thought you were."

He turned and staggered down the steps. Without looking back, he got into his car and sped away.

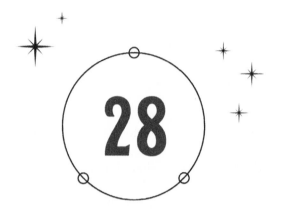

The Witness

Scarlett held me through endless tears, assuring me over and over I'd done the right thing by calling Nicholas out. She told me he probably had no intention of breaking it off with his beautiful girlfriend. If his motives were really so pure, why had he kept her a secret?

We sat on the sofa with a pile of shredded tissues mounded in front of me. "You're lucky," I said with a sniffle. "Warren's a great guy, even if he is a human torch."

She laid her head back and stared at the ceiling. "He is a great guy…"

"Uh-oh," I said at her ambivalent tone. "I hear a 'but' coming."

"It's just that I'm starting to feel like a bit player in my own life." She lifted her head and noticed the confused look on my face. "Everyone else gets to be the star. Everyone else gets top billing."

"You are special," I argued, but she cut me off.

"I know, I know. I'm funny and smart and talented and all that," she said, glossing over the list I recited whenever she faced disappointment. "And we'll see where this goes with Warren, but I'm ready to be the leading lady for once. Hey, are you hungry?" She abruptly switched gears, and I let it go for the moment.

We ordered all our favorite flavors of Chinese food and spent the rest of the night picking through paper cartons of orange chicken and rice noodles and watching *Pride & Prejudice* for the forty-second time. The way Mr. Darcy's hand flexed after helping Elizabeth into the carriage got us every time.

The next day was Friday, so I wasn't missing class in order to lie in bed and wallow in my misery. I shuffled around in my pajamas, occasionally making a stab at doing homework, but mostly Nicholas's reaction to my accusations played on an endless loop in my mind. Each time I thought about it his expression grew more and more repulsed. My phone was so silent I checked to make sure the battery was charged, but of course it was fine. When it finally chimed with a text, I lunged for it, but it was only Jessie checking in. I didn't have the energy to text him back.

Scarlett cancelled a date with Warren that night to stay home and watch Netflix with me. When at last she said good night, I reluctantly retreated to my own room. Endless hours spent staring at the ceiling awaited me as I agonized over my choices. Nicholas had finally opened up to me, but my visions had defined me for so long I couldn't consider someone wanting me for me. I kept reliving the moment his pain had washed through me, trying to understand what it meant. What if I'd completely misjudged him and made a terrible mistake?

Sleep must have come at some point because I was jarred awake to see the glowing bedside clock read 4:07. The world outside my window was hushed, yet something was wrong. Maybe one of my neighbors was having a rough night, and my new empathic radar had picked up on it.

I opened my door to peer into the inky darkness of the common area, but nothing stirred. Figuring my overloaded emotions were getting the better of me, I padded into the dark kitchen without bothering to turn on a light. I'd reached for one of the water bottles we kept under the sink when something flashed through my mind. It wasn't a vision; it didn't last long enough. It was more like a burst of light, there one moment, gone the next.

I stood at the sink, staring into the gloom and wondering if it would come again. It didn't occur to me to be afraid, but when it came again it lasted long enough to glimpse exactly what it was. It sucked the air from my lungs.

It was Alice Ferndale, smiling happily as if into the lens of a camera. Then another snapshot blazed across my brain, this time capturing her in a moment of disbelief. Then another of the doomed enchanter reaching out in terror before plummeting down The Lower 8's majestic staircase. I gripped the counter, wondering how the hell this could be happening.

A soft rattle shook the front door. I muffled a scream as the doorknob jiggled. Someone was outside, checking to see if we'd forgotten to lock the door. I bolted to my room and ripped my cell phone from its charger. Then I dashed for Scarlett's room, locking her door behind me.

It didn't matter how things had been left with Nicholas. He was on speed dial, so I hit the button. Scarlett came awake at the same moment he picked up, groggy but alert.

"There's someone trying to get into the apartment," I whispered urgently into the phone while meeting Scarlett's startled eyes. "I think whoever it is…" I swallowed hard, trying to get a grip on my fear. "I think whoever it is was the last person to see Alice Ferndale alive."

"Hang up, call 9-1-1, I'll be right there." The line went dead.

Scarlett bounded out of bed. "The person who murdered that killer enchanter is here?" she practically squeaked, unplugging her bedside lamp and hefting it like a club. Wearing Hello Kitty pajamas, she didn't look very threatening, but neither of us was going down without a fight.

I relayed the tense situation to the 9-1-1 operator. She must have been trained to keep callers on the line because she wouldn't stop talking, calling me ma'am at the beginning of every sentence. Finally, I threw the phone on Scarlett's bed and focused on what was happening on the other side of the bedroom door. If someone was in our apartment, maybe I could figure out who it was.

I directed my energy into the room beyond but immediately came up against some kind of barrier. I tried again, stumbling back when I realized what was happening.

"It's a sentinel," I whispered. "I'm being blocked." Knowing our intruder was a Nine, I resorted to the last weapon I had. "The Prime Sentinel will be here any second," I yelled, not having any clue if Mr. Silver had picked up on those brief images or not. "The police, too! Get the hell out of my apartment!"

A siren sounded in the distance. Scarlett stood as still as if she were carved from stone, the lamp clutched defensively in her hands. A loud rap came on the door, and we both screamed, the lamp thudding to the floor.

"Miss Wilder," came the calm voice of Akim Silver, "are you well?"

"Blake!" This time it was Nicholas. "Are you in there?"

I rushed to unlock the bedroom door. Both men stood in the glaring light of the common room. Silver gave me a quick once over and then retreated to the front door, which stood wide open. "The police will be here in less than a minute. Mr. Thorne, you stay and take care of Miss Wilder. Do not mention I was here." Then he was gone.

Scarlett grabbed a robe, and I tugged on a sweatshirt seconds before a squad car came screeching up to our building. The three of us lined up on the sofa, and the police came charging in.

It felt like forever that we spent denying any knowledge of why anyone would break into the apartment of two nice girls like us, though it was probably more like thirty minutes. They said it looked like a crowbar had been used to force the lock. While the police took our statements and neighbors stood on the sidewalk grumbling at being woken up by us a second night, Nicholas located an all-night locksmith. The police and the locksmith all finished up about the same time with Nicholas producing a credit card. The Nine definitely owed me for a lock and then some.

The morning paper arrived along with the return of Mr. Silver. Scarlett took one look at the scarred face of the Prime Sentinel and announced, "That's it. I'm done. Thanks for showing up earlier when we were about to be murdered, but I'm going back to bed." She stomped back to her room but paused to throw a glare at Nicholas. "I knew you couldn't be trusted. Go back to London and leave us alone." Her door closed with a bang.

Nicholas and I had barely made eye contact since his arrival, and now the adrenalin that had sustained me for the last few hours had worn off. We all sat at the kitchen table while I shook off exhaustion long enough to tell them about my fleeting encounter with the intruder.

"He was able to block me," I said. "He had to be a sentinel."

"He?" Silver questioned.

"Or she. I don't know." I gave into a jaw-cracking yawn. "There's more. When he or she was outside the apartment, I got a few mental images of Alice. I felt rage, and maybe even guilt."

Silver cocked his head. "Felt?"

"Um, that's what I would guess," I said, backtracking quickly and hoping Silver wouldn't pick up on it. Now definitely wasn't the moment to announce my newly added feature. "Whoever it was, they witnessed her death."

Nicholas glanced at Silver. "Could a sentinel let a few things slip if he's not on guard?"

Silver shook his head. "I've never heard of such a thing."

"What are you talking about?" I asked with impatience. "What about the carnival of death you showed me when I bonded with you, Mr. Silver?"

The Prime rewarded my lapse in discretion with a stern look. "That's because I invited you in."

"Whatever. I'm telling you it happened with Khalia, and it happened again tonight." I was about to ask why I would make up such a thing when it occurred to me Silver must have seen the same thing I did. "Mr. Silver, didn't you see those images of Alice Ferndale?"

"No, I did not."

"Then how did you know I was in trouble?"

He met my gaze with a steady one of his own. "While I can no longer see your visions, I still feel all of your emotions."

I nodded, the last bit of self-control slipping through my fingers. "That's great. Just great. That's fan-fucking-tastic." I shoved away from the table. "Don't forget to lock the door on your way out."

I trudged to my room, wanting to cry but too worn out to produce a tear. As I pulled the comforter over my head, I wondered who had the short end of the stick: me, who had to endure the emotional ups and downs of my love life, college, The Nine, and being pursued by a homicidal sentinel; or the unfortunate Prime who had to watch.

Body Language

Mr. David squinted at me from the front seat of a beat-up Toyota four-door as I came out the front door. He had a five o'clock shadow though it wasn't yet noon, and a cloud of cigarette smoke wreathed his disheveled hair. Silver must have recruited him once again for sentry duty during the few hours I'd been asleep.

Did sentinels track each other in the same way they did other Nines? Had Silver ruled Mr. David out as the possible intruder? And what had been the unknown sentinel's motive? Other than Nicholas and possibly Khalia, no one else had known I could take fleeting glimpses into a sentinel's past or future.

"I'm walking to work," I called, quickly skirting his car. I didn't want to risk being offered a ride and smelling like an ashtray by the time I got to Jitters. His car rolled behind me at a discreet distance as I paced the six blocks.

Saturdays were good days at the coffeehouse; the weekend customers were a different breed from the over-scheduled weekday crowd. Monday through Friday, producing lattes and cappuccinos in less than sixty seconds was almost an Olympic sport. On the weekends people were in a good mood, orders weren't rushed, and the tip jar filled quickly.

After tying on an apron (this one read *A morning without coffee is called sleep*), I joined Al and Olive behind the bar. On the counter was the most bizarre Thanksgiving display I'd ever seen. We had enough space to set out seasonal decorations like the great jack-o-lanterns Cindy had carved for Halloween, but the freakishly large papier mache turkey covered in blue and red feathers and surrounded by tiny figures of pilgrims and Native Americans suggested Godzilla stomping on the fleeing residents of Plymouth Rock.

"Isn't it just the cutest thing?" Olive sidled up next to me but missed my expression of loathing. "Blue and red are my school's colors."

"You made this?" I tried not to sound accusatory.

"I wanted to do my part," she said, wiping down the espresso machine between orders. "Cindy did those great pumpkins, and I heard Al talk about the Christmas decorations he planned to bring in, so I thought, 'Olive, make sure you let everyone know you're a team player.' So there it is!"

Al glanced at me from the other end of the bar, a look of mock horror on his face. He'd have to face that thing every day but was too kind to tell Olive what we'd really like to do with her artwork was burn it and dance gleefully around the flames.

Turning my back on the monstrosity, it was a relief to work; I was that desperate for distraction. Midway through my shift a familiar face appeared on the other side of the bar.

"Hello, Blake," the telepath Marina Novak said aloud. "See? I'm doing better at not ambushing people."

"Much appreciated." I smiled in return. "It's good to see you. What would you like?"

She smoothed down the jacket of the cranberry skirt suit she wore, her pearls peeking out at the neckline. "I've got four showings for a couple who probably need a divorce more than a new house, but who am I to judge?" She sighed. "Better make it a double espresso."

As I whipped up her order, our conversation continued, this time telepathically.

So what's this I hear about your alliance with Jessie McCabe? she asked.

I fumbled the cup, spilling hot coffee across the bar. How did everyone know my business?

Betty Goldberg, the evanescent, that's how, Marina thought. *That woman couldn't keep her trap shut if her life depended on it. She probably started spreading the news Jessie would be your patron the minute she walked out of the club.*

Had that been Jessie's intent? Did he knowingly use her to broadcast word of his claim on me in hopes it might drive Nicholas and me further apart?

Whoa, slow down there, Speed Racer, Marina cut in. *Jessie McCabe is ambitious, sure, but I don't think he's that diabolical.*

I mopped up the bar and swallowed back tears that never seemed far away these days. *I don't know what to think, or who to trust.*

I gave her a quick rundown of what had happened since the night we met, including the job offer from Sutton Sinclair, the disappearance of Selena Flores, the vision of Nicholas with Julia Martin, our resulting fight, and the break-in by an unknown sentinel.

Damn, kiddo, you don't do anything by halves, do you?

Al brushed by me. "Is everything okay here?" From his viewpoint, our silent conversation must look like an animated staring contest.

Marina beamed at him. "Blake is such a doll. I'm practicing communicating through body language. You know that class out at the community center? Can you guess what I'm communicating now?" The attractive telepath shot Al a heated look that despite his many years of happy marriage made him blush to the roots of his gray hair.

"Well, um, carry on," he stammered, scurrying to the other end of the bar.

What should I do? I asked, returning to our private means of communication.

I wish I could tell you, but I only hear what people are thinking in the moment, and that doesn't include sentinels.

So unless somebody was hatching a plot right in front of her, she wouldn't know. I really was on my own.

Not quite, she thought, taking pity on me. *I know Nicholas was genuinely concerned about your welfare that night at Lower 8.*

It felt like a weight had been lifted from my chest. *And Jessie?*

A small line had formed behind the telepath, so I quickly went about steaming her espresso without dropping it this time.

She giggled. *You're way too young to know what Jessie was thinking about you.*

She paid for the coffee and added a big tip before her expression turned serious. *A word of advice, if I may. Pledge to The Nine. It will keep you safe. But think for yourself, question everything, and don't let others define you.* Her lips curled up slightly. *You have more power than you know.*

I stared at her a moment, wondering what exactly she was telling me. She picked up her coffee.

"Nothing can change what has passed," she said aloud. "But for someone who has such unique insight into the future, anything is possible."

That Voodoo That You Do

Scarlett and Warren had textbooks spread across the kitchen table when I walked in the door. Tomorrow would be homework catch up day for sure, but there was no way I could concentrate right then on chemistry and art history, even if I could convince Dr. Hamilton to let me make up the exam I'd missed the day Alice attacked me. If the enchanters Jessie sent to school had done their job, no one would remember the incident, and my absence would be marked as unexcused.

"You'll be happy to know no blood-thirsty sentinels dropped by to murder us while you were out," Scarlett said, not bothering to look up from her book. Warren shifted in his chair, uncomfortable at the sudden tension.

I plunked down at the table. "I'm a horrible friend and roommate, and you have every right to be angry."

She met my gaze with a raised brow. I'd learned long ago apologizing straight away went a long way with her. The problem was, she too had figured out I had her number.

"I mean it this time," she insisted, as if we were already in the middle of a conversation. "We can't just sit here waiting for whatever headcase wants to kill you this week. We need to do something to protect ourselves." Mr. David had silently trolled behind me all the way home, but she was right.

I told them about Marina's visit. "It was like she was saying they need me more than I need them, but I don't know how that can be." There was still so much I didn't understand.

Scarlett flicked her hair over her shoulder. "I like her already."

"Blake, aren't you forgetting something here? Why don't you use some magic to figure it out?" Warren waggled his fingers as if he were casting a spell.

"Magic?" I asked with a smile.

"You know, your voodoo, your mutant powers, your mad skills," he said, his enthusiasm building. "You've got this cool thing you can do, but you act like it's a curse or something. Why don't you look into everyone's futures and see what happens? Maybe you could find out who is really looking out for you, and who just wants another notch on his bedpost." Scarlett shot him a scolding glance, and he grinned. "So to speak."

My best friend and I looked at each other with speculation.

"Warren has a point," she said.

I nodded slowly, thinking it all through. "By the way, Warren, there's something else you should know about that vision I had of you and Scarlett being mugged." I now understood what it meant.

His eyes bulged when he heard about his future attacker lighting up like a Roman candle. "What do we do? I can't go around hurting people, even if they are trying to steal my wallet."

They could probably steer clear of the whole encounter if the two of them avoided walking at night for the next few days, but unless Warren learned to channel his energy, it was only a matter of time before something terrible happened.

"Maybe we should find you an elementalist to help you learn control," I suggested.

He grabbed Scarlett's hand, suddenly excited. "Can we go to The Lower 8 to find one?"

I knew this was coming but didn't imagine it happening quite so soon. Though Scarlett might suspect she'd never get into a club for Nines, I'd hoped her relationship with Warren would be further along before it was brought home that another person in her life was literally going someplace she couldn't follow. Maybe there was a special pass for people like her, those who embraced what made us different without thought to the consequences.

"Let me talk to Jessie," I hedged, but the way her eyes dimmed when they met mine told me she already knew.

"They won't let me in, will they?" She withdrew her hand from Warren's.

"Scarlett…" I had no idea how to comfort her.

She fixed an encouraging smile on her face for Warren's benefit. "You should go with Blake. I'll be here when you get back."

"Tonight?" It was Saturday, and the place would be packed. "Maybe we should go another time. I need another dress. I can't wear the same thing twice in a row."

Scarlett got up from the table. "I'm sure I've got something we can do a quick alteration on." Years of whipping up costumes had made her a fiend with a sewing machine.

Warren rose to his feet and looked at Scarlett. "You can't come?"

She forced a laugh. "Going to a club full of you weirdos is the last thing I want to do. Why don't you go change, and we'll have Blake ready when you get back."

He put his arms around her. "You know this weirdo would rather be here with you than anywhere else, right?"

Her bright smile faded. "Something is happening to you that we can't ignore. You need to go find someone to help us figure it out."

He kissed her hard, as if I weren't in the room. When he finally pulled away, he said, "I like it when you say *us*." He skipped out the door.

It was a wonder Scarlett's closet door never burst off its hinges. Inside was a solid mass of colors and textures, with shoes wedged into every square inch not taken up with fabrics, yet somehow, she found exactly what she sought with very little effort.

"Try this on," she said, holding up something black and lacey, which turned out to be a deceptively sexy dress. Wielding straight pins with professional speed, she soon had it tacked the way she wanted and ordered me to strip.

As the dress pooled around my feet, I said, "You're really okay with this?"

She searched through her sewing basket for a fresh spool of black thread before answering. "You have always been the special one, and I get that." She held up a silencing hand when I would have interrupted in protest. "You will always be my best friend, but I don't know if I have room for more than one of you in my life."

After that blistering kiss, I couldn't believe she meant it. "You'd end it with Warren because he's barely a Nine?"

"No," she said. "I'd end it with Warren because I won't make him choose between me and this whole new world opening up for him. It may sound selfish, but it's my turn to come first."

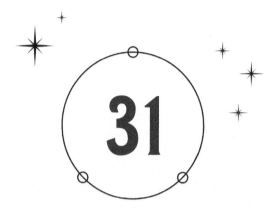

The Girl on the Bed

The eyes peeking through Lower 8's portal squinted at us through owlish lenses. The sentinel on duty tugged open the front door, and we were admitted by a woman who looked like she'd seen her fair share of bake sales and soccer fields. Middle-aged and comfortably padded, she was dressed in a floral dress buttoned up to her chin. Mr. David hung back, his expression of distaste making it clear the nightclub was not in his comfort zone.

"Well, aren't you two adorable," the door sentinel exclaimed, her twangy accent putting her hometown as somewhere south of the Mason-Dixon line. Taking in Warren's awkward stance, she asked, "First date?"

"No!" he blurted. "I mean, we're friends. I have a girlfriend but she's, you know, not interested in coming here."

She nodded sagely. "I understand completely."

"Excuse me," I cut in. "Is Nicholas Thorne here by any chance?" I wasn't sure which response was the one I wanted.

"No, I haven't seen him tonight," she answered with a sunny smile. "But he is a Thorne, so he doesn't need a reservation to get a table." She turned to Warren and held out her hand. "May I?" I'd explained what to expect on the way over, so he quickly obeyed. Her smile slowly faded as she tried to take his measure. "Maybe the other hand?" she suggested helpfully. It took another minute, but at last she nodded. "A new elementalist, I see. Welcome, young man."

She turned to me to repeat the process but dropped my hand the moment we touched, her eyes going wide. "My stars," she said with a shaky laugh. Reaching for two red bracelets, she collected the cover charge without another word.

As we moved away, Warren whispered, "What did you do to her?"

"Beats me," I said, though I knew exactly what had happened. My mind had brushed up against hers, something I now understood never happened to sentinels. The snapshots of her future included a healthy new grandchild rather than anything frightening, but it didn't make my invasion any more welcome.

Making our entrance, I was glad the dress had turned out so well. Solid material covered my assets, but the rest was all transparent black lace. It was also long enough to camouflage the remaining bruises on my knee. No matter what else the crowd might be thinking as we descended the staircase, they had to admit it was a killer dress. The little jeweled evening bag Scarlett had lent me added the right dash of sparkle.

Warren looked like he'd walked thru the gates of Disneyland. The small orchestra played a tango while dancers swayed gracefully on the floor. The waitresses wore sequined tuxedo jackets and matching shorts, and the tables were set with white linen. Overhead the ceiling had been transformed into a brilliant nighttime sky. Occasional shooting stars streaked across the heavens.

He gaped in wonder. "I don't remember there being so many stars out tonight."

"I think that's the work of an evanescent," I said, pleased at the sudden sense of belonging surging through me. I was no longer the wide-eyed newcomer.

He caught sight of the crowd at the bar. "How many of these people are elementalists?"

Jessie appeared just as we reached the bottom step. He wore a beautiful white dinner jacket and bow tie, his hair slicked back into a low ponytail. "Welcome to Old Hollywood night," he said, looking like a subversive Gatsby welcoming us to his private party. "Did I hear you say you are searching for elementalists?"

I made the introductions and explained Warren's newfound skill. Within moments, Jessie had separated me from my companion and pawned him off on a pretty girl who didn't seem to mind. Warren would most likely be single soon anyway, so there was no need to protect my best friend's interests.

"Nicely done," I complimented Jessie.

His appreciative gaze swept over me. "At Lower 8, everyone finds what they're looking for."

I smiled. "Is that printed on the napkins?"

He shot me his trademark grin. "No, but I'm considering making it a well-placed tattoo."

I lifted my eyes to the stars. "Remind me not to ask you open-ended questions. Ever." His warm laughter reached into parts of me I didn't know existed. I'd come here to help Warren, but within three minutes I'd abandoned my charge and let myself be charmed by a man who'd given me little reason to trust him.

In keeping with the evening's throwback theme, he jutted out an arm to escort me across the room. With my hand tucked in the crook of his elbow, he said, "May I say how fine you look in that dress, darlin'?"

"You may," I said with a laugh, resolving to keep a wary eye out for Nicholas. He'd probably hear about my visit soon enough, but I didn't want to be the girl who played one guy off another, especially not in the middle of this particular crowd.

The house table had a discreet *Reserved* sign keeping it vacant, so we slid into the booth. At the bar Marcus sat hunched over a drink, but he showed no interest in joining us.

"If I'd known you were coming, I'd have met you at the door," Jessie said, moving in close until our shoulders touched.

"I didn't know myself until an hour ago," I confessed. "A lot of things surprise me these days."

"Maybe I can help. Ask me anything," he said, dropping an arm along the banquette behind me. "Now that you're under my protection, I promise to answer your questions truthfully."

Layla swung by and dropped off what was apparently now a standing order of a Coke for Jessie and a mineral water with lime for me.

"I don't think anyone has necessarily lied to me," I said after Layla had departed, "but neither do I think people are telling me the whole truth."

He cocked his head in that way he did as if listening to something only he could hear. After a few moments, he said, "Cedric and I agree: you are as smart as you are beautiful." He clicked his glass against mine.

I took a sip. "So you admit it?"

"I admit to not telling you everything I know, but that will come in time."

"How about you start with telling me what you want with me," I said, cutting to the chase. There'd been too much fuss made over the patron thing for it to be as straightforward as they said.

He dropped his mouth to my ear. "Do you really want me to answer that?"

It would be so easy to relax into him, to save the questions for another day, but then I glanced out across the crowded room. A number of faces were turned our way, watching, whispering.

There was a game in play here, and like it or not, I was on the field.

I toyed with the white cocktail napkin under my drink. The club's logo was printed on it in silver. "Why did you name this place The Lower 8?"

His brow arched at the shift in topic. "England has been the base of power for our kind since the beginning."

"Alder House?"

He nodded. "They hand down the laws, and we're supposed to follow without question. Sometimes I think they forget we're real people out here, with reasons for doing what we do. It's like they're the top nine…"

"And you're the lower eight," I finished for him. "That's where I come in, isn't it? If this were a movie, they'd be the empire, you're the rebel alliance, and I'm the droid with the death star plans."

He threw back his head and laughed. "I would hardly compare you to a robot, but yes, it is time that we get more say in our own future, and a powerful voyant on our side adds to our strength."

I wasn't a history professor's daughter for nothing. Stories of political maneuvers and machinations passed as appropriate dinner conversation at our house, including the unfortunate tale of Lady Jane Grey, England's Nine-Day Queen. She was manipulated all the way to the chopping block. I'd always wondered how she could have been so clueless to have let herself be used that way, but maybe she hadn't known enough to fight back.

"What if I decide I don't need a patron?" I asked. The paper napkin was in shreds, hopefully the only outward sign of my agitation.

He sipped his drink, observing me over the rim of the glass. "That's not the way things are done."

I stiffened my spine. "Maybe it's time to try something new."

"Look around you. What do you see?" Without waiting for an answer, he continued. "Outside these walls is the modern world where topics trend, facts are fake, and science has become subjective. But in here, you are one of us. We are a law unto ourselves, and there are traditions that must be obeyed."

I shifted away and turned to face him. "Or what?"

"If you refuse to respect our laws," he said, all playfulness gone, "you cannot expect to be protected by them."

"And yet you named this place The Lower 8 in protest of those laws," I observed.

"I'm telling you the way it is," he said, steel edging into his voice. "Part of our strength is in our alliances. If you refuse a patron, you'll become fair game. Henry Thorne's day is ending whether he realizes it or not. Do you think Sutton Sinclair is the only shark in the water smelling blood? You wouldn't last a month."

I gaped at him. "What century do you people live in? I'm not some kingdom to be conquered."

His eyes glittered. "No, but you're a fool if you think making some declaration of independence makes a damn bit of difference. I can keep you safe, and the only thing I will ask in exchange is your loyalty. If you'll grow up some, I can give you a whole lot more."

I bet someone had told Lady Jane the same thing.

"Maybe I see it differently," I said, bristling. "No one can force me into anything against my will—not you, not Nicholas, and not Sutton Sinclair." I moved to slide out of the booth. "I officially cancel whatever agreement we had."

His hand clamped down on my wrist. "You're making a mistake."

"Let me go," I said, trying to twist away, but he held fast. Jessie practically vibrated with energy, and his touch made our connection even stronger.

"Fine," I said, staring into his remarkable gray eyes. Warren was right. It was time to start looking into the future and getting some answers.

Fair skin intertwined with bronze. Blonde hair tangled on a white linen pillow. A tattoo of some intricate symbol marked the muscular shoulder blade of a man passionately wrapped around a woman.

I'd seen plenty of erotic visions, but they were mostly of my high school classmates. Backseat fumbling or bathroom encounters were so basic and devoid of emotion I would figuratively tap my toe until they were over. This was different. I spied on Jessie, and though I was angry and exasperated to have stumbled upon such a personal moment in his future, I wasn't immune to his beauty or grace.

The vision flashed forward. The couple's pleasure mounted, and I couldn't tear my eyes from his lean, naked form. Long, feminine legs snaked around his waist, pulling him closer. A sigh of longing escaped me, wishing I had the nerve and experience to take what I wanted as easily as he seemed to.

My premonition skipped forward one more time. I'd soon be freed from this vision, much like the couple would find their own moment of release. Jessie grasped the woman's hands, pinning them to the bed as they merged together in a last breathless moment. Then Jessie raised his head, pushed back his hair, and smiled down into the face of his partner.

I froze in shock and astonishment when I glimpsed her face. The girl on the bed was me.

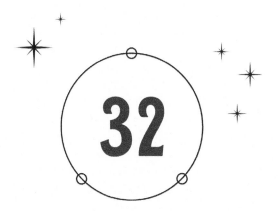

There's Been an Accident

I sat in the dark parking lot clinging to the wheel of the Volvo, holding on as if it were a life preserver in a storm. The shocked look on Jessie's face when I tore from his grasp and charged up the stairs was seared into my mind. There was no way he could know what I'd seen, yet my own expression must have revealed some clue. What if a telepath had picked up on my erotic premonition, and the story got back to Jessie? Or Nicholas? My forehead dropped to the wheel, and I groaned.

An urgent tap came on the window.

"Go away," I said without bothering to look up. I couldn't bear to face Jessie again. The summons came again, and I was surprised to discover Marcus's distressed face peering through the window.

"There's been an accident," he said, his voice muffled by the glass. "It's Nicholas."

Instantly I turned on the ignition and lowered the window. "What happened? Is he okay?"

"I don't know. My dad just called to say something happened to Nicholas at the job site." He shifted on his feet as if there was more bad news. "We also just got a report that Tristan Murrieta has been spotted in Santa Carla." The final suspect, Alice's likely partner, had finally made his move.

I put the Volvo in gear. "Let's go."

He dashed to a gleaming red Porsche. In moments he was racing out of the parking lot, and I was hot on his tail. Tearing down the dark roads, I floored the gas pedal to keep up with him. Images of Nicholas crushed under tons of steel flashed through my mind, and my teeth started to chatter, the dropping temperature penetrating both my heart and the thin fabric of my dress.

Marcus skirted the crew parking area and zipped along a short access road. The Porsche spewed gravel as it lurched to a stop, and I pulled up next to him. Grabbing the evening bag with my phone tucked inside, I jumped out of the car. We went through a small gate set into the long line of fencing, and I ran ahead as he stopped to close it. Giant lights suspended over the pit threw enough light to see we'd come in right behind Sinclair's construction offices.

With high heels sinking into the dirt, I stumbled my way around to the front of the trailers expecting to find a collection of EMTs, but the area was deserted. The offices were dark, and there wasn't any sign of Nicholas or Sutton. I blinked, trying to make sense of it.

Marcus came up behind me, and I turned to him in confusion. It was so quiet I could hear the occasional car drive by. "Where's Nicholas?"

"They're around the side." He gestured for me to follow, and a ripple of his nervous anticipation flowed over me. I backed up a few steps in shock. Marcus had lied about Nicholas being here, and now we were alone on a deserted job site.

He must have seen my expression change because all trace of concern disappeared from his face. "You should have just walked with me," he said sulkily. "It would have been so much quicker. Why are you always so much trouble?"

"I don't mean to be," I choked out, backing up a few more steps in the direction of the exit. "In fact, why don't I just go home, and you'll never have to see me again."

"I locked the gate," he called out as I oozed back a bit farther. A quick glance over my shoulder revealed the entry had been secured with a heavy chain and padlock. He laughed. "What, don't you trust me?"

He started to advance, but I maintained our distance by taking several steps toward the offices. Suddenly, a snapshot of memory blazed across my consciousness. It was an image of Alice Ferndale looking trustingly up at her companion. I knew what it meant.

"You killed Alice, didn't you?" The night was so still I didn't have to raise my voice to be heard. His face contorted with fury.

I took off running toward the catwalk that skirted the pit. Before I could reach it, his hand clamped down on my wrist. I kicked out blindly, and he grunted as my heel dug into flesh. I twisted out of his grasp, but he latched onto my purse. I let it slide off my shoulder, realizing too late I'd also given up my phone and pepper spray, too.

I reached the catwalk and turned toward the main entrance, but he'd anticipated my escape plan and appeared on the walkway several yards in front of me. I skidded to a stop as he rummaged through my purse and came up with my cell phone.

"You want this?" He lobbed it into the pit followed by my bag. "Go get it."

I turned around and ran for my life. It took only a few seconds to realize I'd never outrun him in a race around the pit, especially in heels. I frantically glanced around for another means of escape, zeroing in on the giant metal staircase ahead that zigzagged down into the massive hole.

Racing down the first flight of stairs, I kicked off my heels before whipping around to take the next. Midway down the third, the drumming of Marcus's feet overhead drowned out the pounding of my heart.

Massive cement pillars rose above me like a petrified forest as I burst onto the floor of the construction zone. Barricades of rebar and lumber created a forbidding maze, and slumbering machinery appeared poised to awaken and devour all in their path. I shut down my wild imaginings before resolutely darting into the labyrinth and hopefully in the direction of my phone.

Sutton Sinclair ran a tight ship; tools were safely stowed for the night, and the cement floor had been swept of debris. Only a shovel propped against a wheelbarrow had been overlooked. I paused to reach for the shovel, and it seemed to leap into my hand. Bits of gravel tore at my bare feet as I took off again.

Monstrous shadows created pockets of false security, but I needed to catch my breath. I ducked around the far side of a bulldozer and hid, panting in the gloom. I didn't fully understand Marcus's role in the Alice Ferndale drama, but explanations could wait. The last remnants of the mental bond with Mr. Silver had most likely faded by now, and it would be a while before Nicholas realized I was missing. I was on my own.

Pinpointing Marcus's whereabouts was the only advantage I had against a man most likely familiar with every corner of his father's job site. Clutching the shovel like an unwieldy baseball bat, I reached out with my mind and hoped to encounter the same sensation of resistance as I did the night of our apartment break in. It seemed this wasn't his first attempt to silence me.

I stumbled back against the bulldozer at the unexpected pull of his mind. Marcus must have guessed what I would do because instead of a barrier, he'd thrown aside any mental defenses and welcomed me in. I balanced on the precipice of an abyss for a long moment before the sentinel dragged me into a chasm of dark memories.

The door swung open to reveal Alice Ferndale framed by the nighttime sky. Behind her was the parking lot at The Lower 8, now completely empty of cars.

"You rang?" She wore a wolfish grin as her eyes drank in the sight of Marcus. This was a completely different Alice than the one I'd first met, and it wasn't just because of the bruises left on her face from our encounter in the library.

Marcus opened the door wide. "Come in."

She stepped into the club's little reception area. "What are you doing here so late?"

"Celebrating," Marcus said. "After everyone finally left, I found the last of the bank documents. No more trail of papers leading back to me, plus no more blackmailer. I'm in the clear, and I have you to thank for it."

She preened, lapping up the praise. "Does that mean we can go away now? As nice as your apartment is, I'm starting to feel like a prisoner."

"We wouldn't want that." Marcus opened the interior door leading into the main club and waved Alice through. "Let's open a bottle of champagne, and then we'll be on our way."

The enchanter clapped her hands with delight. "Something expensive? I've never had the good stuff."

"Anything for you." Marcus paused at the top of the staircase, causing his companion to stop as well. "I do have one question though. Why did you go after Blake Wilder in such a public place?"

"A present for you, babe." She looped her arms around his neck and gazed at him lovingly. "Now no one will ever suspect you of anything."

"It wasn't to keep me bound to you forever?" He twisted a lock of her hair around his finger. "If the Prime Sentinel ever catches up with you, you might tell him I put you up to it."

She blinked in mock innocence, failing to hear the low fury in her lover's words. "We're so good together. Why would you ever need another reason to stay with me?"

He kissed her briefly before disentangling her arms. "I don't."

A vicious shove was all it took. A look of complete shock crossed her face just before she tumbled brutally down the stairs. Marcus watched dispassionately as her body came to rest on the floor down below, her head twisted at an unnatural angle.

He trotted down the stairs. Feeling for a pulse he nodded in satisfaction. "You got your wish," he murmured. "Your fate is now forever bound with mine."

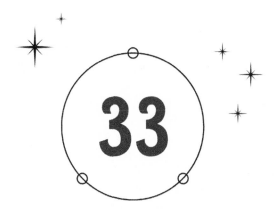

A Death in the Family

"This is all your fault, you know." Marcus's voice echoed off the unforgiving concrete. It was impossible to tell where he was, only that he was near. I could have kicked myself. He'd laid a trap, and I'd walked right into it when I dove into his mind. He'd followed the trail of energy right to me.

"No one would have ever known about my connection to Ashley Norman, or Selena Flores, or Alice if you hadn't pushed your way in," his disembodied voice continued.

I crept to the back of the bulldozer, straining to hear the slightest noise. Fear combined with the skimpy black dress left me chilled to the bone. I gritted my teeth to keep them from chattering,

"That bitch, Ashley, tried to blackmail me, can you believe it?" He was on the move, his voice increasing in volume. "She realized I'd forged Dad's signature on the new loan, and she wanted her share. Money that belonged to me."

I whirled about when the click of a gun came from directly behind me. He'd come around the front of the machine. He pointed the gun at my chest. My shovel made a pitiful shield.

"Then Selena figured out I'd been skimming from the construction payroll," he continued, his expression puzzled and strangely detached.

"What did you do to her?" I asked, fearing the answer.

"Oh, they'll never find her. After you broadcast our plan to the whole club, we took her out to the desert." His expression grew distant at the memory. "It's funny; the only thing she asked for was the life of her dog."

I sucked in my breath. "You killed them both?"

He shrugged. "The stupid mutt ran off into the brush. The snakes probably got him by now."

I struggled for something, anything to buy time. "Suki knew about you and Alice, didn't she?" It explained why she'd been so freaked out by my vision and had made herself scarce.

"Suki?" He paused, considering my words. "Thank you. I didn't know there was another loose end."

Confession time was over. He took aim. In desperation I threw the shovel at him and dove for the dirt. The shot went wild. I scrambled to my feet and ran for the nearest pillar. Another gunshot exploded, biting into the column, and a stinging shower of cement shards tore at my face.

I kept running, and another bullet whizzed by my head. I frantically looked around for another weapon when I spied my cell phone ahead on the ground. I made a mad dash to it, barely even slowing as it seemed to jump into my hand. Leaping behind a pallet stacked with bags of concrete, I ran my thumb across its cracked face. The screen lit up with a selfie of Scarlett and me taken at last year's Outside Lands music festival, but the phone refused to open. A sob caught in my throat.

If I just ran blindly like a scared rabbit, Marcus would eventually get me in his sights. If my cell phone had landed here, my purse with the pepper spray couldn't be far away. It wasn't much of a defense against a gun, but it was all I had. I abandoned my temporary cover with one goal in mind.

The gun went off at the same time my shoulder screamed with pain. I flung myself against another pillar so hard the rough concrete dug into my hands. My face was wet with tears or blood, or maybe both, but if I gave into fear, it was as good as sitting down and waiting for my executioner. A burning anger filled me instead. *How dare you, Marcus Sinclair.* That he had the audacity to think his life was more important than mine, or Selena's, or anyone else's.

I dashed to yet another pillar, but Marcus stepped out of the shadows and directly into my path. I stumbled back. He held the gun aimed almost casually in my direction, as if the bastard knew he'd won and had all the time in the world to finish the job.

We stood like that for endless seconds. Maybe it was harder to commit murder when your victim stared you in the face.

People say your life flashes before your eyes if you know you're about to die, or maybe you're supposed to contemplate your regrets, but neither happened to me. I noticed small details, like how drawn Marcus looked, much older than his years. The tang of curing cement, an earthy smell that reminded me of my dad's botched attempt to repair a crack in our driveway. The steady tapping of blood dripping from my fingertips and onto the rugged concrete. Maybe I reacted that way because I was too pissed off to accept my fate.

I desperately wished Nicholas was there. One look from him, and the gun would fly from Marcus's grip. Shockingly, the gun did exactly that, and both of us stood dumbfounded for a moment. A few seconds later a hefty piece of lumber sailed straight at Marcus, sending him diving for cover.

"Blake! Run!" Nicholas stood on the catwalk overhead.

I dashed back to the stairs and tore up them as fast as I could. I panted like a long-distance runner by the time I reached Nicholas, whose attention was riveted on the pit below where things crashed and banged about. Marcus dodged and staggered, doing his best to evade Nicholas's onslaught of telekinetically guided weapons, but he was already beaten and bloodied. Racing through the now-open gate was Mr. Silver and Sutton Sinclair.

I grabbed Nicholas's arm. "Stop! You're going to kill him."

As if he was in the grip of a fever dream, it took a few moments for awareness to seep in, but then he yanked me into a fierce embrace. I yelped at the pain in my shoulder, but he didn't let go. The others peered over the edge to survey the damage down below.

Marcus's fearful expression changed to one of feigned amusement when he realized we had company. "Well, hello, Dad," he called up with bitter sarcasm.

Sinclair stood tall, his imperious bearing ingrained, but there was defeat in the droop of his shoulders. "What have you done?"

Marcus stumbled to the side of the pit. "What I had to do." He speared his father with a glare. "What you forced me to do."

"I don't understand," Sinclair said, genuinely shocked. "Did you really kill Selena?"

"She told me you were going to marry her." He spit a mouthful of blood onto the concrete. "Think of all that future alimony I saved you."

The elementalist paled as he took that in. "And Kurt?"

The bravado drained from the younger man's face, and he hung his head. "Kurt was an accident, I swear."

Sinclair stood motionless. His hands gripped the catwalk railing as he briefly closed his eyes. When he opened them, they were hardened with resolve. "Just tell me one thing, son: why?"

"Why?" He cocked his head so he could see his father as he spoke. "I gambled, Dad, and just like always, I lost. You told me after the last time you wouldn't bail me out no matter who held my markers, so I did what I had to do to survive. You know all about survival, don't you, Dad?"

"I do," Sinclair said quietly, "and I will survive this." He looked down at the pitiful sight Marcus had become: battered and unrepentant. "You are no son of mine."

Marcus flinched but didn't turn from his father's condemning gaze.

"Mr. Silver, I believe we've heard enough." Sinclair's gravel voice rang with steel. "I will not subject my family to the spectacle of a trial. You will bear witness to the judgment of The Nine."

The air around Sinclair snapped with power. The wood planks bracing the wall above Marcus's head suddenly cracked and splintered.

"Oh, God, no!" I cried, realizing what was about to happen. "Mr. Silver, do something!"

"As a regent, it is within his rights," Silver said, though he too appeared conflicted.

The elementalist tore away at the earthen wall towering over his son. Marcus bowed his head. Boards snapped, and soil tumbled. I turned away as the ground shook and the earth roared. It seemed to go on forever, but then at last it was silent. A massive cloud of dust rose above the tons of dirt and debris that now buried Marcus.

Sinclair stood frozen at the railing, coming to grips with what both he and his son had done. At last he cleared his throat. "I trust, Mr. Silver, that your business here is concluded."

Silver gazed at Sinclair, a look of pity on his usually inscrutable face. "Justice has been served." He turned from the railing. With a last look at the silently grieving father, Nicholas put his arm around me, and we followed Silver out of the gate.

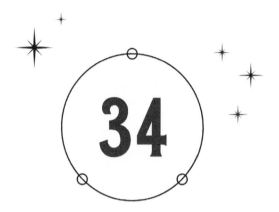

Living out Loud

"It's just a scratch," I said, trying to convince both my audience and me.

The blood had been washed from my shoulder, revealing a deep crease where Marcus's bullet had grazed the skin. The same nurse who'd tended to Khalia's injuries at The Lower 8 sat next to me now. Despite the late hour, he'd appeared at my door about ten minutes after we arrived back at the apartment. He introduced himself as Bob and set up shop at my kitchen table.

"That's quite a gash," he announced. "I'm sorry to say it will likely leave a scar." He wore the same green scrubs as before, as if he were perpetually dressed to leap into action.

"You're lucky to be alive," Scarlett said. She hovered nearby, too upset to sit, while Warren and Nicholas claimed the other two chairs at the table. "Why were you even there?"

"She thought I was in trouble," Nicholas answered. "Jessie McCabe overheard Marcus telling her I'd had an accident at his father's job site." It was more likely one of his spirits had eavesdropped on the conversation, but I was grateful either way. "He called Sutton who then called me."

My shoulder wound stitched and dressed, and my feet washed and bandaged, the nurse turned his attention to my face. His touch simmered with low-grade energy. He was one of us, though perhaps Second or Third Class.

"How bad is it?" My voice betrayed my anxiety. I hadn't dared check out the damage in a mirror, but blood had slowly dripped down the front of Scarlett's ruined dress the entire drive home.

Bob's placid expression gave nothing away as he tilted my chin this way and that, using gauze to wipe away blood, tears, and dirt as he examined my wounds. Finally he smiled. "It's all superficial. I'd say you'll look like yourself again in just a few weeks."

My body turned to jelly as the tension drained away.

"Could I get a towel?" Bob asked.

Before Scarlett could move, a clean dishtowel from the kitchen flew across the room to Nicholas's waiting hand. "Anything else you need?"

"Hang onto her," he directed. "This will sting."

He wasn't kidding. As Bob extracted gravel and cement chips from my abrasions, Nicholas squeezed my hand every time I flinched.

Warren filled the silence that had overtaken us, telling Scarlett, "Did you know there are people who can, like, pull things out of thin air? There was this girl whose dress changed three different times while I was talking to her. Can you believe it?"

"A materialist," Nicholas murmured.

"Yeah," Warren agreed. "And then I met a whole bunch of elementalists. It turns out there are more of us than any other skill. One guy even nicknamed me Fireball. Cool, huh?" He chattered on happily about the tips and tricks his new friends had offered to hone his talent and gain more control, oblivious to Scarlett's growing despair. When she turned away to hide the tears, I feared a fateful choice had been made.

"Warren," she said, interrupting his latest story about the water elementalist who served in the navy and set records for her rapid rise in the ranks. "Would you take a walk with me?" He jumped to his feet, innocent of what awaited him outside.

"Scarlett..." I tried to catch her eye in a silent attempt to urge her to postpone any rash decisions. Guilt washed through me at what I'd put her through, and I knew she was reacting out of fear. Warren was barely a Nine. Letting herself love him would be no riskier than handing her heart to any other guy, and knowing Warren, probably a good deal safer.

She spared me barely a glance as she zipped up her jacket, already retreating into a world of heartbreak. Cutting Warren loose would probably be the most painful thing she'd ever done, and I hoped she didn't regret her choice.

Of course, I was hardly one to give romantic advice. When I'd thought Nicholas had been injured, all my misgivings had melted away. Conveniently forgotten were my suspicions over whether Julia Martin really was in the rearview mirror, as he claimed, along with his motives for wanting to be with me. Even the erotic vision of Jessie, which seemed to indicate I would screw things up with Nicholas one way or another, lost its hold on me.

"All done," Bob announced, breaking into my thoughts. "An evanescent will come by in the morning to minimize your chances of infection and scarring." I'd never thought of myself as a vain person, but I appreciated the cosmetic perk that came with being a Nine.

"Thanks for coming so fast," Nicholas said, shaking the nurse's hand. "Send my father the bill."

"Oh, don't worry. I will." Bob chuckled as he packed up his kit. "Chancellor Thorne and Sutton Sinclair are paying my rent this week. Most appreciated." No one had gone into detail about the nature of my supposed accident. Bob had no way of knowing Sinclair had executed his own son that night, or he might not have brought him up so casually.

Nicholas closed the door as the nurse ducked out into the night. Scarlett and Warren hadn't returned, so we were alone. I was banged up, dirty, and crusted with dried blood; never had I felt less attractive. Yet when Nicholas looked at me, the electricity was immediate. He took the chair Bob had vacated, trapping my knees between his.

"The last time we talked," he said, leaning in so close his face was mere inches from mine, "you accused me of being willing to do anything, including murder, to get you to ally with us. Yet you hear I'm in trouble, and you risk your life to be with me. Why?"

My endurance was at an end. I had no energy for games or verbal sparring. "What do you want to hear? That I died a little when I thought something horrible had happened to you? That I hate not knowing where we stand?" My words tumbled out unfiltered. "That I'm afraid…" My voice caught, but I pushed through the doubts and fears. "That I'm afraid of falling in love, and finding I'm there all by myself?"

His mouth found mine, and the spark between us instantly reignited. My lips were about the only thing on my face not bruised or scraped, and he was exquisitely gentle. After a minute, he pulled back far enough to say, "You don't know how to be anything less than who you are, do you?"

"That's not true," I said, remembering days when I wished to be invisible, and nights longing for my real life to show up.

"It is," he insisted, taking both of my hands in his. "It's one of the reasons I can't stay away. You let yourself feel everything, no matter how messy or painful." His gaze dropped to where our fingers twined. "When my mum died, it was like she never existed. My dad won't talk about her or even tell me how she died. We just stopped setting a place for her at the table." A humorless smile twisted his lips. "And then I realized I was doing the exact same thing to you with Julia. If I just ignored the problem, it would go away."

My family talked over each other at the dinner table, argued over who had to take out the garbage, and laughed ourselves silly at my dad's stupid jokes. We did everything out loud, and I couldn't imagine it any other way.

His eyes lifted to mine. "I'll be heading home soon. What I have to say to Julia shouldn't be said over the phone."

"And then?" I prompted.

"And then I want to come back. To you." He gently squeezed my fingers. "If you'll let me."

I hated being the cause of another girl's heartbreak, but it wasn't like I could erase my feelings for Nicholas. "Are you sure about this? About us?"

He leaned in and kissed me again. "More than you know."

When our lips parted, I said, "Have I thanked you yet for saving my life?"

He smiled. "You had it under control. All I did was toss about a few two by fours."

I regarded him quizzically. "What about the gun? He was going to shoot me."

Now it was his turn to look puzzled. "What gun?"

I shook my head in confusion. "Marcus had a gun." That was now buried under tons of rubble.

"I don't know what you're talking about," he said.

The front door banged open, and both Scarlett and Warren came flying into the room. Tears streaked down her stricken face while Warren gripped the sides of his head chanting, "Ohmygod, ohmygod, ohmygod."

Nicholas jumped to his feet. "What happened?"

Scarlett turned her terrified gaze to me. "The mugger. The fire." Her face crumpled.

I knew exactly what she'd seen. "I had a premonition of a guy with a knife attacking them," I told Nicholas, "but then he burst into flames."

"I think I killed someone," Warren said, choking back sobs.

Nicholas pulled out his phone with one hand and latched onto Warren's arm with the other. "Show me," he said, pushing Warren out the door.

Scarlett had always been the rock I clung to whenever my visions got too frightening or the vicious words whispered in the hallway between classes drew blood. Our roles were suddenly reversed, and I put my arms around her as she cried.

I murmured soothing reassurances that all would be well. The Nine was a law unto themselves, and if anyone could get Warren through whatever came next, it would be Nicholas.

As I stroked her hair, my mind strayed back to earlier in the night, replaying the final confrontation with Marcus. I swallow hard at the question I couldn't shake off: If Nicholas hadn't ripped the gun from Marcus's hand, who did?

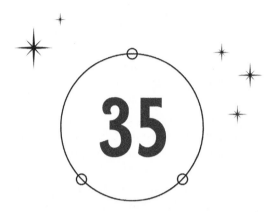

Truth and Lies

I had to give props to Al, the only one working behind the counter when I walked into Jitters the next morning. It was still too early on a Sunday for more than a trickle of customers. He'd just handed off a fully leaded triple skinny latte to a mom pushing a stroller when I stepped up to the counter. He blanched at the sight of my battered face but recovered well. "Dude, what happened to you?"

"Car accident," I said, hoping that would stave off further questions. "Windshield shattered, but no one else got hurt."

The evanescent Nurse Bob called had shown up this morning before the coffee pot had finished perking. A young dad with a toddler on his hip, it took him all of two minutes to work his magic on my various injuries. The red, angry wounds on the left side of my face had been reduced to small scabs while the scrape going from my right cheek to chin now looked more like the creases left by a pillow. My skin still tingled from the accelerated healing.

"What a bummer. Do you need tomorrow off?" Thanksgiving was only a few days away, and I'd only been scheduled for the Monday afternoon shift before Scarlett and I drove home for the holiday.

"That might be best." My arm still hurt from being grazed by a bullet.

I cut a glance at Olive's turkey abomination, which now had more pink coffee stirrers jabbed into its sides than feathers. "Really sorry to be missing out on that," I said with a grin. "By the way, do you mind if I grab a few dog biscuits?" He gave me an odd look but slid over the canister.

I'd called my cell company that morning to reactivate a creaky old phone that had been tossed in a drawer until I got a replacement. It rang when I got back in the car.

I glanced at caller ID. "Hi, Mr. Silver."

"Miss Wilder," he responded. "Are you available to come to The Lower 8?"

"Now?" All I wanted to do that day was catch up on homework, eat cookie dough ice cream with Scarlett, and sleep—though not necessarily in that order.

"Please. I will be leaving in a few hours, and you haven't been fully debriefed."

I stifled a groan. The last thing I wanted to do was relive last night's horrors again, but I'd come to like and admire the Prime. "I'm on my way."

The back door to The Lower 8 had been propped open, and a cool breeze swirled through the empty kitchen as I let myself in. Pushing through the door leading into the club, I discovered I wasn't the only one who'd gotten a phone call that morning.

Two square tables had been shoved together in the middle of the dance floor. Jessie sat at the end of one table, his blond hair tangled as if he'd come straight from bed. Nicholas sat bleary-eyed at the head of the other, wearing the same clothes he'd had on last night. Our eyes met, and the look we shared was worth whatever I had to endure next.

Silver had chosen a chair in the center. He was composed and in command as always, a notebook and pen in front of him. Also in attendance was Khalia, who held the hand of a pretty woman wearing a prim, high-necked dress that made her look like a Sunday school teacher. The last member of the party was a worn, distracted woman I couldn't place, her fingers curled over the keypad of a laptop as she worked.

Layla dispensed coffee cups from a tray, her bright smile at odds with everyone else's somber mood. She set one down at the vacant spot between Jessie and Silver. "Here you go, Blake."

I'd planned to claim the empty chair next to Nicholas, but it would make too much of a statement if I ignored her invitation. I took the designated spot and smiled gratefully as she filled my cup.

Khalia inspected my damaged face. "I can't leave you alone for five minutes, can I, princess?" Other than a line of stitches holding her bottom lip together and two fading black eyes, she'd healed nicely. Maybe an evanescent had paid her a visit as well.

"It's been a rough week," I admitted.

She chortled, the first time I'd ever heard her laugh. "Could be worse. At least you and I are still above the ground."

I smiled weakly. It was too soon to find even gallows humor in the deaths of Alice and Marcus. The young woman next to her extended her hand. A solid hum of energy sparked just under her skin.

"I don't know where Khalia's manners are, but I'm her girlfriend Maisie, enchanter, Second Class." With a sweet smile, milky skin, and manners to burn, she couldn't be more different from the hard-edged sentinel than a kitten from a pit bull. "I attended the aftermath of your battle at the school library. I can personally guarantee not a single one of your classmates will ever know what happened."

I opened my mouth to thank her, but Silver cleared his throat and captured the room's attention.

"Thank you all for coming so early in the day. There is a situation in Brazil I must attend to immediately." His matter-of-fact tone made it sound like jetting around the globe was all in a day's work, which for him it probably was.

Behind him Layla's smile dissolved at the unwelcome news, though I didn't know if her crush on Silver had ever gained traction. Between her and Scarlett, doomed romances were in the air.

I'd stayed up half the night with my best friend. The attack on her and Warren had interrupted the breakup conversation, but the traumatic event had only reinforced her decision. In her usual composed manner, she'd listed all the reasons why it wouldn't work between them, all while listening to the Phantom of the Opera bemoan his unrequited love. It was only when she abandoned logic that she crumbled. The heart wants what the heart wants, even if it did come in a slightly combustible package.

"I'm sorry to interrupt." The older woman who had yet to be introduced didn't sound very sorry. A wireless printer on the bar whirred as she spoke. "The transfer of ownership papers is ready. If I can get a few signatures, I'll be out of your way."

As Jessie signed where the woman indicated, she glanced about the bar. "You're a lucky man, Mr. McCabe. Against my advice, Mr. Sinclair has practically given away his son's interest in The Lower 8."

Jessie scrubbed a tired hand across his brow. "Yep, I'm lucky all right. Only five people and a dog had to die so I could have my bar."

The woman stiffened. With lips compressed into a narrow line, she collected her signatures, witnessed by the Prime, and packed up her computer and printer. Before she could leave, however, Mr. Silver asked the question that had been on my mind. "Is Mr. Sinclair well?"

She unbent long enough to answer. "As well as can be expected. The city has shut down the construction site, pending a full investigation. My client is a wealthy man, but most of his assets are tied up in the new building." As if realizing she'd revealed too much, she clamped her mouth shut.

Khalia looked stricken, which Nicholas picked up on. "Don't worry," he said to her. "You will always have a place with us."

Maybe if he offered stock options, he could seal the deal.

"I believe our business together is concluded, Mr. McCabe," Silver said as soon as the lawyer was gone.

Jessie sipped his coffee. "If it's all the same to you, I'd prefer to stay."

Silver nodded and turned to me. "My apologies for rushing you, Miss Wilder, but I need an accounting of last night's events. Please tell me what happened from the moment you were approached in the parking lot of The Lower 8 by Marcus Sinclair."

I could have gone my entire life without ever talking about it, but there was no avoiding it now. "I think you know it started when Marcus told me Nicholas had been in an accident at his father's job site." I met Jessie's gaze. "Thank you. You and I'm guessing Cedric saved my life."

"Always." His eyes held mine a fraction too long, as if searing me into his memory. An image of his naked body pressed against mine flashed through my head, and I quickly glanced away. Dwelling on my steamy premonition could only lead to trouble, so I determinedly shoved it into a dark corner of my mind. Instead I took a deep breath and began recounting the last thirty minutes of Marcus' life.

My voice came out cool and detached, as if what I told them had happened to someone else. Pretending it was a bad movie starring a girl who looked like me was the only way I'd get through it.

"Did he say where in the desert?" Silver asked when I brought up the fate of Selena Flores and Chico. His pen paused over the notebook, the page almost filled.

When I shook my head, Nicholas spoke up. "The Mojave stretches from here to Las Vegas and beyond. It could be years before anyone finds them."

I had an idea about that but wasn't ready to share it just yet.

The rest of the tale spilled out. Jessie's eyes glittered when he heard my suspicions about Suki, his door sentinel, and her abrupt departure. I finally ended with my fiery premonition of Warren and Scarlett coming to pass, and subdued silence overtook the table.

His pen still poised, Silver looked at me as if there was more to the story. He was right. I'd told them Marcus's gun had jammed, and his nose for untruthfulness had scented out the lie. I met Silver's eyes with an unwavering gaze of my own. There was no way I would reveal my fears I'd been hit with another latent talent.

My wounds would heal, Marcus would be dug out of one grave and buried in another, and if the cold-blooded instinct for survival Sutton Sinclair displayed last night was any indication, the death of his son would be merely a temporary setback. The only lasting proof of treachery, betrayal, and heartbreak came from the scratching of Silver's pen as he decided to let my story stand unquestioned. He dashed off a last few sentences, recording the events of last night for posterity.

"What about Tristan Murrieta?" I asked. "Marcus said he was back in town."

"Indeed." Silver put down his pen. "He did in fact leave the country to attend a funeral, or he would have been exonerated much more quickly. I also relied overmuch on Mr. David. I see now I should not have allowed our bond to lapse, Miss Wilder."

It was almost too much to hope for. "You didn't see a, uh, premonition of mine last night?" Maybe some of my erotic secrets were still my own.

"No, I didn't. Was it significant?"

"Nope," I said quickly before changing the subject. "What about Suki?" If she knew Marcus and Alice were together, perhaps Selena's life could have been saved if the sentinel had told someone what she suspected. Instead, she ran.

"She can't stay hidden forever," Mr. Silver said with confidence. "If she concealed knowledge of Miss Ferndale's and Mr. Sinclair's crimes, she will face justice."

I didn't wish her ill, but neither did I think she should escape the consequences if speaking up could have prevented so much grief.

Finally I asked the question I dreaded most. "Will Warren Hartman be okay?"

"We contained the, ah, evidence," Nicholas volunteered, "so no outside authorities are involved."

"An inquest will be convened," Silver added, "but it's an obvious case of self-defense. He'll be paired with a patron before anyone else is injured."

Silver consulted his watch and closed his notebook. "I thank you for allowing me to dredge up such unpleasant memories, Miss Wilder. Your courage is an asset to our people. I look forward to seeing you at the Declaration."

I straightened up in my chair. "Declaration?"

"Yes," he said, gathering his things. "Once a year, the newest Nines and their patrons gather at Alder House to formally make their pledge."

I didn't stop to consider my words. I had to know. "What if a Nine shows up without one? A patron, that is."

He momentarily froze halfway out of his chair. "To my knowledge, it has only happened once before."

I eagerly leaned in. "And?"

He rose to his feet. "The Nine was required to prove they'd surpassed the need for a patron."

"How did they do that?" I questioned.

Across from me, Khalia cackled. "The same way our people have settled everything for centuries. We fight for it."

I called my parents as I drove home. If I didn't give them a heads up about my injuries before showing up for Thanksgiving, they'd wonder what else I was keeping from them. The irony was that they'd be right to wonder. If they knew how close I had come to death, my life in Santa Carla would be over.

As it turned out, they too were driving. One of my dad's favorite things in life was picking through other people's dubious treasures in garage sales. If my mom wasn't on call, she'd sometimes humor him and go along on his hunts for historical artifacts.

My dad had just scored big. "You should see this antique embalming aspirator I bought for twenty bucks!"

I didn't know what that was, but knowing his fascination with ancient burial rituals, I could guess.

"Go, Dad," I said with enthusiasm. "Now you and Mom have the whole life to death thing totally covered."

"Great," my mom said, her tone dry as dust.

My dad started describing exactly how his new toy would have been used on the dead, so I rushed to cut him off. "TMI, Dad. I've got enough problems without having those images stuck in my head."

"Oh?" He'd picked up on the warning of bad news to come.

"There was a freak accident at school. A window got shattered, and I happened to be right next to it. I'm fine, but my face and arm got a bit cut up."

"Did you need stitches?" Mom asked. "What doctor did you see?"

"I saw a local guy, and only my arm needed stitches."

She had great respect for plastic surgeons and had always drilled into me to never let anyone but a plastics guy touch my face. We chatted a few more minutes about my supposed accident before I asked, "Is Jordan still hiding in her room?"

Dad expelled a breath. "Pretty much. She can return to school after the holiday, and she's keeping up with homework online."

There was something else bugging him. "What is it, Dad? What aren't you telling me?"

"It's Noah," my mom said. It took me a moment to remember he was my sister's boyfriend. "He hasn't called or texted since her suspension."

That sucked, but it wasn't like there weren't ten other guys waiting for her to be single. "I'm sure she'll be fine."

The silence on the other end of the line told me they weren't so sure.

"I'll be home in a few days. We'll figure it out then."

After listening to them tell me to drive home carefully at least three times, I was finally able to say goodbye. Something had occurred to me when we were talking about my sister, but I didn't want to say anything until I knew one way or another. Being a Nine seemed to run in families; the Sinclairs, the Thornes, and the Silvers all proved that, though some more successfully than others. Nicholas had also said most people grew into their talents in adolescence.

What if Jordan had just come into her own as a Nine?

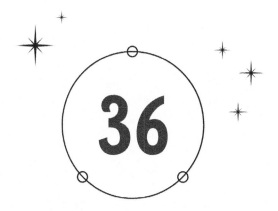

Believe in Me

I stomped out of class stuffing yet another assignment into my backpack. It was like all the teachers had banded together and decided our brains would atrophy if we didn't do a ton of homework during our five days of alleged freedom. I'd started for the parking lot when a familiar voice said, "Hello, Blake Wilder." Nicholas grinned over at me as he matched my stride. "You still walk too fast."

"But I see you're learning to keep up." I hadn't heard from him since we'd parted at The Lower 8 the day before, but he'd probably gone home and slept, just as I had. There was still so much between us that remained uncertain, but now we had time to figure it out. "Want to grab a cup of coffee? Or in your case tea?"

"I wish I could." His steps slowed, and so did mine. "I have to go."

I clutched my backpack to my chest. "So soon?"

He nodded. "My father called. Something's happened with one of the regents."

I pulled him off the walking path. "Is everything okay?"

He glanced toward the road fronting the school as if he were anxious to be on his way. "I'm not even sure myself. I'll know more when I get to Alder House."

"Oh." We were back to the guy who kept everything bottled up. "Well then, don't let me keep you."

As if realizing he was once again retreating into his fortress of solitude, he deliberately stepped closer. "Be patient with me. Please."

I decided on a full-frontal assault. Dropping my backpack onto the grass at my feet, I slid my arms around his waist. "I will, but you have to meet me halfway. You can start by talking to me and telling me what's going on."

"I can do that," he promised, studying my face as if committing it to memory. "I'll call you when I know more."

His hand cupped my cheek as he lowered his mouth to mine. It was the last time he'd kiss me for a while, and I wanted to remember every moment. The moment his lips touched mine the energy unique to us surged. His tongue stroked mine, and I tasted the familiar tang of the citrus and smoke of his favorite tea before all rational thought scattered under an onslaught of pleasure and longing.

And then the premonition struck.

The world was a blur of color and movement before the image sharpened into a sea of people pressed up against some sort of a barrier. Eager, expectant faces peered through a latticework of iron bars and jostled for a better view. It was an arena or a giant cage of some sort, though I could only imagine what kind of animal would need to be confined in such a way.

The picture shifted. With a jolt I saw the cage was no longer empty, yet the creature inside was no animal. Nicholas stood in the middle, turning slowly to take in the cheering crowd. He was dressed head to toe in white as if readying for a fencing match. I strained to hear what had the audience so worked up, but their collective voices bounced and reverberated into a jumble of sound.

The image jumped one more time, and I was seized with fear. Nicholas was now on his knees, beaten and battered. His white clothing accentuated the blood that now oozed from a dozen different wounds. No part of his body had been spared from assault. Even his face bore a small gash on the chin.

Nicholas wasn't leaving me just to break up with Julia Martin. He would be fighting for his life.

I pulled away from him with a horrified gasp, but he didn't let go. He gripped my shoulders.

"What did you see?" he asked, wary and tense.

"You," I said, trembling. "You were dressed all in white inside some cage. There was so much blood..." He instantly released me and stepped back but didn't look as shocked as I would have expected. "You know what that vision means, don't you?"

His expression reflected sadness and resolve. "I still have to go."

It was my turn to grip his arm. "Change your future. Stay here with me." His smile was bittersweet; I had his answer. "There's nothing I can say to keep you here, is there?"

He pulled me into his arms. "Despite what I feel for you, I still have a duty to The Nine." He kissed me again before loosening his grip. "Believe in me the way I believe in you." And then he was gone.

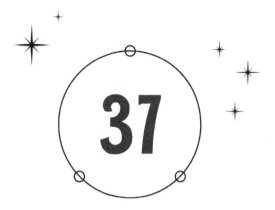

Homeward Bound

Warren sat at the bar nursing a Coke when I trudged down the stairs at The Lower 8. It was early on a Tuesday night and combined with the upcoming holiday, it was quieter in the club than usual. The pool tables were out, and it was a beer-drinking, jeans-and-tee shirt kind of crowd. I took the barstool next to Warren.

"Thanks for coming," he said, his glum expression reinforcing my guess that Scarlett would be the topic of conversation. "Your face is looking better."

Makeup to the rescue. The bartender gave me a nod, and I ordered my usual mineral water with lime. I was actually starting to like it. My drink soared through the air and arrived neatly at my elbow.

We were silent for a few minutes until he blurted, "I think I love her."

At least that made two of them. Scarlett was doing her best to shrug off her feelings for Warren, but I knew her too well to buy it. Since breaking up with him, she'd been living in her pajamas surrounded by a boatload of trendy magazines. When I'd left her tonight, she'd been diligently filling out a quiz titled *Is Breaking Up With Him The Right Thing to Do?*

"I think she loves you too," I said, hoping Scarlett wouldn't be upset at breaking a confidence. If two people cared about each other, then nothing else should matter.

Warren brightened. "So what do I do now? How can I make her understand she means more to me than any of this?" He waved his hand to indicate the Nines dotting the club.

"Tell her that, and if she won't listen, keep telling her." He'd eventually break through her resolve.

"Now?" The hope and optimism on his face was uncomplicated by concerns about a beautiful Irish girl, a possibly lethal premonition, and a fight for independence, but I shoved aside my own worries and nodded. He jumped off his stool and bounded up the stairs.

I sighed, wishing my own situation could be so neatly resolved, but just like Scarlett I couldn't pick and choose what I liked or didn't like about Nicholas. He led a complicated life, and I had to accept I had no control over the choices he felt honor-bound to make. I had to trust in what we felt for each other and hope for the best.

A body slid into Warren's vacated seat. "Hello, darlin'. Drowning your sorrows in a stiff glass of water?"

Didn't Jessie ever take a night off?

"What do you know of my sorrows?" I tried to project an offhand air.

"I know that Thorne has run back to London." He tipped his empty glass in the direction of one of the bartenders, and the glass immediately refilled itself.

I used a straw to poke at the ice bobbing in my glass. "Then you know as much as I do."

"Maybe more." He took a sip of his drink. "One of the regents is dead."

My hand stilled in mid-poke. "What happened?" And why was it Nicholas hadn't shared that detail?

He sipped his drink, drawing out the moment. "Murdered."

I swiveled to face him. "There are nine regents, right? One of each talent?"

He nodded.

Ever since witnessing the violent episode in Nicholas's future, I'd racked my brain trying to figure out why he'd be forced into such bloody combat. A chill went through me at the possible answer. "It was the telekinetic regent, wasn't it?"

Jessie smiled darkly. "Good guess. Rumor has it he was a potential challenger for the seat of chancellor. Now there's a vacant seat on the council to be filled. Know any ambitious telekinetics eager for the job?" He raised a mocking brow. "Christmas has come early for the Thornes."

The following morning, I was hoping for an early Christmas present as well. Scarlett had let me talk her into a detour on our drive north for the holiday. Our alarm clocks had gone off just after sunrise, so even with the added miles we'd still be home in plenty of time to bake the traditional collection of Thanksgiving pies.

"We'll be going completely out of our way, you know." She didn't sound as if she minded though. Warren had been at the apartment when I'd returned home last night. They weren't back together yet, but the way she'd smiled after he'd said goodnight was a hopeful sign.

Our bags were in the car, and Scarlett stood patiently waiting by the front door with the car keys in hand. I'd been tearing the place apart for five solid minutes searching for my phone. Scarlett had called it twice already, but I must have forgotten to take it off silent. I was getting ready to toss the cushions off the sofa for the third time.

I threw up my hands. "Where the hell is my phone?"

Suddenly a blur of silver shot out of my bedroom and into my hand. I froze. Scarlett dropped the keys. With trembling fingers, I regarded the phone I now held.

"How did you do that?" Scarlett's voice was a frightened whisper.

"I think," I said hesitantly, not wanting to scare my best friend more than I already had. "I think I'm a multi."

She dropped gracelessly into the nearest armchair. "What does that mean?"

"Remember I told you about the nine gifts?" At her wary nod I continued. "Sometimes we get more than one."

She smiled weakly. "Great."

"It doesn't have to change anything between us," I rushed to add. "I'm still your weird best friend forever, just with more standard features."

Her eyes met mine. "Features?"

The air was thick with her apprehension. What would she do when she discovered another part of her was mine for the taking? I worked hard to avoid looking into her past or future, but I knew of no such way to shield myself from her most private emotions. The thought of her turning away from me, the cost of being my friend finally judged too high, made the bile rise in my throat.

"Just the telekinesis." The many years I'd spent perfecting my poker face allowed to me to keep my features relaxed. "Most multis have two talents, and in rare circumstances three, so if I get one more, let's hope it's the one that'll let me dream up a new sofa."

A relieved smile crossed her face as she regarded the tired piece of furniture in question. "Maybe something in a nice floral?"

"Floral?" I asked in mock outrage. "Did you skip middle age and go right to old lady?"

She laughed, as I'd hoped, and got on her feet. "Let's go home."

We headed east out of the city, stopping only once to drive through McDonalds for coffee and breakfast sandwiches. Ninety minutes later we arrived at the Desert Springs Animal Shelter. Only a few cars were parked on the cracked asphalt lot behind a tired-looking, single-story building painted in faded beige.

The air outside was at least fifteen degrees warmer than the morning we'd left behind in Santa Carla. Abandoning our sweatshirts, we made our way through the front door. Instantly a cacophony of barks greeted our arrival, as did a young woman with a round face and a warm smile.

"Can I help you?" She sat behind a tall counter. Her tee shirt had a paw print across it with the words *My Favorite Breed is Rescue.*

"Hi, my name is Blake Wilder. I called earlier about—"

"Yes!" she interrupted. "I'm Victoria. Nice to meet you." She rose from her desk. "Come with me." The barking went up a decibel when she buzzed open a door leading into the kennels.

"He's just the sweetest thing but really scared," she said as we walked into the bowels of the building. "We've called the number on his chip repeatedly, but no one's called us back. I'm afraid he's living on borrowed time now. He's been spared because of the holiday, but if he's not claimed by Monday..." Her pained expression filled in the blank.

We passed puppies and adults, large dogs and small. I didn't want to think about what would happen to those who weren't lucky enough to be adopted. She stopped in front of a small kennel. In the very back was a small dog concealed by the shadows. I hooked my fingers through the bars and bent down to his level.

"Chico?" I asked the question tentatively. "Is that you?"

A whine met my ears before the rest of the dog shot to the front of the kennel. The telltale golden ears and white face were there, along with his utter relief at seeing a familiar face. He frantically licked my fingers, and I pulled out one of the dog biscuits I'd swiped from Jitters. He wolfed it down.

"It's okay, Chico." I tried not to get weepy as I thought about Selena. Her last thoughts had been of her beloved dog. The twenty-three animal shelters I'd called before finding a dog matching Chico's description had been the least I could do for her. "You're safe now."

"I take it we have a new dog?" Scarlett asked.

A signed contract and fifty dollars later, the three of us were on the road. Scarlett drove while Chico curled up on my lap and passed out, exhausted from his ordeal. He didn't even flick an ear when my phone chimed with a text.

It was Nicholas. *No matter what happens, just know I meant every word. Even the ones I don't know how to say.*

Dread pooled in my stomach as I thought of the frightening glimpse I'd had of his future and what I thought it meant. Had the grisly moment arrived already? I shot back my own text: *Tell me you're ok.* After another minute I texted, *???*

I stared at the dormant screen until the phone turned off. Scarlett took one look at my face and extended her hand. I took it, determinedly burying the guilt at having deceived her into the deepest reaches of my heart.

When at last we turned into our neighborhood on the outskirts of Salinas, a city with so many agricultural farms it was called the "Salad Bowl of The World," it felt like we'd been away for a hundred years. It almost seemed strange that everything looked the same when I felt so changed. Even our usual parking spot at the curb in front of my parents' one-story ranch-style house waited for us.

We each grabbed a small suitcase from the trunk. "Good luck," I said to Scarlett. She would drop off her stuff at her mom's before coming back to bake.

She shrugged. "It's still daylight. Maybe she's still sober enough to notice I'm home."

My parents descended on me the second I walked through the door. Mom pulled me into a tight embrace followed by Dad wrapping his arms around the both of us, exclaiming, "Group hug!"

Chico hovered at my heels, his tail wagging slowly as he took in his surroundings. Dad was the first to ask, "Who's this?"

"He just lost his owner," I said simply. "She was a friend."

"My first grandchild!" Dad eagerly swooped in and picked up the mutt. The way they looked at each other made me think Chico's feet would never touch the ground again.

Mom inspected my face and then my arm with a professional eye. "If I didn't know better, I'd say these wounds were at least a week old." I would share a highly edited version of everything that had gone on since Nicholas had walked into my life, but that could wait.

"Where's Jordan?" I asked. My parents locked gazes for a moment. Uh-oh.

"She's in her room," Mom said. "Why don't you let her know you're here? Maybe she'd like to come help you and Scarlett in the kitchen."

"Yeah, sure," I muttered, trudging down the long central hall leading to the house's four bedrooms. Jordan's busy social life had never allowed time for such homey pursuits as baking.

A knock on her door went unanswered, so I slowly nudged it open and peeked inside. The curtains were drawn against the late afternoon light, casting the room in semi-darkness. The shape huddled under the covers didn't stir as I came to sit on the side of her bed.

"Jordan?" She didn't budge. I sighed, thinking back to my worry about what it would be like for her if she woke up to discover she was a freak like her sister. My heart went out to her.

The covers erupted, and Jordan bolted upright. Her dark hair was a snarled mess, and the sweatshirt she wore looked like she'd been living in it for days.

"Don't you dare feel sorry for me!" she cried before bursting into tears. That's when I felt it, the energy of her connection, our connection, to The Nine.

"You knew what I was thinking?" I asked, knowing the answer before the question was even out of my mouth.

She nodded, her face a picture of misery. "What's happening to me?"

ENJOY A SNEAK PEEK AT

THE NINE:
Alder House

COMING 2023

The Discovery

I was being watched. It was a cool December day in Southern California, and other than a few parked cars, the employee lot behind The Lower 8 was deserted. The private club exclusively for people with paranormal abilities, known as Nines, wouldn't open for hours, but I'd come to talk with the club's seriously gorgeous owner, the phantomist Jessie McCabe. However, before ringing the bell at the service entrance, I had to deal with my voyeur.

I shook the box in my hand, the contents rattling like a thousand-piece puzzle. "Are you hungry?"

The skinny little cat with dull black fur arched his back in anticipation. He'd darted into the shadows the last time we'd crossed paths, so I'd picked up some kibble in hopes of convincing him humans weren't all bad.

"I'm just going to pour out a bit of this, ah…" I paused to consult the box's label. "…Seafood Feast, and then lunch is served."

I took a slow step in the creature's direction, but he instantly turned tail and ran around the side of the building. The place being a former warehouse, there was nothing over there but the loading dock. It would be deserted at this time of day.

"It's okay, little kitty," I said, trailing him around the corner. "I'll leave some food where nobody will bother you and—" The box of kibble dropped from my hand. As a clairvoyant who'd seen her fair share of violent and shocking moments in other people's pasts or futures, it took a lot to unnerve me.

Maybe that's why I didn't scream at the sight of the dead body at my feet.

The woman was young, late teens or early twenties, with magenta hair razored into an edgy style. Her gold metallic spandex dress was cut low at the top and high at the bottom, and I sagged in relief to see her clothing undisturbed. She lay on her back, clouded eyes staring up at the hazy sky, her mouth stretched wide in a silent scream. There wasn't any blood or visible marks on the body, nor any other obvious reason for her to be lying dead on the cracked asphalt.

She was a stranger to me, but my heart bled for the ones who knew and loved her as a daughter, a girlfriend, or maybe a sister. As soon as I reported her death, it would set in motion a chain of events that would end in grief and sorrow. I already regretted my role in another heartbreak.

With my mind and emotions so preoccupied, my only spare thought went into finding Jessie. As I raced to the back door, it flew open of its own accord. Things moving without me consciously willing them to do so was happening more often, particularly when I was stressed.

So far only Scarlett, my best friend and roommate, knew about my budding telekinetic powers, but if I didn't get them under control, it wouldn't be our little secret for long. She still hadn't learned I was starting to become empathic and often picked up on what other people were feeling no matter how they tried to hide it. It was some comfort that Nines didn't seem to develop more than three talents, but that was still three more than I wanted or needed.

This wasn't my first visit to The Lower 8 during off hours, so the prep cooks didn't pause in their chopping and stirring as I dashed through the kitchen. As expected, I found Jessie hunched over the desk in his otherwise empty office, but since he had the ability to communicate with the dead, he wasn't necessarily alone.

"Man up, Cedric," he said, staring at the empty chair in front of him. "I realize change is hard when you're five hundred years old, but we agreed Harper could stay for a spell because a fresh perspective will do us all some good." He shifted his gaze to the sofa. "But Harper, calling Cedric a 'perpetuator of the patriarchy' is probably not the best way to make new friends."

Jessie caught sight of me in the doorway and shook his head in exasperation. "It's a good thing ghosts are already dead, or there'd be blood on the floor every time a new spirit showed up." He took in my distress and bolted to his feet. "What's wrong?" Well-worn jeans hugged slender hips, and the tight indigo pullover made his shoulder-length golden mane just that much more burnished.

"There's a dead body outside," I burst out.

He blanched. Marcus Sinclair, his former business partner, had murdered a girl last month inside the club, only to then die himself days later at the hands of his imperious father. Jessie had been dealing with the fallout ever since. The last thing he needed was more trouble on his doorstep.

He shook off the jolt and came around the side of his desk. "Show me."

I hesitated when we reached the corner of the building, but Jessie understood my reluctance. "Stay here," he said, slipping around the side. It didn't take long for him to return, his mouth set in a grim line.

"Do you know her?" I asked.

"She tried to get into the club last night, but we turned her away. She wasn't one of us."

The entrance to any place Nines exclusively gathered was always guarded by a sentinel. Their job was to evaluate each person's paranormal connection and refuse entry to those who lacked one. The most important mandate of the ancient society was to keep outsiders from learning of their existence.

"Shouldn't we call Mr. Silver?" The Prime Sentinel, the closest thing we had to a sheriff, had come to Santa Carla when our city had been plagued by a series of paranormal murders. Investigating a dead body found at The Lower 8 would be right up his alley.

"The latest protocols say if the victim of a crime isn't a Nine, we have to call the local authorities." Jessie ran both hands through his hair. "But this is one of those times when I think we were better off not trying to adapt to the modern world."

"Meaning until recently, you'd just get rid of the body and call it a day?" I tried not to sound judgmental, but someone had robbed this girl of her life and her dreams. She deserved justice.

He leveled his gaze at me. "Meaning whenever you mix Nines and outsiders, there's always trouble."

True Detective

Before dialing 9-1-1, Jessie informed his crew of the tragic turn of events, though he tried to be more diplomatic when breaking the news to Gustav, the house materialist. It was Gustav's job to use his talent of transforming matter to change the look of the club on a daily basis, from a country roadhouse one night to Blackbeard's pirate den the next. The dapper Austrian considered his creations works of art, and after taking a look at the magical winter wonderland conjured up for that evening, I had to agree.

"This is *inakzeptabel!*" the temperamental artist cried in a mixture of English and German.

"Gustav…" Jessie muttered, his voice carrying a low note of warning.

The materialist heaved a sigh but waved a hand to halt the snow falling gently from a starry sky. He murmured a few words, and the ice skating pond transformed back into a dance floor. By the time uniformed officers arrived on the scene ten minutes later, they entered a rather mundane-looking nightclub.

Layla, a double empath who could sense moods as well as influence them, hovered in the kitchen as the cooks turned out platters of burgers. The head waitress was dressed for the night as a sexy snow bunny, a tight white mini dress with a fur-trimmed hood and matching thigh-high boots showing off her slender figure. Her spiked pixie haircut was fitting because with her small stature and elfin features, she resembled nothing so much as a magical woodland sprite.

"What's with all the food?" I asked.

She smiled, and a touch of her anticipation spilled over onto me. I'd often been the beneficiary of her optimistic outlook on life, but lately, I picked up on her moods less and less. It was especially odd considering my empathic connection to others seemed to be growing.

"Jessie asked me to feed the first responders," she said, easily hoisting a large tray of food. "He wants to make sure they feel, uh, kindly toward us." Only Layla could turn a murder investigation into a buffet.

"Smart," I agreed, helping myself to a cheeseburger from a second tray. I'd come straight from my last final exam of the semester at Cal State Santa Carla, and my stomach growled. It didn't care that the rest of me was still pretty shaken.

A handful of employees lounged around the bar in the main club, and I took an empty table close enough to be social but far enough away not to intrude. After a minute or two, Jessie pulled up the chair next to mine with his own burger and a large plate of fries.

"Everything okay with Cedric?" I asked. "I heard you talking to him when I first got here." Jessie could see ghosts as well as hear them, and he'd once shared a vision with me of the gossipy English aristocrat who'd been dead since before Henry the Eighth (also a Nine) sat on the throne.

He took a swig of Coke. "He's fine, just a bit prickly about the arrival of our latest spirit, but I can't turn her away just yet. She's sixteen and only recently passed."

My hand froze over my plate. "What happened?"

"Harper won't talk about it, nor will she share enough personal information for me to start digging." He shook his head. "She won't even tell me her last name."

My heart went out to the ghostly girl. "My sister is sixteen. Try to be patient."

"*You* were sixteen not too long ago," he pointed out. "How bad can it be?"

"I was never sixteen." My childhood ended with my first visions of loss and betrayal.

He still hadn't touched his food. "Maybe, but you seem to be handling today's drama pretty well."

His words caught me off guard, provoking memories of the countless times I had been judged and scorned for not handling it well at all. Every vision of pain and tragedy left its mark; today's horror would stay with me forever.

He laid his hand across mine. "Hey, it's alright, darlin'. You don't have to explain yourself to me."

Maybe not, but with so much attention on how my voyancy could be useful to so many within The Nine, no one had given any thought as to what opening the floodgates of my mind could do to me.

I took a steadying breath and met his gaze. "Every terrible thing I see, whether it's in a vision or dead on the ground at my feet, becomes part of me. I can't help it, it's just who I am. All I can do is try not to let it change me too much."

His gray eyes darkened as the price of my gift fully registered. "Every time I think I have you figured out, you say or do something that puts me back at square one." He smiled, deliberately shifting gears. "Well, I don't know about you, but I'm starving." He bit into his burger, and after a moment, I did the same.

"As much as I enjoy the pleasure of your company," he said, reaching for the fries, "I'm betting you didn't stop by for a late lunch."

I hadn't, but easing into the reason I'd come didn't make it any less painful or embarrassing. Finally, I blurted, "I wanted to know if there's been any news from Alder House."

Jessie's eyes crinkled as he regarded me with sympathy. He knew there would be only one reason I'd ask about the latest happenings at The Nine's home base in England. Nicholas Thorne, the son of The Nine's chancellor and my supposed boy-friend, had returned there two weeks ago and then promptly dropped off the grid. It didn't help that the last time I'd seen him, I'd had an unnerving premonition of him involved in some kind of bloody fight.

I'd first met Nicholas when he came to Santa Carla with the purpose of introducing me to the world of The Nine, but business between us had quickly turned personal. I hadn't known of his girlfriend's existence the first time we'd kissed. My cheeks warmed with a flush of guilt at having come between them, but he'd sworn his relationship with Julia Martin had been over for a long time. He'd only flown home to make it official.

He had rung a few times, the last to let me know he'd ended it with her. She'd taken the news well, he said, even agreeing they'd stayed together more out of habit than any real passion, but after that, he became a ghost.

My calls now went straight to voice mail, and there were only so many times you could have a one-sided phone conversation before feeling the sting of rejection. The last message I'd left for him was several days ago, and I'd resolved there would be no more. The next move was his. If he'd changed his mind about us, chasing after him would only make it that much worse.

"Love sucks, doesn't it?" Jessie said.

The kitchen door swung open, admitting a grim-faced woman in her mid-thirties wearing a navy pantsuit over a white tee and black running shoes. Her dark hair was pulled back into a no nonsense bun, and her only makeup was an understated lipstick that blended in with her light brown skin. A uniformed officer at her side pointed first to me and then to Jessie before withdrawing.

I'd seen enough *Law & Order* to bet she was a homicide detective. She took her time scrolling the screen on her phone, followed by casually patting her jacket pockets to come up with a notepad and pen. Her unhurried, deliberate manner clearly signaled she had all the time in the world to sweat us for details, so we might as well do everyone a favor and cut the bullshit right from the start. She must have decided I was first on the list because her eyes fixed on me as she approached.

"Blake Wilder?"

"Yes, ma'am." I'd never had much contact with the police but figured respectful was the way to go.

"Come with me." Without waiting to see if I followed, she beelined to a table on the other side of the dance floor, well away from the others. Once seated, she examined my face as if my life story could be found in the faint pink pockmarks still healing on my left cheek, evidence of a near miss by a bullet. Make-up would have covered them, but I'd had finals on my mind that morning, not a police interrogation.

"Why do I know your name?" she asked. It wasn't said in a curious manner, like someone saying you looked familiar before trying to figure out where you'd met. This was accusatory.

While she might recognize my name, it wasn't because it had appeared in any arrest reports. "I had a near miss last month at the Sinclair building site, but another man was killed."

"That's right," she said, though I got the impression she'd known the answer before asking the question. My suspicions were confirmed with her next words. "Then you had a problem with someone breaking into your apartment. Did they ever get anyone for that?"

"No," I answered, and they never would. The person who'd pried open my front door in the dead of night was now dead himself.

"Does trouble make a habit of following you around?" Her eyes narrowed if she were gauging just how much of an inconvenience I might be.

I bristled at the insinuation. "Look, I'm just a college student who dropped by today to visit a friend. I didn't kill that poor girl out there, and I don't know who did. May I go now?"

Satisfaction oozed from her pores at having goaded me out of my polite façade. "We're just getting started. I want to hear everything you did since you woke up this morning."

We proceeded to spend a very dull ten minutes together until one of the officers mercifully interrupted us. He handed the detective several items zipped into clear, plastic bags before retreating back through the kitchen. She glanced them over before calling out, "Jessie McCabe?"

Jessie stood, poured himself another glass of soda from the bar, and then ambled over as if he too had all the time in the world. No one was going to one up him in his own place. The detective gestured for Jessie to take a chair.

"Hello, Mr. McCabe. I'm Detective Bree Navarro." Since she hadn't felt compelled to introduce herself to me, the ambling must have worked. "You the owner here?"

"Yes, I own The Lower 8," he said easily.

"Why aren't there any security cameras? You have a secret for keeping out the miscreants you'd like to share with the other bar owners in town?"

The Prime Sentinel once told me the risk of having camera footage outsiders could use to identify members of The Nine outweighed any possible security benefits, but I kept my mouth shut.

Jessie shrugged. "We've never had a problem before."

Navarro slapped a driver's license encased in plastic on the table in front of us. "Do either of you know this girl?" From her picture, Paige Greenway had been a pretty, twenty-two-year-old brunette with a penchant for big hoop earrings. Her address was local, so it was unlikely she'd stumbled upon Santa Carla's industrial district by accident.

Jessie and I both shook our heads.

Navarro's phone chimed, and she stopped to read whatever was on the screen.

"The coroner," she informed us, "puts the victim's time of death at sometime between eleven p.m. last night and one a.m. this morning. No cause of death yet, though the expression on the girl's face made it look like she'd seen a ghost." I didn't dare glance at the phantomist to see what he thought of that observation. She eyeballed us again. "Where were you two last night between the hours of eleven and one?"

I was home asleep while Jessie was here at the club, which we both told her. The detective didn't seem pleased with our answers, but other than confessing to the murder, I got the feeling nothing we said would make her happy.

"One more thing," she said, focusing on another baggie containing a square scrap of white paper embossed with silver printing. It was one of The Lower 8's cocktail napkins, and there appeared to be a phone number inked across it. "This was found in the victim's purse."

She picked up her cell and dialed the number. Inside Jessie's pocket, his phone started to ring.

Follow Owl Hollow Press on social media or subscribe to our newsletter at OwlHollowPress.com for the latest news and updates on The Nine, a nine-book series by Kes Trester.

Or find out more about Kes Trester and her other books at KesTrester.com

Acknowledgements

No time spent writing is ever wasted. This book is proof of that.

When I first decided to take on the challenge of writing a book, I spent two years immersed in every relevant online course available at UCLA Extension. My days were spent producing television commercials and raising a young family. My nights and weekends were devoted to dreaming up stories, creating outlines, writing and revising various scenes, and then attempting to string them together into chapters. The concept for this book can be found in one of those early, muddled attempts at cobbling together a story.

My original scribblings may be lost to time (or at least buried on some forgotten laptop), but the idea of a young clairvoyant who'd seen so much yet experienced so little never left me. Finally, in between promoting one book and waiting to sell the next, I knew the time had come to tell Blake's story.

Along the way I have been blessed with the most understanding and supportive family. My husband, Fred, is my biggest cheerleader and proudly pitches my books to most everyone he meets. My son, Luke, has followed my footsteps into the entertainment industry and reads my work with a film producer's discerning eye. And my daughter Jordan, who lent her name to a character you will soon come to know, is now a Hollywood publicist orchestrating my PR.

I must also give credit to my big brother, Robb Sullivan, an A-list film editor and my own personal story editor extraordinaire. He vets my outlines for pacing issues and missed opportunities, and then pours over each word of my manuscripts in much the same way he analyzes each beat of a movie. There are directors who won't shoot a frame until Robb has critiqued their script. Lucky me, he's stuck with me for life!

Equally valued by most successful writers are trusted readers. No book of mine goes out into the world without first being read by the incomparable Fiona McLaren, a friend, fellow writer, and now an amazing editor who always finds time for me; the talented Jen Marie Hawkins, an accomplished author and dear friend who has elevated Southern wit to an art form; Jan Wieringa, who many a night came straight from a film set to help her godchildren with their homework, and now feeds my author's soul by texting her excitement as she reads my books; and Dete Meserve, a rockstar in film, television, and publishing who knows the power of casting wishes upon the waves.

I'm also blessed to have a wonderful team behind me every step of the way. Addison Duffy at UTA, who read an early draft of this book and called me at home on a Saturday night to say how much she loved it; and Kim Lindman of Stonesong Literary, who I hope I keep amused with my endless plotting and planning.

A special thank you to my friend, the gorgeous Khalia Frazier, who cheered me on through endless reps and then let me steal her name (the real life Khalia is a lot nicer than the fictional one!).

And finally, a thank you to you, dear readers. The fantastic emails and messages I received after publishing A DANGEROUS YEAR have often encouraged me to stay at my computer long after the dogs have packed it in and gone to bed. Words cannot express my joy and gratitude that you have chosen to take this journey with me.

A native of Los Angeles, Kes Trester's first job out of college was on a film set, though the movie's title will remain nameless because it was a really bad film. Really.

As a feature film development executive, she worked on a variety of independent films, from gritty dramas (guns and hotties) to steamy vampire love stories (fangs and hotties) to teens-in-peril genre movies (blood and hotties).

Kes produced a couple of independent films, both award-winners on the festival circuit, before segueing into television commercials. As head of production for a Hollywood-based film company, she supervised the budgeting and production of nationally broadcast commercials (celebrities, aliens, talking animals!) and award-winning music videos for artists such as Radiohead, Coldplay, and OKGO (more celebrities, aliens, and talking animals!).

Kes' contemporary novels are cinematic, fast-paced, and above all, fun. Her well-received debut novel, the young adult boarding school thriller A DANGEROUS YEAR, has been optioned for film/television. She is a four-time Pitch Wars mentor and an SCBWI Susan Alexander Grant award winner. When she's not writing, she can usually be found in the company of an understanding husband, a couple of college-age kids, and a pack of much-loved rescue dogs.

Find Kes online at KesTrester.com

#THENINE

Made in the USA
Las Vegas, NV
14 October 2022

57221110R00173